THE
RED SCORPIONS

VOLUME 2

The Taste of Vengeance

Chinedu Innocent Okafor

Published in Nigeria in 2015 by
GiPi Publications, Abuja
Plot 701 Mabushi, Cadastral Zone B6,
P.O. Box 7881 Wuse,
Abuja

First Published in Brazil, 2005

ISBN-13: 978-978-53198-6-6

Chapter 24

Bambam returned to the campus after spending some months in the hospital. One night, Ezenwa got into his room and saw him conversing with his room mates. There was a feigned friendliness on the faces of Ezenwa's room mates. They laughed arduously at Bambam's ribald stories. Ezenwa knew they were scared of Bambam. On the campus, the fear of Bambam was the beginning of wisdom. To display any kind of animosity or repulsion towards him would be like stroking the embers of hatred. And to be hated by Bambam was the best way to attract his attention. Nobody attracted his attention and remained unruffled. For this, Ezenwa's room mates laughed animatedly and tactlessly at the stories Bambam told them, to the magnitude that Bambam himself was puzzled by their hilarity. They greeted uninteresting stories with resonant laughter and falsified enthusiasm. At a time, David started dosing, but when his room mate laughter resounded all over their block, he was startled, and started laughing too. Bambam had seen him sleeping, and knew that the laughter was only to keep up appearances. He wanted to ask David why he laughed, but then, Ezenwa came into the room. The relief on the faces of his room mates at his entrance was pitiable. It was exactly like what he saw at the tap the day Bambam slapped him. Bambam greeted him jovially like an old friend.

'*Ol boy* I have been waiting for you for the past two hours, where were you?' Bambam asked.

'I visited my girlfriend,' Ezenwa replied jokingly.

'Can you come to my room now. I guess we can talk in seclusion there?' Bambam asked.

'I don't know your room,' Ezenwa lied.

'Block A5 room 205,' Bambam said and left the room.

'Now you see what you have brought on yourself and on us. People would start thinking we are cult members,' David complained to Ezenwa.

1

'Everybody is free to think what he wishes. Misgivings of people would never worry me,' Ezenwa replied and went after Bambam.

Bambam was waiting for him in front of his room. The moment he saw Ezenwa coming into the Block, he opened his door and held it for him to enter.

'Thanks once again for saving my life,' Bambam told him. And for attempting to snuff it out, Ezenwa mused.

'I am sorry for that incident at the tap. To tell you the truth, I became ashamed of myself when I saw you at the hospital,' Bambam apologised once again.

'Don't worry yourself, it is nothing. I just did it out of impulse. I couldn't watch like others while somebody dies. My conscience would torment me,' Ezenwa replied.

'That's a good conscience, quite unlike mine,' Bambam said. Ezenwa laughed, and wondered how Bambam would have reacted if he knew that the person on whom he was pouring gratitude was the same person who had taken his life to the brink of extinction.

'All the same, I did not call you just to thank you. I want to tell you things you don't know.'

'Things like what?' Ezenwa asked, puzzled.

'It was your girlfriend that shattered the head of one of my best boys,' Bambam said, and stared at Ezenwa to observe the impression his statement made.

'So the boy is your boy?' Ezenwa asked.

'Yes, and you would have been dead by now if not for that attack on me.'

'Dead?' Ezenwa asked and gaped at him in astonishment.

The discussion he overheard between Jack and Bambam that night he stabbed Bambam became clear to him. He started shivering again. He was really the person Bambam had told Jack to murder.

'Yes dead,' Bambam repeated, 'but that would have been after she had been violated and maimed. But somehow, I was attacked, and through your help she bought her freedom.

2

But I am still trying to know who wanted me dead.' Ezenwa remained silent.

'Would you like to become a Red Scorpion?' Bambam asked. Ezenwa winced. He had imagined that their discussion must come to that, but had no ready answer to give. However, he would not be cowed to get involved in nefarious things, or give answers that might compromise his freedom.

'No, I don't want to get involved in cults. I don't need it,' Ezenwa replied, a little scornfully.

'Perhaps you are right,' Bambam said. 'You don't need it now, because nobody will molest you again on this campus as long as I am alive. As far as I am still a student, you do not need anybody's protection, except God's, if you would allow him.' Ezenwa smiled. To be under the protection of Bambam was a step towards freedom, although in the intricacies of cult life he would be vulnerable to the schemes of Bambam's enemies.

'Thanks,' Ezenwa said with smiles.

'Another thing,' Bambam continued, 'tell your woman to stop moving about alone at night. I have been trying to contain the anger of some boys in other cults. I don't know how long I would be able to keep them in reins. I have been doing it because of you.'

'I don't understand, she was never alone,' Ezenwa said, a little surprised.

'I know that you and your friend always follow her at a distance, but that would have stopped nothing. Initially, they were afraid to molest her, because they know I would not like it. They knew you took me to hospital, and that I owe you the debt of protection. But she cannot continue to taunt them. Besides that, there are other things you need to know,' Bambam said. Ezenwa waited patiently to know what Bambam would tell him. Bambam lifted his pillow and brought out three pictures.

'What is this?' Ezenwa asked and took the pictures from him, looked at them, and shouted.

'How did you get these?' he asked.

'Don't be angry, no harm has been done yet. Only few people have seen them,' Bambam replied.

'But why?' Ezenwa asked, on the brink of tears. Someone had photographed Nneka where she was bathing. She was completely nude. Ezenwa seethed with explosive rage.

'That my boy whom she attacked with empty bottles did it, but could not do anything with them without my permission. I have restrained him many times, and apologised on her behalf. I have even paid a large sum of money to mollify his anger. But each time his friends taunt him, he comes back to me seeking permission to retaliate. But as long as I don't permit him, he will not do anything. My only fear is that he might pay other cults to do the job for him. And in such circumstance, I would not hold him responsible. He could import boys from another university to do it for him. I would only know when the deed has been done. So I believe it is better to prevent such incident instead of reacting when it has happened.' Ezenwa listened with rapt attention. The nude pictures of Nneka before him gave him a fretful foreboding of what would likely happen. He had underestimated the powers of cult boys.

'So what do I do?' Ezenwa asked Bambam.

'You need these, as I will not always be following you around,' Bambam replied, lifted his mattress again, and brought out two revolvers.

'One for you and one for your friend,' Bambam said with a grimace.

'Which friend? Nneka?' Ezenwa asked, astounded.

'No, not her, Nya... Nya... I can't pronounce his name.'

'Nyadiba?'

'Yes, that's the name. I like him. He is intelligent and cautious. He acts with restraint.'

'How do you know?' Ezenwa asked again, baffled by Bambam's accurate surmise of Nyadiba's character.

'I studied him to know if he had the characteristics of treachery. You know, somebody that might betray you. You know, on this campus, treacherous friends kill more than proclaimed enemies.'

'You are accurate in your guess. He is intelligent and cautious,' Ezenwa agreed.

'Yes, some of my girls have tempted him. One had deliberately insulted him. If it were you, you would have slapped her immediately, but he only smiled and went away. One thing that gladdens my heart is that he is not a coward. As I am talking to you now, he is still scheming to lure the girl into his web. He is very cunning,' Bambam explained, and extended the revolvers to Ezenwa. Ezenwa took the guns and thanked him.

'Don't worry about ammunition,' Bambam said, 'I will always replenish your stock whenever you want.'

'I am more worried about these pictures,' Ezenwa said sadly.

'Don't be worried. Here are the negatives too. Be assured that nobody is going to do anything again with these pictures here. But they can photograph her again.'

'How did they do it the first time?' Ezenwa asked.

'One of the girls in her hall did it for them. Just tell her to stop bathing at rush hours, and not to waste time whenever she goes to the bathroom.'

'Thanks, I am very grateful,' Ezenwa said and stood up.

'That's all right. Should you encounter any problem, don't hesitate to tell me,' Bambam added.

'Before I forget,' Ezenwa said, 'I saw a tin of scorpions at the abandoned building. Is it yours?' Bambam frowned. Ezenwa saw his discomfort, guessed his worry, and added, 'I went back there to see if I could find anything with which to trace your attackers, then I saw the tin.'

'Yes it is mine. Where is it?' Bambam asked feebly. He now knew that Ezenwa must have discovered a lot of things about him. But the way Ezenwa spoke to him still showed him that Ezenwa was a person he could trust, so he became less worried about what Ezenwa must have discovered.

'I hid the tin under my bed,' Ezenwa said.

'Thanks a lot. I have been searching for it everywhere.'

'But what are you going to do with scorpions?' Ezenwa asked, a little scornfully. He knew what the scorpions meant, but wanted to know if Bambam would offer more explanations.

'If you had looked well at them, you would have seen the red dye on them. We don't attack anybody unless we first send a live red scorpion as a warning to the person.'

'Come and take them tomorrow.'

'No, I would like you to bring them to me. I can't be coming to your room so often. It is not good for you, and I am yet to identify the person who wanted to kill me. I have to be careful, else they would get me again. But here,' he indicated his room, 'I am not vulnerable.'

Nneka wept lavishly when she saw the pictures of her nakedness. Ezenwa had guarded it jealously and made sure that she saw them alone.

'Stop crying,' he consoled. 'What would you have done if these pictures had confronted you on the notice boards of the university. Would you have committed suicide? Now you understand what I meant when I said that there are animals too in this university.'

Nneka was too dazed to talk. She had never in her life thought that she would be scourged by anybody to the extent of exposing her nakedness to the public. And to think that another girl like her had done it for a boy to castigate her was a shame to womanhood. She continued to cry. Ezenwa was touched. For a timid girl who was so conscious of her beauty like Nneka to be chastised with her nakedness by a boy she resented must be perpetually agonising. Ezenwa cuddled and consoled her. She allowed herself to be cuddled and caressed. He pulled her to sit down on his legs. She willingly sat down on his thighs. Slowly, the fire of his passion was ignited. She felt the turgidity in his groin and got up from his body.

'You have to go now,' she said, smiling. He sighed, yet relieved and happy that her smiles had returned.

'I will see you tomorrow. Remember what I told you. Don't go out with anybody at night. A girl took your nude pictures, and she would, without scruples, decoy you out for them,' Ezenwa said and started moving towards the door.

'I now understand what you have been saying,' Nneka said, still smiling.

Ezenwa had scarcely counted three steps towards the door before somebody started tapping on the door.

'Yes, who is there?' Nneka shouted. Ezenwa moved back and sat down again on Nneka's bed.

'It's me,' a male voice replied. Seeing Ezenwa beside her, Nneka felt protected and unlocked her door. A boy, outrageously ugly and nauseating with dirtiness, came in quickly into the room. Nneka was infuriated by the intrusion and wanted to reprimand him. Ezenwa winked. She understood and remained silent.

The boy was the ugliest thing Nneka had ever seen in her life. His head was abnormally large with a conspicuous large ears. His lips jutted out like appendages to the mouth. He attempted to intimidate Ezenwa and Nneka with a stern posture. But the aggressiveness of his demeanour augmented his ugliness. Such ugliness was unpardonable. Worst of all, against all decency and moderation, he wore dark goggles at night in a room with a dim light. Nneka guessed immediately that he must be a fool. Perhaps he had heard that she was a new student and wanted to try his luck too. It seemed nobody had told him what had been happening to boys who came to her with intimidation.

As Nneka and Ezenwa were still admiring the boy's ugliness, Lucy came in too and saw the boy sitting on her bed. She lost her restraint and told him to get up. As she was still talking, other room mates came in too and started making comments about the boy, right there, before his eyes. The boy was not deterred. As if Ezenwa did not exist, the boy started talking, without tact or style, about his love for Nneka. Unlike other boys who usually sat close to Nneka and spoke in whispers, the boy sat down on Lucy's bed and said everything he wanted to say loudly. Nneka's room mates laughed at every word he uttered. Ezenwa, after listening to him for a while, sighed and left the room.

From the boy's speech, Ezenwa deduced that he was not a threat, and did not worth his attention. He would find a way to scare him away later, but for now, he allowed the girls to amuse themselves with him. He was surprised that a human being could be so repulsive. Nneka's room mates, in spite of their caution and civility, could not hide their revulsion. Ezenwa walked down leisurely back to his hostel and never thought about the boy as a threat.

Ezenwa had to give Nyadiba one of the revolvers. He went to Nyadiba's room, tapped gently on the door, and waited for the response. Nobody responded. He peeped through the keyhole. The room was dimly illuminated. He tapped again, but no response came from within. He put his ear to the keyhole. A soft melodious female voice filled his ear. He paused and contemplated on what to do. He wanted to speak with Nyadiba, but not in the presence of anybody. The subject of their discussion needed extreme caution and prudence. He was on the verge of desisting from intruding into the room, but reasoned that the girl could be a visitor to Nyadiba's room mates. In this case, he would be obliged to ask Nyadiba's room mates where Nyadiba had gone. He tapped on the door again.

'Who is there?' Nyadiba asked with anger.

'It's me,' Ezenwa replied. Nyadiba unlocked the door.

Ezenwa went in suspiciously, and was surprised to see the girl lying on Nyadiba's bed. He smiled, and was short of asking Nyadiba what he was doing together on the bed with the girl. He would not have felt any contrition in embarrassing Nyadiba with vulgar comments. It had been their way since their childhood, but the girl would not understand. And for her sake, Ezenwa sacrificed a rare opportunity.

'It seems you are busy, I will see you tomorrow,' he said and started moving out of the room, with the vulgar smile still on his face.

'Not as busy as you think,' Nyadiba replied and started an introduction. 'Kate,' he called the girl, 'this is Ezenwa my friend, Ezenwa, here is Kate my sweetheart. Ezenwa and Kate laughed and grabbed each others hand with ardour.

'She is a pretty girl,' Ezenwa said. Kate giggled.

'She is pretty, but some people are bent on snatching her from me,' Nyadiba said ruefully.

'Snatch? Who?' Ezenwa asked angrily.

'It is not true,' Kate interjected, 'just because Pastor Jerry saw us on the way down and stopped to greet me, your friend started sulking.'

'Do you know anything about any Pastor Jerry?' Nyadiba asked Ezenwa.

'No, but if the guy is a pastor, I don't see why you should worry yourself. He is a man of God. So he is not a threat.'

'Man of God my arse. You should have seen the lewdness in his eyes and the vulgar stare he gave to her breast.'

'Nyadiba! Stop defaming a man of God!' Kate shouted and started laughing hilariously.

'I would rather rot in hell than have him help me to heaven,' Nyadiba chided.

'I will tell you about him tomorrow,' Ezenwa said and left the room. He knew that if anybody like that resided on the campus, Bambam must know about him.

Chapter 25

Jeremiah Nwankwo was a fraudulent student popularly called Pastor Jerry. He had been studying and attending classes as a student of the Department of Sociology, but not on the merit of any matriculation. After many years of unsuccessful attempt to get admission into one of the universities in Nigeria, he came illegally to the University of Nigeria Nsukka, and started attending classes as a student of Sociology. Nobody knew of his illegitimacy until after four years of gratuitous studies, and he was about to graduate with his mates. The Department of Admissions discovered the scam, and wrote a letter to the Department of Sociology, alerting it on the existence of an unqualified student in the department. With this information, the Head of the Department of Sociology sent him away from the Department.

Unmasked, but not discouraged, Jerry left the Department of Sociology and went to the Department of English, where he studied illegally for another three years before he finally passed the Matriculation Examination. He was admitted legally with Nyadiba's set. All the years Jerry was in the university appeared wasted on the surface, but the knowledge he had acquired could never be expunged from him. Academically, he was almost ahead of every student in his class.

When he established The Hope of Heaven Christian Church, it was only to lend credence to his fraudulent character, and nothing in the spirit and principles of Christianity. Contrary to the modesty and morality of Christianity, Jerry's congregation thrived on nudity and eroticism. Many students believed that the church was a church of fashion and liberty, and thus, Jerry's congregation was made up of mostly those whose tenets of Christianity were malleable. Pastor Jerry and his church cared for nobody's soul. As some students would say, Jerry sold souls to the devil.

'Why a church?' Ezenwa asked Bambam.

'He has been in the University longer than he should. And when he was legally admitted, his parents distrusted him and stopped funding his studies, so he has to look for a source to fund his studies. With his gift of oratory and skills in drama, what else would give him the money more than a church filled with wilfully gullible people.'

'Is he making a lot of money?' Ezenwa asked.

'You should have known that by what you saw. That car you saw, where did you think he got the money to buy it? But it is not a thing to worry about. You should only worry about him if he sees you with your girlfriend.'

'Does he snatch other peoples' girlfriends?'

'No, he does not snatch them, they run after him. You know girls like comfort. With his car and constant flow of money, he can have any girl he wants.'

'He is after my friend's girlfriend,' Ezenwa said.

'How? Did he tell her anything?' Bambam asked.

'Yes, he saw them coming down here, stopped and greeted her.'

'Does she know him very well?'

'No, she said that she had only seen him once when he visited a member of his church in her room.'

'Didn't he invite her to the church?' Bambam asked, a little surprised.

'He invited them, the girl and Nyadiba,' Ezenwa replied.

'This is what I wanted to hear.'

'Why?' Ezenwa asked, astounded.

'It is his mode of approach. Do you know that he has taken almost all the girls in his church to bed? He has seen the nakedness of every girl in that church. We have been setting a trap for him with one of our girls, and he is following the bait. Very soon the trap will catch him. And he won't escape.'

'Do you think that Nyadiba should not honour the invitation?' Ezenwa asked.

'No, he should go. His absence would make things easier for Jerry. Nyadiba should go. Tell him to keep his girl always by his side. Jerry is as cunning as a snake.'

'I might go with them. Nyadiba begged me to go with them,' Ezenwa hinted. Bambam stared at Ezenwa and laughed.

'Will you go with your girlfriend?' Bambam asked, still laughing.

'I have not told her to go with me.'

'If you happen to go with her, tell me everything that happened when you come back,' Bambam instructed.

'Do you think Jerry would chase her?

'Think?' Bambam asked with a wry gesture of the face. 'He must chase her. If he is the Jerry I know, he must do everything possible to get his hands on your *babe*. But don't worry. If the *babe* likes you, Jerry would be rebuffed. But rarely has he been rebuffed.'

'I want to go because Nyadiba needs my company, you know, just to keep his spirit up, not that I like the church.'

'I know. Of course, to like that church you have to be depraved. Is it not the church where boys and girls go only to dance and caress themselves erotically?' Bambam asked. Ezenwa grimaced and stood up.

'I have to go. It is already late to be walking around alone,' he said.

'Where is the gun? Bambam asked.

'Here,' Ezenwa lifted his jacket to show Bambam the gun he tucked into his trousers.

'With that you don't have any problem. Just fire some shots and run away before you could be identified. Your assailants would run too. Nobody wants to die.'

'That's all right,' Ezenwa said and started moving towards the door, but turned again. 'Another thing,' he said and sat down again. 'One ugly boy intruded into my girlfriend's room two days ago, do you know him?'

'Describe him,' Bambam said. Ezenwa gave him a vivid description of the boy. Bambam laughed heartily.

'Bully, that's his name. He is a fool, but not dangerous, although he could be deadly if your *babe* follows him into his room. Don't worry about him. He is quite harmless. He follows women about and amuses them. Whenever they smile back at him, he savours the gesture for a whole week. If I were you, I will tell her to show a little interest in him. You know, hold his hand, joke with him and call him endearing names. There will be a time she would need somebody as a shield. That time, instead of showing yourself to your enemies, you allow Bully to cover you, and perhaps get the bullets first. Then you will know where the bullets come from, and plan your own defence. In this university, there is always a need for a shadow. Allow Bully. Instruct your girl to be good to him, then he would be happy and do your dangerous walks for you.'

'That's all right,' Ezenwa said, reflecting on the wisdom in Bambam's advice. Bambam was intelligent, but dangerous too. Ezenwa had never thought he needed anybody to use as a shield. Now that Bambam had suggested it, he would tell Nneka to encourage Bully.

It seemed Ezenwa could not do anything again on the campus without first telling Bambam. He liked Bambam. But from what he had heard of him from Nyadiba's room mates, it would be better to stay away from him whenever he could, else he would one day be involved in a gunfight over something he did not know. Besides getting involved in a duel, he did not want to be seen as Bambam's loyalist.

Nneka had been waiting for Ezenwa's arrival, although unsolicited menacing visitors no longer inundated her privacy. But since the previous night Ezenwa left her room while that ugly boy was still there, she had been fuming about the way he left her unprotected with the boy. She would tell him how she felt by such arrant negligence. What if the boy had meant to harm her? Of course, he would tell her that he had given her a dagger, and that he expected her to resort to the use of it. Well, they would talk about that. It was time she told him that she was not Brutus. Nneka was still sulking when Ezenwa tapped on the door.

'Who is there?' she asked furiously.

'The idiot you are waiting for,' Ezenwa replied. Nneka walked briskly to the door, trying to maintain her furious countenance. She wanted him to know how she felt, and was not in the mood for his humour.

'Hmm, You look like a person who has eaten raw yam,' Ezenwa chided as he stepped into the room. What is the problem?'

'Why did you leave me with that ugly boy?' Nneka asked angrily.

'Mind your words, the boy is not ugly,' Ezenwa replied.

'What do you mean?' Nneka asked, baffled.

'A man is ugly only when he is poor. That is the only time his ugliness would be noticed,' he explained.

'I am not in the mood for your jokes. Why did you leave me with him?' she asked again.

'You are annoyed because the guy looks like a poor boy. That was why you and your room mates were making fun of him. If he were a rich guy like Pastor Jerry, all of you would be killing yourselves to jump into his bed.'

'Pastor Jerry? Do you know him?' Nneka asked, shocked.

'Yes. Why do you ask?'

'He came here this afternoon.'

'Here! To do what?' Ezenwa asked, enraged.

'I don't know where he saw me and followed me. I heard a knock on my door and opened it. He came in and told me that he is Pastor Jerry of Hope of Heaven Christian Church. I was alone, and before I could say anything, he sat down on the bed.'

'And what happened next?' Ezenwa asked, seething with anger.

'He told me that he likes me, and would like to know me intimately. I was astounded. I could not say anything before Sandra came in. He invited us to his church and left. Here are the invitation cards.' Ezenwa stared at the invitation cards. They were the same card Jerry gave to Nyadiba's girlfriend.

'But why does he invite only women?' Ezenwa asked Nneka. She stared at him and blinked.

'You ask as if I am his wife. How would I know why he invites only women?' Nneka replied.

'Do you want to honour the invitation?' Ezenwa asked tauntingly.

'Me? Go there? For what?' Nneka asked, perplexed that Ezenwa should even think about that possibility. Then, carefully and mirthlessly, Ezenwa told her about Pastor Jerry's encounter with Nyadiba and his girlfriend, and what he learnt from a friend about Jerry. He was careful not to mention Bambam's name. A word about Bambam would have frightened Nneka and made her suspicious of Ezenwa and everything he did.

'Do you want to go to the church?' Nneka asked surprised.

'We shall go.'

'You and who?' Nneka asked.

'Both of us,' Ezenwa replied.

'Nobody will see my legs inside that church. Even if I die and somebody takes my corpse to that church, I will get up and run away.'

'You don't understand. I want you to go with me. I want him to see you with me just to scare him away. Besides that, Nyadiba's girlfriend was invited too, and she insisted on going. Nyadiba did not want to go. But he is afraid his girlfriend would fall for Jerry if he allows her to go alone, so he begged me to accompany them.' Nneka did not like the idea, but was obliged to accept Ezenwa's proposal, just to satisfy him, but not without adding biting remarks to her acceptance.

'I will go with you. Perhaps you want to hand me over to him too, the way you handed me over to that ugly boy last night.' Ezenwa laughed.

'I have told you that a man is never ugly unless he is poor. If he is rich, nobody will see his ugliness. In fact, I wanted to tell you to encourage the boy,' he added.

'What do you mean?' Nneka asked with a wry countenance. Ezenwa then told her what he heard about the boy and begged her to encourage him with pretences.

'What if I end up falling in love with him,' she asked jokingly.

'As long as it is your desire, I will not interfere,' Ezenwa replied.

It was Sunday morning. Ezenwa woke up early and prepared elaborately for the hypocrisy at Pastor Jerry's church. He had woken up with a frazzled mind, and would have jettisoned Pastor Jerry and his church from his mind if not for Nyadiba's interest. Moreover, he had compelled Nneka to accompany him, and knew that she must have been ready and waiting for him. Thus he prepared hurriedly and went to Nyadiba's room. He was surprised to see Nyadiba already waiting patiently for him.

'What women would do to men in this world is yet to be seen,' Ezenwa chided.

'I don't understand,' Nyadiba replied with smiles. He knew the jeer was meant for him.'

'Yes, I know you would not understand. But I know that you did not sleep last night, because you were thinking about Jerry and your *babe*. That's why you woke up so early to prepare. If not for her, you will still be sleeping, waiting for me to come and wake you.' Nyadiba understood the jest, but merely smiled and stood up. Together they boarded a taxi to Eyo Ita Hall and were surprised to see Nneka still on her bed in her nightgown.

'Look at this girl,' Ezenwa shouted. 'What's wrong? Are you not going with us?'

'Honestly I am very tired. If there is a way out, I would like to rest.'

'No, there is no way out. Prepare and let's go and dance the bizarre orchestra,' Ezenwa urged. Nneka sighed and started preparing, but slowly and without enthusiasm.

'What about Kate?' Ezenwa asked Nyadiba.

'I am going to call her,' Nyadiba said and left the room.

Nneka wore a short black skirt and a white blouse. Ezenwa stared at her and sighed.

'Why did you sigh? Don't you like my dress,' she asked.

'I like it, but I think the skirt is too short. In fact, I don't blame those following you about like vultures. You invite them too.' She smiled mirthfully and sat down on the bed beside him.

'You want me to go to Pastor Jerry's church. Don't worry, you are going to compete with him over me. I am going there to distract him. Sandra told me about him last night.'

'If I see him within twenty yards of you, I will strangle him. But beware of what you do before the anger of God falls on you. Don't go there just to tempt a man of God,' Ezenwa jeered. Nneka laughed again, and threw her arm across his shoulder.

She knew that Ezenwa could kill anybody out of jealousy for her, and when it was a notorious pastor, he would just be too glad to eliminate him. Ezenwa could even lay down his life to protect her. This had been one of her greatest worries. But for now, she needed to quieten Ezenwa's mind and expunge the jealousy the discussion about Jerry had ignited in his mind. She got up from the bed and sat down on his legs, knowing full well that she could take liberties with him in her room with her three room mates still dozing peacefully. She had been tempting him in this way whenever she felt she was safe. He remained silent and thoughtful. She pushed him down on the bed and started kissing him. He had never made any resolute and lustful approach towards her. He had been wondering what her reaction would be if he attempted any sexual conduct with her. He knew she would not reject his overtures, but he did not want to make any move that would elicit misgivings from her about his interest. In matters of sex, Ezenwa was imperviously rigid. Seeing Nneka as she was, innocent and pure, gladdened his heart. Perhaps it was that unsullied purity that bound him to her. She continued to kiss him. His groin became turgid, and he responded by an attempt to touch her indecently. She stood up immediately.

'We are going too far,' she said and smoothed her skirt. That instant, Nyadiba tapped on the door.

'We are coming,' Ezenwa said and straightened his rumpled cloth. Nneka opened her door, greeted Kate animatedly and asked why she liked Jerry's church.

'Not that I like the church, but he is my friend, and he has invited me many times. I can't continue to refuse the invitation all the time.'

'Do you mean that Jerry is your friend?' Nneka asked and made a derogatory gesture with her hand.

'Yes and no, in the sense of intimate friendship, he is not my friend. But I know him and we often chat,' Kate replied.

'He was here last night, and I could only compare him to a dog,' Nneka said, an allusion meant to warn Kate.

'That's his business,' Kate said with a wave of the hand. If Kate was piqued by that allusion, she did not show it.

Chapter 26

Hope of Heaven Church had no designated building as a church. The congregation met regularly for their worship at the main hall of the Faculty of Arts building. Pastor Jerry had rented the hall for all the Sundays of the year. Every Sunday, a big board in front of the building, with the inscription "Hope of Heaven Christian Church" indicated the presence of the church.

That Sunday, Jerry came very early to the building with some members of the church to give the hall the tidiness it required. He had distributed more than a thousand invitation cards and was of the hope that at least half of his invitations would be honoured. Thus he did not want to disappoint his new guests. He had made extra effort to select the prettiest girls in his congregation to usher in the newcomers. His girls wore white blouses and short erotic black skirts. None of them could bend down to pick anything on the floor without exposing her pants. This was one of the attractions of the church, the celebration of nudity.

Ezenwa, Nneka, Nyadiba, and Kate walked majestically into the church. Nneka wasted time in preparation, thus they arrived when the church was already filled to the brim. There were two men on the altar, Jerry and a guest pastor. Pastor Jerry was saying prayers with outstretched arms. His eyes were unblinkingly focused to the entrance of the church. Ezenwa and Nyadiba walked in first, followed by Kate and Nneka. Jerry knew Nyadiba, Kate, and Nneka, but had never seen Ezenwa, so he paid no attention to him.

Nneka's arrival had her unique influence on everybody in the church. Jerry's prayers that moment could have been anything but prayers. He was hypnotised. He lacked concentration and started mumbling and jumbling his words. It seemed he was praying more to Nneka than to God. He was carried away so brazenly that some people were unable to hide their disgust and embarrassment.

There were few empty seats inside the church. Ezenwa and Nyadiba stood at the back and compelled Nneka and Kate to move up to the front and look for a space to sit. But there was no empty seat in the front row too. Somebody called them from the middle and pointed at two empty seats. Kate moved first, followed by enchanting Nneka, who deliberately swung her hips tantalisingly. In truth, even an impotent man would have his potency restored just by a look at her.

Ezenwa fixed his gaze on Jerry. Jerry had started saying incoherent things the moment the sensuality for Nneka supplanted his sensibility. Abruptly, he turned his back to his congregation and faced the wall of the altar. Ezenwa laughed.

'What is it? Why did you laugh?' Nyadiba asked.

'Look at Pastor Jerry,' Ezenwa replied.

'What happened to him?'

'He had an erection while staring at Nneka, so he turned to the wall to hide the erection from the congregation.'

'Are you sure?' Nyadiba asked.

'I saw it clearly.'

'Why didn't you tell me on time. I would have indicated it to Kate too. She thinks Jerry is a good pastor. Imagine the embarrassment, a pastor having an erection while praying for his congregation.' Jerry turned abruptly again and faced his congregation.

'Go and tell Nneka to move again, I am sure it will happen again,' Ezenwa told Nyadiba. Nyadiba went to Nneka, whispered into her ear, and pointed at the altar. Jerry stared at Nyadiba without any glint of decency. Nneka got up again, walked up to the front of the church, whispered to one of the ushers, and started walking back sensually. Ezenwa and Nyadiba fixed their eyes on Jerry's groin. Suddenly, the erection started again, jutting out glaringly. It seemed some people saw it too and started murmuring. Nyadiba ran to Kate, whispered into her ear and pointed at Jerry's groin. Kate bowed her head shamefully and pushed Nyadiba away.

Ezenwa continued to whisper to Nyadiba, pointing at Jerry. The guest pastor must have guessed what was happening, and acted quickly. 'This is the time for healing and exorcism,' he said and took the microphone from Jerry.

'I think it will be better if these pastors exorcise themselves first,' Ezenwa whispered to Nyadiba.

'If anybody in this church needs exorcism, it is Jerry,' Nyadiba replied.

'Let's wait and see what is going to happen.' Ezenwa suggested.

'Close your eyes and call down the *Holy Spirit*,' the guest pastor instructed. Jerry started walking round the altar with his eyes firmly shut, muttering indistinctly. The whole congregation joined in what they called a prayer. The hall resounded with absurd brouhaha. Some bleated like goats, others cackled like hens. The guest pastor shrieked and hopped on one leg, moving forward and backwards, thrilling everybody. The noise grew in intensity. Ezenwa covered his ears with his hands. He had never experienced such absurdity. Half-naked girls jumped up and down, making incoherent sounds, and exposing their nakedness.

'What kind of god listens to this noise?' Nyadiba asked Ezenwa.

'A deaf god. They have to shout for him to hear. Since he does not want to listen to honest prayers, perhaps faked ones may interest him,' Ezenwa replied.

'What if he does not hear this noise?' Nyadiba asked.

'Someone else would act on his behalf,' Ezenwa said. It seemed the pastor heard what Ezenwa said. He hushed the congregation imperiously. The once mutinous crowd became dead quiet.

'While we were at prayer, the *Holy Spirit* whispered to me,' the pastor said, 'there is a girl here who had been having acute headache. The *Holy Spirit* said that it is not an ordinary headache. It is a kind of headache caused by evil spirits who are bent on harming her for her faith in the Almighty God. We shall pray for her now and destroy the work of the evil one. The girl in question is sitting at the back row.' He pointed at the back row, and three girls came out at the same time. The pastor pointed at one of them. 'Yes, it is you, you have the description

I got from the *Holy Spirit*. The *Holy Spirit* said that your name is Jane,' the pastor said.

'No, my name is not Jane, my name is Ann,' the girl said and turned to go back to her seat.

'Ok, it is still the same thing,' the guest pastor said, 'Ann or Jane. Your name may be Ann, but the *Holy Spirit* knows you as Jane. The way of the spirit is different from the way of men. He knows each of us by a different name.'

'What is the meaning of the names we assume at baptism if the *Holy Spirit* does not recognise it?' Nyadiba asked Ezenwa.

'Shhh, allow them,' Ezenwa hushed him.

'I don't understand,' Nyadiba persisted, 'Just the noise here alone is enough to give somebody a headache.'

'Do you question the wisdom of Jerry's *Holy Spirit*?' Ezenwa asked sceptically.

The girl walked up to the altar and knelt down before the pastor.

'I want you to stretch your hands towards this our sister and pray for her and deliver her from the burden the devil loaded on her head, which has been causing the headache,' the pastor instructed and stretched his hand too. The hall erupted in another round of brouhaha. When the prayer stopped, the pastor started a song. Everybody started dancing, except Ezenwa and his friends.

Suddenly, the pastor hushed the congregation again and said, 'while we were praising God, the *Holy Spirit* told me that there is a barren woman here. If she would come out for prayers, an angel is waiting here with her baby, and would give it to her immediately.' The congregation applauded hilariously.

'What part of the church is the woman sitting?' Nyadiba asked Ezenwa.

'The *Holy Spirit* did not say. Perhaps the *Holy Spirit* does not know if there is a barren woman in the church, so he did not say where she is sitting,' Ezenwa whispered.

'If she would come out for prayers?' Nyadiba commented.

'The angel would give her the baby,' Ezenwa completed.

'And if she did not?'

'The angel would go back to heaven with her baby,' Ezenwa concluded. The pastor waited for a while, and nobody came out.

'It seems the *Holy Spirit* has forgotten that he is in a university campus,' Ezenwa whispered to Nyadiba, 'and that almost all the girls here are spinsters, and being spinsters, they would not know if they are barren.'

'The *Holy Spirit* got it wrong this time,' Nyadiba agreed.'

'No, he is not wrong, he only made the mistake of speaking to a guest pastor who came from a district where barren women seek miracles to end their woes, thus he assumed there must be barren women here too. If it were Jerry, the *Holy Spirit* would not make that mistake. He would have known the kind of problems inherent in a university campus,' Ezenwa explained. Nyadiba wanted to say something, but Ezenwa did not allow him.

'Stop talking, or do you want the *Holy Spirit* to afflict you with dumbness?' Ezenwa asked. The guest pastor stood up and pointed at those sitting at the back row of the church.

'It seems he has spoken again,' Nyadiba said, laughing.

'There is a girl here, she is under the influence of demons,' the pastor said. 'The *Holy Spirit* has just ordered that we liberate this daughter of Abraham. Let the girl come out now.' A girl started running towards the altar. 'Praise the lord!' the pastor shouted.

'Alleluia!' the congregation chorused.

'Sister what is your name?' the pastor asked her.

'My name is Mary Magdalene,' she replied.

'What? Mary Magdalene?' the pastor asked.

'Yes,' the girl answered.

'Why did you choose the name of a sinner. The bible said that Mary Magdalene was a prostitute, and that seven demons had gone out of her. And for you to have taken her name, you attracted the demons that came out of her,' the Pastor explained.

'But Mary Magdalene was the first person to whom Jesus appeared after his resurrection,' Nyadiba told Ezenwa.

'Shut up!' Ezenwa said, 'how can you question the wisdom of a man of God? What is your other name?' he asked Nyadiba.

'Paul,' Nyadiba replied.

'Don't you know that as far as these charlatans are concerned, the demons that possessed Paul when he stoned Stephen to death can possess you too, here and now?'

'So I need exorcism?' Nyadiba asked.

'Jerry's *Holy Spirit* will arrange that with you, so that when the exorcism starts, you will know what to do to make it seem real.' As if Ezenwa was part of the plan, his words were manifested in the exorcism of Mary Magdalene. Jerry, his guest, and his congregation stretched their hands towards Mary Magdalene and started shouting and screaming their prayers. In accord with what she planned with Jerry, she fell down and started rolling down the hall, screaming. Jerry and his guest ran after her and showered mutinous prayers on her. Perhaps tired of rolling, she stoop up and staggered back to her seat. The guest pastor started a hymn, and his gullible followers joined.

'Why should one fall down when demons are being exorcised from one?' Nyadiba asked.

'It happened in the time of Christ. And if it does not happen like that now, it would look as if the exorcism did not work,' Ezenwa replied.

'Praise the lord!' the pastor shouted again.

'Alleluia!' the congregation choroused.

'We thank God for delivering our sister from the grips of demons,' the pastor said. The *Holy Spirit* was about to speak to him again, and would have spoken. But it seemed the *Holy Spirit* had concentrated his messages on a guest, to the ire of the owner of the church. Jerry whispered something to the pastor and took the microphone from him.

'It seems the *Holy Spirit* is going to speak to Jerry now,' Nyadiba commented.

'He has already spoken, Jerry is about to tell us what he told him,' Ezenwa jeered.

'Perhaps the *Holy Spirit* told him something about Nneka,' Nyadiba teased.

'And this church, with the whole congregation, will be burnt down today,' Ezenwa threatened. Jerry had been following the activities of his guest pastor. Only few things the pastor did fitted into Jerry's plan. The fake exorcism was Jerry's plan. Nneka was the utmost thing in his mind, and nothing had been done to hoodwink her. As far as Jerry was concerned, if nothing was done to decoy Nneka into his hands, his effort that day would be without value. And if he did not intervene, as he did, his guest would waste precious time in faking miracles, and Jerry's craving would remain unattended.

Jerry knew his desires, and some members of his church knew them too. They had seen him staring at Nneka a while ago and some of them were waiting to see what he would do about her. Nneka saw him staring at her again after he had taken the microphone from the guest pastor. She deduced that he was about to say something about her. She frowned and waited for him. The frown on her face warned Jerry. He wanted Nneka and did not want to scare her away from his church. Thus he turned his attention where he thought his motives would not appear questionable to Nneka. He went for Kate first.

'While we were singing, the *Holy Spirit* whispered to me,' Jerry said.

'I told you!' Nyadiba exclaimed.

'There is a boy here with HIV. The boy is aware of this, but he is afraid. The *Holy Spirit* has revealed it to me, and is waiting to cure the boy before the HIV develops into AIDS. I want the person to come out and receive his healing now. Praise the lord!'

'Alleluia!'

'This is going too far. Who will agree to play this part,' Nyadiba asked.

'Let's wait and see,' Ezenwa replied. Jerry waited for a while, and nobody came out. He walked up and down the hall, and told the congregation to pray so that the *Holy Spirit* would divulge more information about the person. The prayer started again. The dance started too. The oddity was heightened this time. Jerry bent down and started moving backwards, groaning like a person in pains. Then he stood up all of a sudden and raised his hand. The prayers stopped. Jerry was gifted with more adroitness for fraud than the guest pastor. The way he controlled the emotions of his congregation had a mark of ingenuity. Everything he did seemed real.

'I got a shocking revelation from the *Holy Spirit* now,' he said. 'The *Holy Spirit* said that the boy could not be healed, but that his soul could still be saved. If he dies, there is a great chance for him to get to heaven. But the most important thing the *Holy Spirit* revealed is that there is a girl about to be infected with this virus. The *Holy Spirit* is now warning the girl to stay away from the boy. Now brother,' Jerry said gently, 'we are going to pray for you and commit your soul into God's hand. Even if you die, your soul will be saved.' Everybody started looking askance. Nobody knew whom he was addressing.

'You,' he pointed at Nyadiba.

'It is you he is talking about,' Ezenwa told Nyadiba.

'If he is talking about me, then he is a mad man,' Nyadiba said unperturbed. Jerry shut his eyes again and started muttering what he called prayers of revelation.

'It seems the devil wants his soul in hell, and has made him obstinate,' he uttered. 'We shall not allow this among the children of God. Our mission is to save souls. If the devil is here with us, we shall expel him and give the soul of our brother to God.' Nyadiba did not move from where he was sitting. Jerry called out some boys sitting in the front row and spoke to them in whispers. Cunningly, they walked down to the back of the hall, blocking every exit from the hall. Two people stood beside Nyadiba and Ezenwa.

'Bring him up,' Jerry ordered. Four strong hands grabbed Nyadiba's two arms and started dragging him towards the altar. He grappled with them, but his resistance lacked impact. Ezenwa attempted to rescue his friend. He held Nyadiba's leg and started pulling him back. Jerry said something and pointed at Ezenwa. Four boys dashed towards him. He left Nyadiba's leg, eluded them, and ran out of the church.

Afraid that something must be brewing to encompass her, Nneka looked left and right, and jumped out throw the window on her left.

They laid Nyadiba on the altar, pinned him down with their hands and immobilised him. He kept shouting that he has no disease.

'Don't worry about that,' Jerry told him. 'My only joy is that your soul will be saved after this'. Nyadiba kept struggling and complaining. Jerry called his guest pastor, and together they bent down over Nyadiba and exercised, in the words of Ezenwa, their spiritual ineptitude on him.

'Go and tell your god that he is a stupid god,' Nyadiba shouted, still in captivity. Everybody in the church had joined in the prayer. Even those who were holding him down shut their eyes and shouted their prayers too. Their saliva rained down on his face like waters of baptism. When he noticed that if he continued to struggle, they would continue to hold him down, and would continued to baptise him with their saliva, he stopped struggling and shut his mouth. That was a great error. The congregation believed immediately that their prayers had exorcised the demon of obstinacy in him, and for that, he stopped to struggle.

Kate covered her face with her hands and started weeping. She too believed Nyadiba stopped struggling because the demon of obstinacy had left him. Jerry saw her, and knew that he had triumphed. He told those holding Nyadiba to leave him. Grinning, Jerry said, 'go now and thank God that you have been saved. Nyadiba got up, threw a glance at Kate, saw her countenance, and knew that she had swallowed Jerry's deception. Sorrowfully, he left the church, but promised Jerry another encounter.

Nneka ran to the entrance of the church, and met Ezenwa where he was looking for a weapons to invade the church. She had her dagger in her handbag, but intuition and the fear of dire consequences of Ezenwa's possible action held her back from offering the dagger to him. She knew Ezenwa well and knew that nothing at that moment could have restrained him from stabbing Jerry to death if he could get his hands on that dagger. Ezenwa was still looking for weapons, planning how to rescue Nyadiba before they saw him coming out of the church.

'Now everybody believed that I have AIDS,' Nyadiba cried.

'Where is Kate?' Ezenwa asked.

'She is still there,' Nyadiba uttered tearfully.

'Did she believe Jerry?' Nneka asked.

'She is crying, I think she believed him,' Nyadiba replied and shook his head sadly.

'Let's wait for them and see what will happen after the dismissal,' Nneka suggested. They walked to the post office opposite the church and sat down on the pavement. They heard Jerry telling the congregation to dip their hands very deep into their pockets and make their offerings.

'The measure you give is the measure you will receive. And remember that God loves a cheerful giver,' Jerry said.

Ezenwa guessed that the service would end immediately after offering. The money from the offering was the main reason for the establishment of the church. The offering lasted for almost an hour, then the service came to an end. People started coming out, but Kate remained inside the building.

'What could be happening?' Nneka asked.

'How would I know,' Nyadiba replied. 'If nobody else is inside the church, I would have said that Jerry has started doing his act right there, but there are still about two people within.' Nyadiba was still talking when Jerry came out of the church, holding Kate's hand. He walked to his car. Kate followed him as if she was hypnotised.

'Let's attack him now and burn his car,' Ezenwa suggested.

'No, it is not now. We have to plan it so that we don't get into trouble,' Nyadiba cautioned. Jerry opened the side door for Kate and she entered. He threw a quick glance at Nyadiba and drove away.

'His next target is you,' Ezenwa told Nneka.

'If I see him in my room again, I will stab him,' Nneka warned sternly.

Undaunted, but wary, Bambam had started going into the dilapidated building again to smoke his Indian hemp. His assailant was still unknown, and other cults were still on red alert, waiting for the reprisal they knew must come. This fear of retribution grew daily. Cult members were distressed and restless. That was the peril of cult membership. Any member of any cult was a potential victim. And until there was a reprisal, they would continue to live in grisly fear, clustered and encumbering themselves in specific rooms. Notorious ones disappeared completely from the campus.

Ezenwa had nothing to fear, except for those on whose toes he might have stepped on while protecting Nneka. He was not bothered either. Anybody who attempted any ignominy towards Nneka should take whatever would come to him. After what Pastor Jerry did to Nyadiba, Ezenwa was prepared for any kind of malicious defamation from anybody at any time, and was prepared to stop it if he could. Since the day of that incident at Jerry's church, Nyadiba had been walking about the campus with the stigma of a HIV carrier. Ezenwa knew that Bambam had heard about the incident, but was waiting for him to come and discuss it with him.

Still incensed by Nyadiba's ordeal at Jerry's hand, and anxious for vengeance, Ezenwa groped for his way in the darkness to Bambam's room. Perhaps the trap Bambam set had caught Jerry and Bambam did not know.

There was light inside the room. Ezenwa tapped on the door and called Bambam at the same time. Bambam opened the door and held it for him to enter.

'I heard your friend is a HIV carrier,' Bambam said and laughed in a comic way that sometimes gave him the appearance of an imbecile.

'That's why I came to see you. You have been laying traps for Jerry, perhaps you can do with what my own trap has caught,' Ezenwa said.

'No, it is not that way. My own trap caught him last night,' Bambam said, 'but we don't have the time now. I forgot to tell you that this university is very tough. The examination starts early next month, and you need to study hard to pass. I was about to come to your room to tell you this. From what I saw, you have wasted a lot of time running after that your girlfriend to the detriment of your mission here. You know that you have a major mission besides her. So I think it is time you give attention to your studies, else you fail woefully. As for Jerry, I am going to leave everything for next semester. I know whom I am after and who is after me. When we come back from holidays, we shall settle our scores.'

'You mean I should abandon my girlfriend?' Ezenwa asked, astonished.

'No, that's not what I meant. I want you to dedicate more time to your studies than you are doing now, so I want you to leave the hostel and move to a place where she would be free to visit you any time she wants. Where she can sleep if she likes. Now, she can't study anywhere without being disturbed by cult boys, and you would continue to waste your time trying to protect her.'

'I can't rent a house outside the campus, it is very expensive,' Ezenwa complained.

'I have a boys' quarter attached to one of my lecturer's house. I paid for it last year but have not lived there. You can live there if you want. It will help you a lot,' Bambam offered. Ezenwa smiled and thanked him. There, he would have all the time he needed with Nneka. He still remembered the ugly circumstance that brought Bambam into his life, but he had continued to thank providence for throwing Bambam at him. The University of Nigeria Nsukka offered accommodation to students, but those who detested communal life rented houses outside the campus. The most coveted, admired, and greedily sought were the boys' quarters attached to the residencies of the university lecturers within the campus. Tenancy in a boys' quarter offered complete privacy and profound tranquillity. To live in a boys' quarter in the University of Nigeria Nsukka was a prerogative of the rich. Ezenwa had never imagined that he would ever be blessed with such possession. Nneka would have the opportunity to visit him at all hours, and they would study as they used to do, without intrusions from cult boys. With

Bambam, in the eyes of Ezenwa at that moment, the unimaginable could happen.

Chapter 27

Ezenwa packed into the boys' quarter, but was still afraid that something might happen to Nneka on the way from her hall to the boys' quarter. He sought a way to avoid such misfortunes. At first, he was confused and distressed, and was unable to find a solution until Nyadiba advised him to engage the services of one of the cyclists on the campus. The cyclist would bring Nneka to his room daily, and Ezenwa would pay him at the end of every month. That seemed to be the solution to the problem. But when he met the cyclists, they were not interested performing such duties. Only one of them had the patience to listen to Ezenwa's distressed solicitation. And as he bargained with Ezenwa, he saw Nneka coming towards them, smiling. He became enchanted. Ezenwa smiled back.

'Is she the person you want me to bring to you every day?' the cyclist asked.

'Yes,' Ezenwa replied. A look at Nneka's smiling face that moment could force any man to grant any request she made, just to continue seeing that face.

'Is she your girlfriend?' the cyclist asked.

'No, she is my sister,' Ezenwa tactfully lied.

'In that case, I will do the job free of charge,' the cyclist offered. Ezenwa smiled inwardly. Here was a man who had been insisting on an outrageous fare. Just a look at Nneka's face, he decided to do the duty free of charge.

'No,' Ezenwa refused. 'I want it to be a deal so that there would be no room for failure.'

'I accept,' the cyclist replied. Ezenwa thanked him and went away with Nneka.

As long as Ezenwa remained a student of the university, he could confide in Bambam in matters of security and remain unruffled. People said that Bambam was a devil, but Ezenwa had started liking him even in his devilry. However, certain thoughts sometimes taunted him that Bambam might be after his girlfriend after all. These thoughts often left him disconcerted and gloomy. Yet he did not stop to confide in Bambam. After Bambam had given him the advice about his mission in the university, and followed it up with the gift of a tenancy in a boys' quarter, Ezenwa almost worshipped him.

He had accepted Bambam's advice and studied diligently. And when the examination came, it was not as difficult as he had thought it would be. Perhaps it was because he studied assiduously and made up for the lost time.

On her part, Nneka's classmates saw her as a girl whose beauty got in the way of academic proficiency. She was denigrated as academically incompetent. Some even thought that it would be abysmally unjust for God to bless her with such exquisiteness and academic aptitude at the same time. Some students wished that her good fortune ended in her beauty.

The examination had ended two weeks after it started. Students started going home for holiday. Contrary to Ezenwa's expectation, the holiday was only for a period of two weeks. He had hoped it would be up to a month. Nevertheless, two weeks were enough for him to rest and sleep with his eyes closed, after three months of rigorous studies and frenetic foreboding over the safety of Nneka. In the village, his anxiety over her safety would stop for a while.

He travelled back to the village for holiday together with Nyadiba and Nneka, just the same way they left the village. Their parents received them like heroes from a war. For Nneka's parents, the fact that she was their only child made her presence in the house, though fleeting, a source of immense joy. Nyadiba's mother received him with smiles, and his father received him with an embrace and exacting questions about his lecturers and their ideas about the Second World War and Hitler.

Ezenwa's parents were not at home when he arrived. His grandfather embraced him with smiles and a pat on the back.

'Nnaa!' Uyanna exclaimed, 'how was your studies?' he asked.

'Not difficult, only that I was often hungry,' Ezenwa replied.

'I know you would always be hungry. And you did not bother to visit home at all?'

'I was unable,' he replied. He was unable to leave the campus because he was afraid that Nneka would be molested. He preferred to live with austerity than lose sight of Nneka for a day.

Ezenwa stayed at home two days and did not see Nneka. In the morning of the third day, he became restless and desperate to see her. Before the evening of that third day, he could no longer endure her absence, and decided to visit her. He knew that he liked Nneka, and always liked to be with her, but the intensity with which he desired her on that third day frightened him. He had never imagined that Nneka had that kind of frightening and unrelenting influence on him. He only prayed that nobody in his family, especially his grandfather, would notice his restiveness and ask him questions.

Nneka, on her part, was tormented by Ezenwa's absence too, and would have visited him if not for the fear of his grandfather, whose legendary powers had generated a lot of misgivings in the town, inducing a lot of unimaginable and mysterious fears where none should have existed. She knew that her parents would soon discover her obsession with Ezenwa, and it would become a source of anxiety to them. To eschew this anxiety, she started mollifying their minds about him with scary stories of cult boys, and Ezenwa's exacting and unrelenting fights to protect her. She made great effort to make them see the necessity of keeping Ezenwa as a friend. The story made a great impression on them that when Ezenwa visited her on that third day, Nneka's parents received him like her Guardian Angel. Her mother embraced and thanked him with tears. Her father spoke to him almost like an equal. Nneka was astounded by their effusion of affection, and was happy that her stories had done the magic. She was almost convinced that if her parents were later to catch her in any sexual misconduct with Ezenwa, they would look away, and pretend as if nothing had happened.

'Why didn't you bother to visit me?' Ezenwa asked Nneka.

'Who said I did not bother?' Nneka asked in return. 'I was almost at the end of my forbearance. I wanted to come, but was afraid of your grandfather,' she replied. Ezenwa smiled mirthfully.

'Why are you afraid of my grandfather?' he asked.

'I don't know, people said that he speaks with spirits, and that he could turn a human being into an animal,' Nneka answered. Ezenwa grinned.

'It is not true,' he said. 'He is the best man I have ever known in my life. I would like you to meet him and form your own opinion of him, and forget about the opinions and misgivings of other people.'

'You mean I should come to your house?' Nneka asked fearfully.

'Yes, what is wrong with that? Am I not in your house now?' Ezenwa asked overbearingly.

'Ok, it is not a problem. I will come tomorrow, but be sure to be at home,' Nneka warned. He conjectured what her reaction would be if she came to his house and did not see him. She would be dead with fear before anybody could ask her any question.

They conversed intimately and unencumbered by Nneka's parents. After two hours, Ezenwa stood up to go.

'So soon?' Nneka asked.

'What do you mean? I have been here for two hours,' Ezenwa replied.

'Hours? It seemed like minutes.'

'I am sorry, I can't help it. If I stay a minute longer, my grandfather would not like it,' Ezenwa said as he sauntered out of the house.

'Why? Doesn't he like me?' Nneka asked, perturbed.

'I had never heard him say that he hates anybody, so why should he start with you?' Ezenwa asked, 'besides that, he doesn't know that I have come to see you.'

'Why then would he be annoyed with you?'

'I don't know. You can ask him when you come,' Ezenwa replied, laughing.

'Would he answer if I ask?'

'Yes, why not. You will be surprised that he is not what you think he is.'

'All right, until tomorrow,' Nneka said.

They were already about five hundred metres away from her house before she noticed the distance she had gone. She stopped, bade him farewell, and started walking back in haste.

'Why the haste,' he asked.

'I have to help my mother in the kitchen,' she replied.

'Wait, I have a favour to ask you,' Ezenwa pleaded. Nneka stopped and waited for him to talk. Ezenwa went close to her and grabbed her two hands.

'I am not going to let you go unless you kiss me,' he said.

'What has come over you?' she asked, amazed. 'Have you forgotten that we are in the village? Or do you want my name to be announced in the village church, and I would be asked to make a public confession?'

'It's nobody's business,' Ezenwa replied.

'For you, it is nobody's business. But for a woman, it is everybody's business.'

'I won't leave you unless you kiss me,' he insisted.

'Please leave me,' she pleaded. 'Holding my hands is already a scandal, or have you forgotten what happened when we were preparing for the Matriculation Examination. This time it would be worse, because the villagers would conclude that I have gone to the university and slept with all the boys that came my way, thereby lost the sense of shame.'

'It is....' She did not allow him to finish what he wanted to say before she pulled her hands away and started running back to her house. He stood there and stared at her departing figure.

Nyadiba was in Ezenwa's house when Nneka came. She knocked gently on the gate and waited. 'It is her,' Nyadiba told Ezenwa.

'Who?' Uyanna asked.

'Ezenwa's wife,' Nyadiba said jokingly. Uyanna turned to Ezenwa, looking aghast.

'But you did not tell me you are married?' Uyanna asked Ezenwa.

'I will tell you later. But do this for me first: tell her that I have gone out, then frighten her. She is afraid of you. I want to see her reaction,' Ezenwa begged Uyanna, and dashed into the house with Nyadiba. Nneka knocked again on the gate.

'Who is there?' Uyanna asked. 'Come in, the gate is not locked.' Uyanna's voice alone produced goose pimples all over Nneka's body. With a trembling hand, she pushed the gate and came in. Her beauty dazzled Uyanna. It was with great effort that he suppressed the urge to reciprocate her smiles and greeting.

'Who are you?' he asked sternly.

'I am... my name is... is Ezenwa at home?' she mumbled with fear. Every part of her body was shaking. Ezenwa and Nyadiba observed everything from their hiding.

'I did not ask who you are looking for, I told you to identify yourself,' Uyanna said again, this time with a wry face and a harsher voice. Nneka started shaking, and inadvertently dropped her handbag.

'My name is... my name is Nneka,' she stammered.

'It is not true. You are a spirit and I am going to turn you into a vulture,' Uyanna threatened. She gasped and her eyes became misty immediately.

'Let's go out before she urinates in her pants,' Ezenwa told Nyadiba.

'That's if she has not urinated already,' Nyadiba said as they emerged from their concealment. Nneka saw them and ran to Ezenwa, screaming. Uyanna started laughing.

'Stop screaming, nobody is going to turn you into a vulture,' Ezenwa told her, trying to allay her fears and make her calm. She hid behind him and peeped at Uyanna. It was only when she saw Uyanna laughing that she stopped shouting. Then it became obvious to her that Ezenwa and Nyadiba had planned the joke. She sighed and started pouring insults on them.

'I am sorry my daughter,' Uyanna said, 'your husband told me to frighten you.' Nneka shifted coyly.

'He is not my husband,' she said bashfully.

'Then what am I to you?' Ezenwa asked.

'You are an idiot to me,' she replied, still furious for the joke they played on her.

'She is afraid of you grandfather,' Ezenwa told Uyanna. She said that you eat with spirits and turn people into animals.'

'It is not true my daughter. The truth is that I am making adequate use of the intelligence God gave me to help humanity.'

'God? Do you believe in God?' Nneka asked, baffled. Uyanna laughed.

'That's one error of judgement everybody in this town makes. They mixed up things and concluded that I don't believe in God. But tell me, who is God?' Uyanna asked. Nneka did not have any knowledge of God beyond what she learnt from her Christian catechism, and she proffered it.

'God is a spirit. He is great. He existed by himself and has no beginning or end.'

'Good,' Uyanna said. 'Now tell me, what is spirit?'

'Spirit is a living being, which we cannot see, hear, or touch,' Nneka answered.

'Very good, you have answered well,' Uyanna said. 'If I eat and talk with spirits, and God is a spirit, then why do you think that I do not believe in God.'

'That is not the issue,' Ezenwa interjected. 'I sometimes get confused by some things you do.'

'Like what? Uyanna asked, baffled that Ezenwa misunderstood him too.

'Like offering sacrifices at the shrine of Udo,' Ezenwa replied.

'Yes it is true. You often come to the shrine of Ogwugwu in front of my house,' Nneka accused too.

'No, don't be hasty,' Uyanna pleaded. 'I will explain everything clearly to you. But you must tell me one thing. Who is Udo and who is Ogwugwu?'

'They are idols made by man from wood,' Nneka replied.

'And worshipped as God,' Ezenwa completed.

'And you, what do you think?' Uyanna asked Nyadiba.

'I don't know,' Nyadiba replied.

'You are right by saying that you don't know, because you don't really know,' Uyanna commended Nyadiba. 'Your friends said what they were told, and that is where their knowledge ended. Now listen,' he said slowly and almost inaudibly as if he was about to divulge a mysterious secret to them. 'Udo is a name of a man, a slave who was captured when our ancestors fought with Umuohi people. It was at a period when neighbouring towns besieged our town with wars. So it happened that valiant men were always fighting to defend the town, while cowards stayed at home with the women. Unfortunately, it was also the period when our women were flagrantly unfaithful to their husbands.

Some invaders had invaded our town. They burnt our houses, stole our yams, stole our livestock, and whatever they could lay their hands on. As if these things were not enough, they took some women away, including the king's first wife and his beautiful daughter. The king's daughter was the most beautiful girl in the region, just like you,' he pointed at Nneka. Nneka giggled and covered her face with her hands.

'Where you there that time?' Ezenwa asked.

'No, it was in the days of my great grandfather,' Uyanna replied.

'Then how do you know that the king's daughter was like Nneka?' Ezenwa asked.

'Because nobody could be more beautiful than this,' Uyanna replied, pointing at Nneka again. She smiled timidly.

'Are you...?' Ezenwa wanted to ask another question, but Nyadiba did not like the interruptions.

'Oh! Ezenwa stop that. I want to hear the story. Please continue,' Nyadiba pleaded.

'As I was saying,' Uyanna continued, 'the incident was tragic. The king could not bear the loss of his wife and his beautiful daughter. And to make the matter worse, nobody knew where the invaders came from. The king assembled the most valiant men in the town, sent them after the invaders, and told them not to come back to the town without his daughter and his wife. They left the town and came back after two years of fighting. Happily, they returned with some women including the king's daughter and his wife, but they were devastated in spirit when they got back to their homes.

'What happened? Why were they devastated?' Nneka asked.

'Their wives have defiled themselves with adultery and got illegitimate children when their husbands were away at war. The joy of a successful campaign was supplanted immediately by the anguish of betrayal. Infuriated, the warriors went back to the king and demanded that these illegitimate children be exterminated with their mothers. The king refused to accede to their entreaty, and told them that the children born behind their backs represent a generation of our people. He asked them what would happen to the town if they kill those children, and were later attacked by their enemies when it would be the turn of those children to fight for the town; the whole town would be destroyed. Of course, the warriors thought that the cowards at home were the fathers of the illegitimate children. They were unaware of the fact that the king himself was the father of almost all the children. One of the warriors argued that the children were born by cowards who could not go to war, and that the children would become cowards like their fathers, because cowards beget cowards. The king argued too that none of the children would be a coward if valiant men trained them. The warriors accepted the king's verdict and went home.

At that time, Udo was a slave owned by the community, and he slept at the Village Square opposite the king's house. He knew the women who slept with the king while their husbands were at war. He knew when the affairs started and when they ended. He could even say with frightening clarity the favourites of the king, and how many times each of them slept in his house. You know that to raise a child born by an unknown father was the most humiliating thing for an Igbo man, and worse still when that child was in a position of patrimonial inheritance with the man's biological children.

Udo knew that the warriors were curious to know the fathers of their illegitimate children, so he went to them, and bargained to divulge the origin of their bastard children upon the payment of a huge sum of money. Out of curiosity, the warriors paid Udo, and were shocked to know that the king was the father of almost all the children. They grudged, but kept quiet.

It happened that Udo was an astute businessman. His condition as a slave did not impede his dexterity in business. With the large sum of money he collected from the warriors, he started trading. His wealth grew immensely, almost in proportion to that of the king. And with the wealth, he became numbered among the wise men of the town. His status as a slave diminished. The king became jealous of him, because many people started going to Udo for counsel instead of the king.

The influence of the king continued to dwindle in the eyes of the people until Owa people, our neighbours on the west, invaded our town. The king sent for the warriors. They came, but without their weapons. This baffled the king, and he asked them if they wanted to fight with bare hands. One of the warriors summoned the courage and told him that they would not go to war, because they were afraid that he, the king, would take their wives if they leave them and go to war. Another told the king that they had married new wives after he had defiled the old ones, and that they would not let him defile their new wives. "They are still new and young", was what one them told the king. Others agreed. The king was distressed. He did not know that the warriors knew that he was the father of their children.

Unable to convince them to fight, the king conducted an investigation, and discovered that Udo divulged the secret. He called the leaders of the town immediately, and told them that he had decided to make a deity that could detect and punish unfaithful wives. He said this to allay the fears of infidelity on his subjects, and convince them to go to war.

'What about men who would be unfaithful to their wives?' Nneka asked.

'It is not a crime for a man to be unfaithful to his wife. It is the woman's infidelity that counts,' Uyanna replied mischievously.

'Please stop interrupting him,' Nyadiba said angrily.

'So the king told his warriors what he has decided to do,' Uyanna continued, 'they accepted, but as you know, deities are made with human beings.'

'How?' Nyadiba asked.

'To make a potent deity, a human being must be buried alive and a shrine erected over his head.'

'Why do they use human beings?' Nneka asked.

'Because they needed their spirits,' Uyanna replied.

'How?' Nyadiba asked.

'When a person is being buried alive, he will be afraid to die, and will be making agonising struggles to free himself. His soul will be filled with bitterness and hatred for those who are burying him. Thus he will start cherishing the thoughts of vengeance. And when he is finally buried, that desire for vengeance would make him impure to appear before God. The spirit will become what the Christians called demon. It will continue to roam about the world, causing disasters and taking vengeance on those who killed him.'

'How does the deity work?' Nneka asked.

'Being a spirit, it would no longer be bound by space or time. It can be anywhere it wants to be, just by desire. A simple thought about him calls his attention. So when those who killed him come to that spot where he was buried, that fury for vengeance brings him to the spot immediately. But unfortunately, it has no body, so it cannot avenge physically.'

'What happens next?' Nyadiba asked.

'As you know, nobody goes to a deity without an item to be used in a sacrifice. And what is sacrificed to every deity is always what the person who was buried likes when he was alive. When he comes with the zeal for vengeance, and sees his favourite food, the desire for the food rises, and the desire for vengeance subsides. The intensity of the desire for two things

42

cannot be equal. Desire for one thing must always be greater than the desire for other things. When the worshippers have pacified the ire of the spirit with the food, it will be disposed to listen to whatever the chief priest would say. It likes the food, and would want to eat it, but cannot, because it has no body. The sacrifice is the only bait to attract it. Have you ever heard the words used in offering sacrifices?' Uyanna asked. They did not answer. It seemed nobody knew. 'Ezenwa you must know. You have gone to many shrines with me,' he told Ezenwa.

'I know he knows. Pagan!' Nneka said and laughed.

'I was a little boy then, I have forgotten everything,' Ezenwa added.

'When offering sacrifices,' Uyanna continued, 'the priest of the deity starts with praises of the deity, making references to it as a god and a protector, at the same time, throwing the food at the shrine. This makes the spirit glad. The praises will mollify its anger against the people. Being an impure spirit too, it immediately accepts the praises and honour meant for only the Almighty God, and goes ahead to do whatever they begged it to do.'

'How can it do what they want since it has no body?' Nneka asked.

'No, tell us what happened to Udo first,' Nyadiba countered.

'When the king told his warriors his intention,' Uyanna continued, 'they accepted, but maintained that they would go to war only when the deity has been made, and its efficacy tested. As you know, the king needed a human being to make the deity. He was a wise king who knew the hearts of his people and knew how to get there. He told them that he was going to use his first son, the heir to the throne, to make the deity. The people rejected the proposal. Besides being the heir to the throne, his son was one of the most valiant men in the town. He was a warrior with distinction. The people did not want to lose him. The king then told them to bring another person to be used. Some people told him to buy a slave and use the slave.

With that suggestion, the king got exactly what he wanted. He told them that the war could not wait for him to buy a slave. Some people insisted on buying a slave, and wanted to go in search of one, others wanted somebody among them to sacrifice his son. As nobody would ever agree to sacrifice his son, the king made a proposal to them. He told them that there was a slave among them whom they could use. Everybody remained calm to understand what he meant. One of the warriors told the king to explain exactly what he meant. The king told them that he had decided to use Udo to make the deity. Tumult broke out immediately. Udo was a rich man, and had made a lot of friends. His friends wanted to protect him. Some people who did not like Udo agreed to the king's proposal. Udo's friends asked the king why he had decided to use Udo. The king told them that Udo was a slave, and belonged to the community, and that besides being a slave, he had the skill to detect women who were unfaithful to their husbands. This skill, he told them, would remain with him even as a man, he would be excellent as a god. With that, there would be no need to test his efficacy. The warriors understood immediately what the king meant.

After the king's explanation, his words swayed the hearts of many. The opposition to his proposal died as quickly as it started. Before the end of that day, Udo was buried alive. And the people went to war.'

'But is he doing what they needed?' Nneka asked.

'Perfectly,' Uyanna said, 'it is from Udo that we got the *Nkedione*.'

'What is it?' Nneka asked.

'It is a black thread, which the priest of Udo gives to men who think their wives are in love with other men. The man receives the thread with a promise to come back and show his gratitude to Udo if he catches his wife and his lover. The thread is then hidden at a place where the woman would walk across it unknowingly. After that, the husband takes the thread back to Udo's shrine. From that day onwards, if anybody who is not the woman's husband meets her sexually, his penis will be glued firmly inside the woman's vagina. And they would remain inseparable until the priest of Udo makes the atonement sacrifices.'

'What will happen if the priest did not make the sacrifice?' Nneka asked.

'The two lovers will die,' Uyanna replied.

'This is strange,' Nneka said.

'Can you get the thread for me?' Ezenwa asked.

'What do you want to do with it?' Nneka asked, alarmed.

'For you,' Ezenwa told her.

'You are mad,' she shouted and struck him playfully with her handbag. Nyadiba and Uyanna laughed.

'No, you cannot use it on her, she is not your wife,' Uyanna told him.

'Now tell us,' Nyadiba pleaded, 'how does a deity work, since it has no body?'

'Yes, that's what I wanted to know,' Nneka added.

'It is true that he has no body, but he has accomplices in man,' Uyanna explained.

'I don't understand,' Nneka said.

'Man by origin was meant to be higher than these impure spirits whose urge for vengeance, and sometimes greed, has turned into demons,' Uyanna said. 'Man, from creation, has the grace of the Almighty God at his disposal, but through his impure thoughts and bad deeds, he severed the connection to the grace of God, and brought himself to the level of these spirits. And through greed and insatiable wants, especially the urge for vengeance, man sometimes descends lower than these spirits. In error, man called them *gods*, and gave them dominion over himself, thus became victim of their wiles. When one asks a deity for a favour, the deity, being a living spirit, would start weaving a web that could bring about the desires of the supplicant. It achieves this by inspiring thoughts in the minds of people whose actions could bring about the desires of the supplicant.

'So a spirit can only inspire a thought in somebody, and does not force the person to obey?' Nneka asked.

'Yes, it cannot force anybody to obey. Nobody, not even the Almighty God, meddles with the freedom he has given to man at creation. But the thoughts these spirits inspire are always very strong, and sometimes irresistible for those whose minds are not fortified by virtues. That is what the Christians call temptation,' Uyanna explained.

'What about those who use human beings for money making rituals, is it by inspiration too?' Nyadiba asked.

'Like I said earlier, these spirits are impure, and are attracted by impure desires. Greed is an impure desire. When somebody wants something desperately, these spirits would read his thoughts, and make suggestions to him. And being bad spirits, the suggestions they would make must always be bad, just like a bad tree that produces bad fruits. Only a man under their influence would think of using another human being for rituals.'

'Does it mean that anyone could be a victim of the powers of these spirits?' Nneka asked.

'No, not everybody. If you keep your thoughts and deeds pure, they cannot come close to you. Your pure thoughts automatically link you to the Almighty God, who is purity itself. His power would be transmitted to you through that link. And when you have that link, these impure spirits will always run away from you.'

'When you go to these deities, don't you call them god, don't you put yourself below them?' Nneka asked.

'Formally I did, but when I learnt about them and their nature, I stopped. Now they obey my commands with fear.'

'What do you mean by fear? Are they afraid of you?' Nyadiba asked.

'Yes, every impure spirit is afraid of me,' Uyanna affirmed.

'Why are they afraid of you?' Nneka asked.

'Because I have purged myself of greed and all impure desires. I have a direct link to the Almighty God. I have the knowledge of their nature. I know the words with which I can torment them.'

'Torment them? What words? Please tell me,' Nneka pleaded.

'You mean you don't know?' Uyanna asked, baffled.

'Yes!' they all answered.

'And you claim to be Christians?' he taunted.

'But we don't know,' Nneka maintained. Uyanna gaped at them in astonishment.

'Tell us please,' Nyadiba pleaded.

'The words are only two,' Uyanna said.

'But we don't know them. Tell us please,' Ezenwa begged.

'JESUS CHRIST! that's all,' Uyanna said finally.

'Oh, I know it, only that my faith is not strong. But as you have said it now, my faith will get stronger,' Nneka said.

'I know it too,' Nyadiba said, 'but how do I use it?'

'Just call "JESUS CHRIST" with faith, and the bad spirits would start shrieking.'

'But you said something earlier about repelling them with good thoughts, I don't understand,' Ezenwa said.

'You remember that I told you that God is supreme and almighty,' Uyanna said in response to Ezenwa's last question. Being almighty, he can do everything. He has no beginning and has no end. He is goodness to infinity. If one links himself to him, one shares in his immensity and power. It is like connecting to a power generating plant to have electricity in your house. And with the electricity, you can operate different machines in your house. But the only wire to connect to God is good deeds and good thoughts. And the only way to carry out good deeds is by helping other people. With these, greed would be defeated. And you will have the attributes of God, and no similarity with the impure spirits. Only then can you repel them.'

'I don't understand,' Nneka said.

'Let me explain it clearly,' Uyanna said. 'For example you are a very beautiful girl. There is a force, a kind of great power God attached to your beauty, but you don't know. If you use your beauty to attract men, indulge in sexual activities with them, and collect gifts from them just to adorn and take care of your body, then you are using this force in a negative way, for selfish ends. You cannot be selfish unless you are greedy, and greed is a sin that taints the soul greatly. With that, you will have similarity with these impure spirits. Naturally, that alone can attract them to you. You will be detaching yourself from the Almighty God, and the power that came with your beauty would die. Then you will no longer be impenetrable to the inspirations of these demons. But if you keep yourself pure by not indulging in any sexual conduct, you can, just by the power of your will, command man and spirit, and they will obey you instantly. The more you resist the advances of men, the closer you get to God, and the closer you get to God, the more your will power grows.'

Ezenwa had started seeing changes in Uyanna's religion. He knew Uyanna was hitherto against every tenet of Christianity. Now, telling them that Jesus Christ tormented demons baffled him. He wanted to confront Uyanna with the accusation, but decided to wait for Nyadiba and Nneka to go before he could challenge him.

'But Grandfather,' Ezenwa interrupted him, 'there are things you do that I don't know how such things happen.'

'Like what?' Uyanna asked.

'When I was a child, you always know when something bad will happen to me, why?'

'I still know now, but since you are an adult, I cannot interfere in your life and impose my will on you. If I do that, I will lose that power. But to answer your question, you know that God's knowledge is infinite too. He gives it to anybody who asks for it.'

'How can one ask for it?' Ezenwa asked.

'You don't necessarily have to start praying and begging for it. It has already been given to you, but you need to create a space in your soul for it. And when it enters, you have to nurture it with good deeds and good thoughts.'

'I don't understand,' Nneka said, 'please explain it well.' Uyanna remained still and thoughtful for a while, then smiled.

'Go and bring a stone for me,' he told Ezenwa. 'Bring a handful of sand,' he told Nyadiba. They brought the items he required, and thought that he was about to perform a magic. 'Get a cup of water for me,' he told Ezenwa. Ezenwa brought the water. 'Now observe carefully what I am going to do,' Uyanna said, and poured the water on top of the sand. The soil absorbed the water. He poured the water on top of the stone. It touched the stone and glided off. 'Did you understand what happened?' he asked.

'No,' they said simultaneously.

'The sand absorbed the water because it has openings through which the water entered. That is exactly how the gaps we create in our souls permit the power, knowledge, wisdom, and favours from God to get into our souls when they are empty, and are not occupied by malice, greed, pride, sexual desires, vengeance, jealousy and other soul debasing tendencies. The stone has no space where the water can enter. That is exactly what happens to a soul filled with envy, pride, jealousy, greed, urge for vengeance, malice, selfishness, and sexual desires. And you know that selfishness does not leave any space for any virtue to come into the soul. Just as it wants to possess everything alone, it occupies every space in the soul alone. Don't you know that whenever we ask God for any favour, he gives it immediately, but his only means of communication with us, the soul, is always occupied with things contrary to his nature. His favour comes, and seeing no space through which it can enter, bounces off and goes over to an empty soul. No favour from God goes back to him after he has granted it.'

'I now understand,' Nneka said.

'I haven't finished,' Uyanna said and continued. 'The power to know what will happen in future is with God. And if one's mind is devoid of all these vices I mentioned, especially selfishness, which is the root of every vice, one must know what would happen in the future, because the knowledge is already with God. And one has a link with God through good deeds and good thoughts.'

Nneka seemed to be getting tired of the discussion. She looked at her wristwatch and stood up. 'I can't believe I have been here for three hours,' she said.

'What have you to do at home?' Ezenwa asked her.

'I have to help my mother to perform some chores.'

'I hope you are no longer afraid of me?' Uyanna asked her.

'I still have many questions to ask you. Until you explain everything to me, I will continue to be afraid of you,' she replied.

'Suit yourself, I am always at your disposal. Ask me whatever you want to know,' Uyanna said with smiles.

'Let's see her off,' Ezenwa told Nyadiba. Nyadiba got up reluctantly. He wanted to stay and continue the discussion with Uyanna, and at the same time, wanted to go with Ezenwa and Nneka. Nevertheless, he followed his friends.

Nneka did not have the time to visit Ezenwa's house again during the holiday. Her mother became sick with malaria, and she became occupied with the household chores. When her mother recovered, it was already two days to the end of their holiday.

Ezenwa visited her regularly. Sometimes he visited her together with Nyadiba, and helped her in some of the household chores. When it was time for them to return to the university, Nneka's mother was no longer worried about her safety. She had seen the tenacious dedication with which Ezenwa went about Nneka's interests.

Chapter 28

Ngadi was a debased professor of the Department of Microbiology. At the age of forty-eight, he was still a bachelor. There was a rumour that he had been exploiting and abusing female students sexually, but nobody had ever had the effrontery to make a formal accusation against him. He had noticed Nneka in his class the first day she attended his lecture. Her beauty was irresistible. Ngadi wanted her as he had wanted and exploited many female students. But being a crafty man, he did not want to approach Nneka flagrantly and give affirmation to the yet to be substantiated informal accusations some students had been making against him. He only noted her registration number.

Stories were rife in the university that Ngadi's evaluation of female students after every examination was always on their performances on his bed, and not on their performances in the examinations. Nneka heard these stories the first day she attended his lecture, thus she endeavoured to stay out of Ngadi's way. In spite of these efforts to stay away from him, students of the department continued to tell her that it was only a matter of time before she succumbed to Ngadi's wiles. As they predicted, it came earlier than she anticipated.

After the first semester examination, Ngadi searched for Nneka's papers and marked them, hoping that she would be a laggard, and from it, found a pedestal on which he would stand to manipulate her. Nneka's performance astounded him. It was overwhelmingly excellent that he could not see any way to classify her among the failures. If she had failed, Ngadi would have been very happy to post her result on the notice board, and pray that she continued to fail. But he knew from past experiences that brilliant girls like Nneka always fussed over their results, especially when they knew that they performed very well in the examination. The way Nneka carried herself, Ngadi knew that she would not waste any time before accusing him of sexual exploitation if he dared classify her among the failures. If she accused him formally, the university authority would request for her papers. How would he explain her failure with such an excellent performance? He pondered on this for a while, and decided to withhold her result.

Nneka searched for her result on the list of results Professor Ngadi posted on the notice board, but did not see it. 'What could have happened?' she muttered and searched all over again. 'God!' she exclaimed. 'What am I going to do?' she muttered again and started trembling. She knew that the absence of her result on that list would inevitably bring her in contact with the man she had been dreading. She started weeping.

One of her classmates, a boy, who had come to check his result too, saw her distress, and advised her to take the complaint to Ngadi.

'Go to his office?' Nneka asked, alarmed.

'What else would you do?' the boy asked.

'I can't do it,' Nneka replied.

'You must do it,' the boy insisted, 'the absence of your result could have been a mistake, and there is no way to correct it unless you inform him.' Nneka remained silent. The boy knew the game Ngadi wanted to play with Nneka, and knew what the result would be. His insinuation that it could be an omission was just to allay her fears, and compel her to seek her rights. Then he added, 'I know what you are afraid of.'

'If you know, why did you tell me to go and meet him?' Nneka asked, offended.

'I will go with you, if you want, but I won't go into the office with you. My presence in the vicinity will prevent him from using force on you,' the boy offered.

'Please come along,' Nneka pleaded, and they started walking to Ngadi's office.

When they got to the office, Nneka knocked gently on the door. 'It is open,' Ngadi replied. She turned the knob and went in. 'Yes, can I help you?' Ngadi asked.

'I did not see my result on the list of published results,' she replied.

'Sit down first,' Ngadi told her. Nneka sat down, but continued to stare at him.

'You don't have to worry about your result,' he said. 'You are a beautiful girl, and I have a special grade for beauties like you. You only have to say yes, and the best grade would be yours.'

'That's not what I am talking about,' Nneka said.

'What are you talking about?' Ngadi asked sternly.

'I have taken the examination sir,' she said, 'I am not talking about future examinations.' Ngadi frowned. He knew that Nneka would be difficult to get. He had to soften her.

'Well,' he said. 'If you took the examination, why didn't I see your papers?'

'I took the examination sir,' she insisted.

'But I did not see your papers. Please if you would not mind, I have a lot of things to do,' Ngadi said and opened the door for her. Nneka was astonished. She wanted to knell down and start begging him. 'Get out!' he ordered. Nneka jumped up from the seat, and almost ran out of the office, weeping. The boy who had accompanied her to the office shook his head in dismay and started consoling her.

Inside his office, Ngadi smiled happily. 'When next she comes, she would make the proposal herself,' he murmured.

Ezenwa, in his chaotic mind, tapped on Bambam's door. He was agitated by Nneka's report and was in a rage. If it were a case of another student, he would not have been flustered. But a professor! How would he solve the problem?

Bambam delayed to respond. Ezenwa thought that he was not in the room and asked where he could be at that time of the night. Bambam heard his voice and unlocked his door. Ezenwa saw the revolver in his hand and started shaking with fear.

'I was seconds away from pulling the trigger, then I heard your voice,' Bambam said.

'But why?' Ezenwa asked, alarmed.

'Some people are after me. There was an attempt on my life again this evening. When you knocked I thought they have come back.'

'Thank God you did not fire,' Ezenwa said.

'What is the problem? Tell me and get away as fast as you can. This room is not safe for you at the moment,' Bambam said impatiently.

'It is my girlfriend.'

'What happened?'

'There is a professor in her....'

'Professor Ngadi? He withheld her result?' Bambam completed. Ezenwa looked aghast.

'Yes. Do you know something about him?' he asked.

'I know many things about many people. When I saw your girl, I knew that nothing would stop Ngadi from attempting to exploit her. I have been waiting for you to bring this report. It is not a problem. That's the man's style for intelligent girls. If she were a dullard, her result would have been the number one to be published. But don't worry, tell her to go back to him next week.'

'Everything would be all right? Would he release her result?' Ezenwa asked, unconvinced.

'He will release her result,' Bambam assured. Ezenwa stared at him in amazement, confused on what next to do. If Ngadi would become obstinate, he did not know what else Bambam would do, and was afraid to ask him. He sighed once more. Bambam saw his exasperation, but it was not the time to console or play soft with anybody. His life is in danger too.

'Go! Go now! Run away! There is danger here,' Bambam told Ezenwa impatiently. Ezenwa opened the door, came out quietly, and started running, glancing back repeatedly to make sure nobody was following him. He knew Bambam would not kill him, but as everywhere was enveloped in darkness, they might take him for Bambam and shoot him.

Nneka had eaten the rice she saw in the pot, and reclined on Ezenwa's bed, mulling over the events of her life. Ezenwa tapped gently on his door.

'Yes, who is there?' she asked.

'It is me,' he replied. She got up, unlocked the door, and noticed that the perplexity on his face was no longer there. A confident restorative smile had replaced it. She wanted to ask him what happened, but he spoke before her. 'Go back to Ngadi next week. He will show you your result.'

'I don't understand. How can I go back to the man again after what happened to me today?' she asked.

'Don't worry. Just go. You will see your result, and he will never attempt to molest you again.' Nneka gaped at him. There was something unfathomable about Ezenwa. It seemed like magic. She wondered for a moment if he had inherited some of his grandfather's powers, but reasoned that such powers were not hereditary, and that if he had, she would have known. Sometimes, she got worried that she trusted him more than she trusted God. She wanted to know how he made these things happen. But he had often told her to listen to only what he was willing to tell her, and not be inquisitive about things he was not willing to reveal.

'But...but,' she wanted to argue again.

'There is no "but" about it. Go back to him next week and see your result!' Ezenwa insisted. She wanted to speak again, but heard the sound of the motor cycle. She picked her handbag and started moving towards the door.

'Why not sleep here today?' Ezenwa asked. She giggled. Ezenwa had never made any serious sexual advance towards her. She was well aware that he had been suppressing his sexual urge. So many times she had wanted to ask him how he felt about such sexual restraints, but could not muster the courage to indulge in such discussions. What would happen if she asked him and he wanted gratification? She knew she could never refuse his request. Is it not Ezenwa who had taken every kind of risk to protect her? If he wanted her, she would abandon herself to him willingly. But since he had not made an attempt in that direction, she could not tempt his forbearance by unnecessary curiosity. She had been praying that God should continue to keep his reins on him.

'Please Ezenwa, let's not subject ourselves to useless temptations. You know what will happen if I sleep here,' she begged.

'Nothing will happen,' he said with obstinacy.

'That's what you think. Please I want to remain a virgin until I marry.'

'Go, go, the cyclist is waiting for you,' he said and almost pushed her out of the room. She laughed and ran out of his room, thanking God for the day he created Ezenwa. It seemed he was created just for her.

She came back to Eyo Ita Hall in a lively spirit. Her room mates had seen her distress in the afternoon, and were baffled and piqued that she could not confide in any of them. It irked them that Ezenwa was the only person on whose side she felt safe. They started gossiping about her strange behaviour that afternoon, suggesting and analysing possible causes of her distress.

'It could be pregnancy,' Sandra suggested.

'Yes, it must have been pregnancy,' Uju agreed. 'If not pregnancy, what could have made a girl weep like that and wanted only her boyfriend?'

'It might not be pregnancy. It could be any other thing. Do you think that the only problem of a young girl is unwanted pregnancy?' Lucy asked Sandra.

'What else could have been her problem? I don't know what you think she is? A Saint?' Sandra asked.

'No, I am not saying that she cannot get pregnant. Why not? Is she not a woman? But I want you to understand that she is not as wild as you are painting her. She is our room mate, and we all know that she had been behaving very well,' Lucy maintained.

'Yes, Lucy is right Sandra,' Uju agreed. 'No other girl on this campus would have all these boys running after her and still keep a cool head. It is not easy. I agree she is not a Saint, but she merits commendation. Even if it is only for keeping to her boyfriend alone. Such decency from a beautiful girl like her is a miracle.'

'What beauty?' Sandra asked, choking with jealousy. 'Is she the most beautiful woman on earth?'

'Come on Sandra. Why are you jealous? Have you seen her naked?' Lucy asked and turned to Uju. 'Do you know that the first day I saw her naked, even as a woman, I was only able to control myself with great effort.'

While they gossiped, Nneka stood outside the room and eavesdropped on everything they said about her. What she heard discomforted her. That was one of the complaints she had taken to Ezenwa that evening. People were always watching her and analysing every move she made. She sighed and turned the doorknob. Her sudden appearance dried Sandra's next comment on her lips. She twitched.

'I know you must have been wondering why I was crying in the afternoon,' Nneka said. They were startled by her direct hit at the subject of their discussion. 'Perhaps I am pregnant,' she said and watched the embarrassment on their faces with amusement. Lucy and Uju guessed that she must have been eavesdropping, and thanked God that they were benevolent in their opinion of her, while Sandra was effusively malicious. 'My problem has nothing to do with pregnancy,' Nneka said and went ahead to tell them about her encounter with Professor Ngadi.

'Was that why you were crying?' Sandra asked, surprised.

'Yes, is it not a matter for tears?' Nneka asked.

'No, it is not,' Sandra said. 'If I were you, I would be rejoicing. Do you know the number of girls after that unmarried professor? Even if you don't marry him, just allow him to take you to bed once in a while. You have nothing to lose. You will pass all his examinations excellently, and whenever you have any problem with another lecturer, he would intervene on your behalf.'

'Hmmm!' Uju exclaimed. 'Why do you advise somebody to accept that kind of proposal?' she asked Sandra.

'Why not?' Sandra retorted. 'Is she a kid. Haven't you had sex?' she asked Nneka. Nneka only stared at her in amazement. For Nneka, that a girl could be flagrantly indecent was a sign of acute depravity, and for a university undergraduate, it was a detestable absurdity. She made her loathsomeness of such oddities known to Sandra immediately.

'I am not like you Sandra. You can do whatever you like with your life, but please never in your life again give me that kind of advice. I hate it,' she said sternly.

'I can't believe it. Are you a kid?' Sandra asked.

'A kid or an adult, what is the difference?' Uju interjected. 'You want her to satisfy the sexual desires of all her lecturers to make good grades in examinations.' Sandra turned and stared at Uju. Sandra had been sulking inwardly when it became obvious to her that Nneka eavesdropped on their conversation, and heard her malicious comments about her, while Lucy and Uju passed leniently as good people. She also knew that neither Lucy nor Uju would have rejected the professor's proposal. It piqued her that they were arguing hypocritically against her advice, and portraying her as an obsessively immoral person. Unable to bear the hypocrisy, she tongue-lashed Uju.

'Why do you pretend to be what you are not? I know you would have gone out of your way to tempt the professor. Why are you pretending to be the Virgin Mary?' Sandra asked Uju scornfully. Uju was incensed by her comment.

'Sorry Sandra,' Uju replied, 'if you don't have morals, do not think that nobody else has it.'

'Morals! Who is talking about morals? You? Uju? 'Sandra asked.

'Yes, me, I am talking about morals,' Uju replied.

'How can an abortionist talk about morals?' Sandra asked. 'Where were your morals when you had your abortion?' Uju winced. She was hurt immensely. Her face became cloudy.

She became pregnant from her first sexual experience in the university. Still naive, it had distressed her. She confided in Sandra. Sandra helped her to get the pregnancy aborted, and the deed had remained a secret between them. Now, because of a useless argument, Sandra divulged her friend's most guarded secret before her room mates, and before Nneka, whom Uju had always wanted to sell a posture of decency. Unable to bear the perfidy, Uju stood up, poked her forefinger in Sandra's face and said, 'yes, I might have had an abortion, but my body is not mercantile like yours. If you came to this university to whore, don't expect everybody to join you. Continue hawking your wares. Nobody is admonishing you for that, but please don't corrupt Nneka. She is still innocent.' Sandra stood up too. The argument degenerated into a brawl, and was about to turn into a duel. Lucy, being the oldest person in the room, with the help of Nneka, intervened to avert the impending fight.

'Stop this nonsense!' Lucy shouted.

'Please Uju, lie down on your bed and sleep,' Nneka pleaded. She was sympathetic to Uju, because it seemed Uju got the worst of the brawl. Her most guarded secret had been divulged.

Indeed, Uju had felt bad because she thought she was the only person with the abysmal stigma of abortion hanging on her neck. If she knew that Sandra had had abortion three times, she would not have been mortified. If she knew that Lucy had aborted twice, perhaps the gloom on her face would have been lifted. But grieving, she lay down on her bed and started weeping bitterly. Only innocent Nneka was distressed immensely by the abortion story, perhaps because of her innocence and inveterate morality. It would have been a pleasure to see the shock on her face when she would discover the rate of abortion in Europe, America, Australia, and other developed countries of the world. When she wanted to sleep, the abortion story distressed her. She started pondering on the selfishness and turpitude that led to abortion. Her innocence revolted, and she decided to ask Uyanna about it when she got home on her next holiday. She could not imagine why people should kill unborn babies, as they would kill insects, or remove malignant tumours, just to be free to indulge in pleasures. She started thinking. She remembered that one of her lecturers had formed a Human Rights Association and she had registered as a member. But what was the use? What right does an unborn baby have? Animal rights? She had heard about organisations that defended animal rights too. But apart from churches, none of these organisations defended unborn babies. It was all selfishness. If it were not selfishness, why should a human being indulge in pleasure and later reject the consequences of that pleasure. That was the problem of the world. Selfishness! Uyanna was right. What was the need of all these organisations? Organisations for the rights of this and the rights of that! Yet their results remained a heap of wrongs on the left. For Nneka, abortion was only a lamentable exhibition of Stone Age barbarism. What a noxious irony to hear that the countries that legalised abortion were the countries the whole world referred to as developed. Where was the development if their laws permitted heinous savagery that wild animals would recoil from? For a while, she pondered on the love with which wild animals protected their young. She pondered on the relief human beings felt after aborting their babies. She began to cry.

It was on a Friday afternoon. Nneka got back to her room very tired. Her lectures that day were protracted that she did not even have time for lunch. And Professor Ngadi was one of the lecturers.

She had been uneasy from the moment Ngadi came into the class, and she remained restless throughout the duration of the lecture. Her eyes were completely fixed on her book as she took down his dictations. She knew that he glanced at her from time to time, but she completely avoided his gaze. She also knew that he wanted an opportunity to talk to her.

When Ngadi told the students, after the lecture, to come to his office and choose the topics for their weekend research, Nneka knew it was only a ploy to speak with her. Instead of giving him that opportunity, she abandoned the research topic and went back to her room. She was very hungry, but too tired to go to the canteen. Since none of her room mates was available to buy food for her, she lay down on her bed and slept. She woke up when her room mates came into the room and started chattering. Then she looked at her wristwatch and shouted. It was already dark. The cyclist was already waiting for her, and she did not like to keep him waiting always. Ezenwa too would be agitated if she delayed. She started preparing hurriedly to go and see Ezenwa, perhaps eat with him. Little did she know that something terrible was waiting for her on the way.

.

Chapter 29

Ben Jack was a sex maniac. He had been involved in many rape cases, but had never been arrested by the police, or punished by the university authority for such impropriety until his last victim decided to take him up. That last case nearly sent him to jail if not for the involvement of the Red Scorpions. Jack was a member of the Red Scorpions' hit squad, and the Scorpions would never fold their hands and watch one of their leaders sent to jail. They intervened immediately. They kidnapped the daughter of the high court Judge, and threatened to murder her if Jack was jailed. The Judge, out of fear, did their wish and freed Jack. That perversion of justice was glaringly obvious to everybody. His last victim wept bitterly and resigned her quest for justice in the hands of God. She had done what others could not do, took the stigma associated with rape, and yet did not get the justice she deserved. However, she prayed that Jack would one day rape himself into trouble.

His real name was Benjamin Njakili, but he was popularly called Ben Jack. No woman had ever gone into his room and came out unmolested. He was soft spoken. His appearance had a deceptive suavity that when he spoke and smiled, his maniacal nature would be hidden under a captivating gentility. It was not that he could not convince women to have sexual intercourse with him. No, he only derived joy in humiliating and inflicting injuries on them. He did not enjoy sexual intercourse unless it was done against the woman's wish.

From the first time he saw Nneka, he had never stopped nursing the ambition of luring her into his room one day to rape her. On Nneka's first day in the university, Jack had tried to captivate her with smiles, but failed. When it became obvious to him that she would never succumb to smiling faces, he came with intimidation, thinking that every new student would succumb to intimidation. But that night when Nneka attacked him with empty bottles, he noticed that there was no fear in her eyes, and that his intimidation would not shake her. When he paid another girl living in the room opposite Nneka's to take Nneka's nude pictures, it was only a ploy to decoy Nneka into his scheme. Unfortunately, Bambam came back from the hospital and confiscated the pictures.

Ezenwa would not have attracted Jack's attention too if it were not for that attempt he made to defend Nneka that night. Since then, Jack had kept him under keen observation. From his observation, he discovered something about Ezenwa that started frightening him.

Nobody in the university, not even cult leaders, could befriend a girl like Nneka and keep her to himself alone without being molested. Every day Jack expected to hear that Ezenwa had been shot or stabbed. But nothing of the sort happened. To add to his confusion, Bambam himself begged him, and even gave him some money, to forgive and forget Nneka. Initially, he had thought that Bambam wanted Nneka for himself. He obliged and stayed out of her way. But day after day, he continued to see Nneka and Ezenwa, and each time he saw them, the urge to rape her increased.

The friendship between Bambam and Ezenwa was not a puzzle to Jack. All cult boys on the campus knew that Ezenwa was the person who rescued Bambam and took him to hospital that night Bambam was attacked. Jack knew this too. But in his weirdness, he refused to accept the fact that the help Ezenwa gave to Bambam was enough to stop Bambam from possessing a girl as pretty as Nneka. And if Bambam was unable to take Nneka from Ezenwa, from Jack's deduction, it only meant that Ezenwa was a strong fellow too, and that he must have somebody very strong behind him, somebody stronger than Bambam, under whose shadow Ezenwa paraded Nneka all over the campus without fear. Jack could not believe that Bambam did not want Nneka. Moreover, Jack had been baffled by the rare courage Ezenwa exhibited that night he went into the dilapidated building to rescue Bambam. All these fed his fears about Ezenwa.

Indeed Jack did not know why Bambam was still hesitant over Nneka. The beauty he saw in Nneka could not be sacrificed by anybody on the altar of gratitude, and while

Bambam hesitated, Jack decided to make another attempt that would be shrouded in discretion that neither Ezenwa nor Bambam would ever suspect his involvement. He contacted Nneka's cyclist.

The cyclist, initially, did not agree to participate in the crime. Ben Jack knew that he could not succeed unless the cyclist agreed to participate. He used coercion to get the cyclist into his plan. The coercion failed. He resorted to threats, and then back to coercion, but the cyclist remained obstinate.

'What do you hope to gain by refusing to take part?' Jack asked the cyclist.

'She pays me, and I am used to her. In fact, she is like a sister to me,' the cyclist replied.

'A sister!' Jack said scornfully and laughed. 'How much does she pay you?'

'It is not a matter of how much she pays,' the cyclist argued.'

'Tell me,' Jack insisted. 'I will pay you twenty times of whatever she pays.'

'It is not about money,' the cyclist maintained.

'What is it about?' Ben Jack asked sarcastically. 'You should be ashamed of yourself,' he taunted the cyclist. 'Every evening you go to her hall, pick her up, and take her down for another guy to *bang*. And when he finishes, you go there again and take her back to her hall. Are you not a man? What is wrong if you *bang* her too? Have you ever dreamt of laying your hands on such a beauty? Let's do it. I will *bang* and you will *bang* too. After that, you can disappear from the campus. You can do your cycling outside the campus.'

The cyclist remained silent. Indeed, he had never stopped lusting after Nneka. On few occasions when her body brushed against his body while they were on the motor cycle, he savoured the sensation for a long time. One evening, Nneka wore a mini skirt, and in the process of climbing on the motor cycle, she exposed her pants. The cyclist saw it, and that image had never left his memory.

From the silence of the cyclist, Ben Jack knew that he had made an impression on him, and continued. 'Yes, how can you be doing that kind of job for a small boy? Or are you castrated?' The last question swayed the cyclist into his plan. If it would be the last thing he did and died, he would never regret death. Anybody who heard that he died because he raped Nneka would not call him a fool. Who could resist such beauty?

Nneka wanted to put on her shoes, but felt they were dirty. She took the rag she always kept under her bed and started cleaning them. That instant, the cyclist hooted his horn impatiently. She wore the shoes hurriedly with the dirt on them and ran down the stair.

The cyclist bent down the motor cycle for her to climb, but she hesitated and continued to stare at him.

'What's the problem?' the man asked.

'It seems I forgot something, something I need now?'

'Today is the last day of the month, I hope you have not forgotten my money?' the man said jokingly.

'Yes, it is the money. Thanks for reminding me,' Nneka said and ran back to her room. What she actually forgot was her handbag, which contained the money and her dagger. She wanted to take the money and hurry back to the cyclist, but felt that searching for it inside the handbag would waste her time. She took the handbag.

'I have got your money,' she told the cyclist when she returned. He laughed, and started his motor cycle. Nneka sat down, and he zoomed off.

The moment they left the neighbourhood of the hostels, Nneka asked him if he had been waiting for a long time. The man remained silent. He had always talked garrulously every time he took Nneka to Ezenwa's house. Nneka asked him the question again, but he did not answer. She became bewildered and tried to imagine what could be the problem. She nearly asked him if he had any problem bothering him, but decided against it. She knew quite well that nobody had immunity against sorrows and grief. Whatever problem he had was not Nneka's concern. Since he had not told her that he had any problem, it would be impolite to ask him. However, in her generosity of spirit, she decided to add more money to his monthly fare, perhaps such gifts could alleviate the burden on his soul.

The motor cycle was moving very slowly. The haste Nneka saw in the cyclist when he was waiting for her in front of her hall had gone. She did not know why he was moving extraordinarily slowly.

They had just left the vicinity of the Faculty of Pharmaceutical Sciences, one of the areas where streetlights still functioned on the campus, and moved into the neighbourhood of the Faculty of Physical Sciences. From the Faculty of Physical Sciences to the Faculty of Engineering, down to Ezenwa's house, was in complete darkness. As they got close to the Department of Civil Engineering, just after the Faculty of Physical Sciences, Nneka saw when the cyclist bent down. She did not know what he did. The motor cycle jerked and stopped.

'Get down,' the man snapped. Nneka jumped down immediately. She was frightened by the hostility in his voice. If she could see in darkness, just a look at the cyclist's face that moment would have given her the fright of her life. The rigidity of his countenance made him look like a different person from the cyclist Ezenwa contracted. Nneka heard his venomous voice, and was hurt by it. She was unable to see any reason for such sudden aggression. Even if the man had a problem in his family, it had nothing to do with Nneka.

She looked around her. Everywhere was covered by darkness. There were flashes of light from cars going up and down the avenue, but they were not constant. She knew that nobody could do anything to her on the road. If she shouted, people at the University Library could hear her and come to her rescue. Besides that, she could hear voices of students at the Department of Civil Engineering some metres away.

It was only when he saw the cyclist touching one part of the motor cycle after another, without any concerted effort to fix the problem, and at same time, glancing furtively at an abandoned building behind the Faculty of Physical Sciences, that she became wary. All his acts were acts of a person trying to buy time, as if he was expecting somebody to emerge from the darkness. Nneka wanted to run away. But she reasoned that the man alone was incapable of doing anything to her on the road. If they were two, she thought fearfully, they could gag her, and push her into the gutter. The gutter was very deep that lights from passing cars could not illuminate it, and whatever would happen inside the gutter would happen without interference from anybody. With a gag on her mouth too, whatever sound she made would be stifled. She remembered cult boys. If they had paid the cyclist to betray her, there was no chance for an escape now. Her heart started palpitating heavily and rapidly. She started trembling. For precaution, she dipped her hand inside her handbag and unsheathed her dagger. 'Whatever you planned won't be easy,' she mumbled, clutching the dagger with her hand still inside her bag.

She heard footsteps behind her and turned, but was too late. She wanted to shout, but Jack, completely masked, covered her mouth with his hand. He had been hiding inside the gutter, waiting for the time when the road would be free of cars.

With his hand over her mouth, every sound she made was stifled. She bit him, and expected him to remove his hand. But Jack was obstinate. She held her dagger firmly.

'Let's get her away from the road quickly,' Jack told the cyclist. The cyclist bent down to lift her legs from the ground. She kicked him in the face. He fell inside the gutter. She dropped her handbag and stabbed blindly at her assailant. Jack screamed, and released her. The cyclist did not know what happened. He heard the scream of his partner and saw Nneka free of Jack's grip. He started coming towards her again. Nneka waited for him to get closer.

Another flash of light came from a passing car. The cyclist saw Ben Jack bleeding profusely, groaning, and clutching his sprouting intestines. The blood stained dagger in Nneka's hand was very conspicuous to escape his notice. He abandoned his motor cycle, and started running towards the University Library. Nneka did not contemplate chasing him. She removed her shoes, picked her bag, and started running down to Ezenwa's house.

Ezenwa had been be waiting for Nneka. He was worried that she had unusually delayed. His mind was filled with premonition of disaster. He wore his shoes hurriedly to go and look for her. He had hardly stepped out of his house before he saw somebody running towards him. Fear gripped him. He wanted to hide, but instinct warned him to get armed first. He dipped his hand into the waistband of his trousers and brought out his revolver. The running person slowed down his pace. Ezenwa noticed that it was a woman. It must be her, he thought, and hid his gun.

Nneka got to him and threw her arms around him, gasping for breath. Ezenwa saw the blood stained dagger and recoiled.

'What happened? What happened?' he asked in quick succession.

'Give me water,' she replied. He led her into his room and gave her a cup of water.

'What happened?' he asked impatiently. 'Did you kill anybody?'

'I don't know if he is dead,' she replied.

'But what happened? Who did you stab?' he continued to ask.

'I don't know. I did not see his face. It was dark, and he wore a mask.'

'A mask?' he shouted.

'Yes a mask.'

'Calm down and tell me what happened,' Ezenwa pleaded.

'I think I am cursed, but you would not believe me. I think it would be better for you to stay away from me before you get killed too.'

'Shut up!' Ezenwa barked. 'This is not the time for stupid talks.' Nneka took a deep breath and told him what happened.

'That's all right. You did the right thing. I am very proud of you. This is exactly what I expect from you, not foolish talks about curses. I am going out now. I will lock you inside the room. You have to sleep here, because I might not come back on time. If anybody knocks on the door, don't respond, unless it is Nyadiba. And if they try to open the door by force, put out your head through the window and shout. My landlord will hear you, and will come to your rescue.'

Bambam was coming out from the shop in Block A3 when he saw Ezenwa. He knew Ezenwa was going to his room, but did not call him. The anxiety on Ezenwa's mind was too heavy that he did not recognise Bambam. Bambam allowed him to move on, and followed him.

Ezenwa knocked on the door and identified himself, but no response came from within. He sighed and turned to go, then saw Bambam coming towards him. 'What happened?' Bambam asked. Ezenwa, breathing rapidly, told him punctiliously everything Nneka had told him. 'Did the guy die?' Bambam asked.

'She doesn't know. She ran away from the scene,' Ezenwa answered impatiently.

'That's very good. If she had remained there, it would have been a different story.' Ezenwa continued to tremble. 'Hold yourself. You look as if death is after you,' Bambam told him. 'Nothing has gone wrong. Calm down yourself. I will get them. Go back and stay with her. I will get back to you tomorrow,' Bambam said and started laughing merrily. Ezenwa flinched, and was extremely bewildered by such joyful disposition he saw in Bambam that moment. Bambam did not show any sign of repulsion from the story Ezenwa had just told him. Was he involved in the attempt? Ezenwa did not know, and would never know. The serenity on Bambam's face confounded him. It was as if Ezenwa had told him that Nneka stabbed a dog. Bambam was ruthless indeed, Ezenwa agreed.

Ezenwa started descending the steps slowly and fearfully, still wondering where Bambam got the fortitude to exhibit such jocularity after listening to such a gory story. He wanted to hurry back to his room immediately, but decided to inform Nyadiba too.

Nyadiba was reading a book he had borrowed from the University Library. His room mates were all awake when Ezenwa came into their room. The countenance on Ezenwa's face spoke so eloquently that Nyadiba's room mates did not guess twice before they understood that he was in distress. The cause of the distress, they guessed too, could never be far from cult assaults. Since that day Ezenwa rescued Bambam from the dilapidated building, they knew that he had embroiled himself in a cult intrigue, and they waited with trepidation for the day his doom would come. They only prayed that the incident should happen far away from their room. Now, with the perturbation they saw on his face, they knew the time had come. They gaped at him, waiting to hear the story of his eventual doom.

Ezenwa had wanted to tell Nyadiba the story before his room mates, but the anxiety on their faces made him wary. Since he did not yet know if Nneka killed her assailant, telling the story before anybody he did not trust could endanger Nneka's life on the campus. He took Nyadiba outside the room and told him everything. The story irritated Nyadiba.

'Why won't they leave that girl alone!' Nyadiba exclaimed angrily.

'I don't know. If I tell you that I know, I am lying. But I think it is because some people think they own this university. So they want every girl to be at their beck and call. Well, they are wrong about Nneka,' Ezenwa replied and made a move to leave the building.

'Do you want me to go with you?' Nyadiba asked.

'No, Bambam may want to get a message across to me, and naturally, he would come to you,' Ezenwa answered. Nyadiba understood. He had been carrying messages from Bambam to Ezenwa.

Nneka was still weeping when Ezenwa came back. She was no longer hungry. The thought that she might have killed somebody was tormenting her. She had been wondering how many more adversaries she would encounter before she would be free like other girls. Her first act of violence was on Solomon, then the boy she attacked with bottles, and now this. All these distressed her and obliterated the pangs of hunger she had been enduring.

'Still crying? Why?' Ezenwa asked.

'I am afraid I have killed somebody,' Nneka answered.

'No, stopping thinking about that. Would it have been better if they had raped you?'

'I was not sure they would have succeeded. I should have waited to know what they wanted to do to me before I stab him.'

'Your reasoning sounds stupid to me,' Ezenwa said angrily. 'If they had tied your hands behind your back before they started, with which hand would you have stabbed? And you are not sure they were not going to kill you. Can you swear that it would have ended only in a rape? What if they had wanted to kill you for rituals? I think you did something that is worthy of commendation. Very soon we shall know the identity of the assailant, and know if he is dead or alive. If he dies, I am sure nobody will miss him. Dry your tears, and please stop crying. Go and wash your face.'

Consoled and convinced, Nneka wiped her tears, and went to wash her face. She did not ask where Ezenwa had gone, or whom he had gone to see. But from previous incidents, she knew that whoever he had gone to see was powerful and reliable. Sometimes she shivered with fear when she imagined him joining a cult.

The cyclist returned to where Jack was groaning in pain. The sight was gory and sickening. He was tempted to abandon him and run away, but decided against it. If Jack died, Nneka would tell the police about him too, and he would not escape. He got a taxi and took Jack to the hospital

Bambam rushed to the scene of the incident, and saw nothing but a pool of blood. He could not confirm from that if the person was dead or alive. He ordered his most loyal boys to search all the hospitals in the vicinity for anybody with a knife wound.

Jack was already asleep when two boys from Bambam came to the hospital. They did not get close to him before they identified him. Before anybody could ask them any question, they were already out of the hospital and back to the campus.

Bambam tapped on Nyadiba's door. The sound was too weak that only somebody awake could hear it. Nyadiba knew it was Bambam. He always came at midnight when his room mates were already asleep, and any time he knocked, he always did it gently so that he would not wake those already asleep. His manner of knocking was unique, just three weak and spaced taps. Nyadiba unlocked the door. Bambam made a sign to him to come out of the room. Nyadiba followed him. Bambam told him to go and tell Ezenwa that he had identified the assailant. 'He is still alive,' Bambam whispered and went away immediately.

It was midnight. Nyadiba wanted to keep the message until the next morning, but remembered the anxiety he saw on Ezenwa's face. Only this information could assuage his friend's agitated mind. He took his revolver from his wardrobe, moved into the darkness, and ran all the way to Ezenwa's house.

Nyadiba knocked loudly on Ezenwa's door. Ezenwa was startled. He jumped up from the bed. Nneka got up too, shaking. Ezenwa's revolver was hidden under his mattress. He wanted to retrieve it, but did not want Nneka to see it. While he hesitated, the knocking resounded.

'Who is there?' Ezenwa shouted angrily and lifted the mattress hurriedly.

'Who were you expecting?' Nyadiba asked. Relieved, Ezenwa left the mattress and opened the door for him. 'The guy has been identified. He is alive,' Nyadiba announced on entering inside the room. With that information, the throes of hunger that had abated returned to gnaw at Nneka.

The cyclist disappeared from the campus. Bambam's boys were unable to trace him. Ezenwa did not have much information about him too. He did not even know his name. Bambam told Ezenwa to send Nneka to enquire about the man from other cyclists. Ezenwa doubted if other cyclists would divulge any information to Nneka.

'Her face alone would make them divulge more than she required,' Bambam assured him. Ezenwa enlisted Nneka's help.

Nneka walked majestically to a cyclist whom she had always seen conversing with her cyclist. The man knew that Nneka's cyclist had been absent from the campus, but did not know why. When he saw Nneka, his face lit up.

'Hello Pretty,' the man said. 'Where are you going? Come let me take you there. Peter has stopped coming to the campus.' So his name is Peter, Nneka mused.

'Where is he?' she asked with feigned gesture of disappointment.

'I don't know, but I saw him yesterday.'

'Do you know his house?' Nneka asked.

'No, but if it is something very important, I can ask other people.'

'Please do,' Nneka replied. The cyclist got down from his motor cycle and started asking other cyclists the location of Peter's house. Some minutes later, he came back to Nneka.

'His house is behind Saint Victor's Catholic Church at Onuiyi,'

'Any number?' Nneka asked.

'No, but they said it is the only house directly opposite the church, but be careful if you are planning to go there. They said that his wife is a tiger, and would tear your beautiful face into pieces if she sees you with her husband.'

'Thanks! Don't worry about me,' Nneka said and went back to her room. If Nneka knew who needed the information Ezenwa told her to get, she would not have involved herself in it. And if Ezenwa knew a bit of Peter's life history, he would not have given the information to Bambam. Unfortunately, they did not know.

Chapter 30

Peter was born at Enugu. His father was a poor coal miner, and his mother was a daughter of another poor coal miner. His parents got married when they were still very young. It was in the days the Colonial Masters managed the coal mining industries. Miners were paid wages that hardly sustained their families.

Peter's father was blessed with a big family. He had five children; two boys and three girls. Peter was the youngest in the family. His father never had enough money to take care of his children. They were always famished, and none of them went to school. Peter's three sisters were still very young when they got married to men of equal fortune as their father. His elder brother became an apprentice to a carpenter at a very young age. When his mates were yet to be weaned from their mothers, Peter was already learning the textile trade from his father's friend, Mr Udemba, who lived at Kano. The textile business was a lucrative business at that time, and would have guaranteed the decline of poverty in Peter's family.

Mr Udemba was a wealthy textile merchant. Many boys were learning the trade from him, and Peter was the youngest among them. Feeble and sickly, Peter's duty at the shop was never more than taking messages from Mr Udemba to his wife at home.

Mr Udemba's wife had no other job except cooking and procreation. Mr Udemba did not buy the lunch they ate at the shop from food sellers in the market. His wife prepared the lunch at home everyday. It was Peter's duty to go home at midday and bring the food for Mr Udemba and other boys at the shop.

One afternoon, he was waiting to take his master's food to the shop when two other apprentices ran into the house in distress. Mrs Udemba was bewildered by the sudden arrival at home, when they should be at the market. She asked them why they came back.

'*Awusas* are killing Igbos at the market,' one of them replied.

'Where is my husband?' she asked in panic.

'We don't know. Everybody ran away when they started looting our shop,' the second boy answered. Peter was scared to death. He dropped the basket of food he had lifted, sat down on a stool, and began to cry. That was the beginning of the grisly pogrom of 1966 that later led into a gruesome Civil War.

Many Igbos escaped from the market, and ran to the safety of their houses at Sabongari, an area reserved for strangers. The killings did not stop by nightfall of that first day as the Igbos had thought. Instead of abating, it suffused to every part of the city. That was when the Igbos became aware of its gravity. But it was already too late to do anything. They had been surrounded. With the participation of the Nigerian Police and the Army in the conflict, the killings attained a frightening sophistication and a horrifying magnitude. The killers invaded the strangers' area, and started killing those who had taken refuge inside their houses.

Mr Udemba had escaped from the market, and ran back to his house. He locked himself and his family inside the house, praying that the murderers would not remember them. But all of a sudden, they heard voices in front of their house. Peter and one of the boys sneaked out of the house, and went to the gate. The gate was firmly locked, but from a hole on it, they peeped, and saw their street littered with cadavers, a gory sight. Peter started crying again, but Izundu, his companion, hushed him.

They were about to run back and hide inside the house when they saw some people with machetes jumping into the compound from the western wall of the compound. Peter and Izundu ran to the opposite wall, and jumped into their neighbour's compound.

Their neighbour was an Hausa man and a Moslem. He was not at home. His two wives, perhaps already sick with the sight of dead bodies littering the street, hid peter and Izundu inside their houses. From their hiding place, Peter heard the noise in their master's house. They heard Mr Udemba's voice as he pleaded for mercy, and his wife's pathetic and distressing screams. Unable to remain impassive, they came out of their hiding, and saw their protectors looking across the wall into their master's compound. They went nearer.

Peter saw the killers when they dragged out Mr Udemba from the house, and brutally severed his head from his trunk. His wife was heavy with pregnancy. Before Peter's eyes, one of the killers lacerated her belly with a sword, and cut the unborn baby into pieces before cutting off the woman's head too. He saw his master's two daughters, nine and seven years old, raped to death by their father's killers. The sight was sordidly grotesque and nauseating that the women who hid Peter and Izundu started crying and pouring curses on the murderers.

Benumbed by what they saw, Peter and Izundu were too frightened to continue hiding inside the womens' houses. They did not know what else to do, or where else to go. The women inferred their dilemma and promised to help them escape at night.

At midnight, when they thought the road would be clear, they came out of the house. But the road was not free. So many people were still moving about, looting, raping, and killing. It seemed nobody paid attention to Peter and his partner because of their ages, and perhaps their boldness. The killers could not believe that anybody of Igbo origin could come out of his house at that time of the night, let alone two small boys. They looked at Peter and his companion and looked away.

There were mutilated and dead bodies everywhere. What haunted peter, and would continue to haunt him for the rest of his life, was the manner pregnant women were disembowelled. He had never stopped wondering if the perpetrators derived joy from such gruesome savagery. That day was the first time Peter perceived the unpleasant odour of blood.

They walked without glancing back until they were well out of the city, then they stopped and debated on what they should do. His companion wanted to wait outside the city until the killings stopped. But Peter had seen enough horror that he decided to walk back to Eastern Nigeria, a distance of about three thousand kilometres. Izundu objected to such a venture.

But when he saw Peter's determination to walk, he decided to walk home with him.

They walked for two days and were able to get to the outskirts of Zaria, another city of Northern Nigeria. It was at Zaria that they saw a lorry approaching. It was overloaded with passengers. Peter and Izundu assumed that it was going to Eastern Nigeria. They waved frantically. The driver saw them, and deciphered that they must have escaped the pogrom. He stopped. Peter and his companion climbed into the lorry hurriedly.

When the lorry moved into the city of Zaria, it ran into another holocaust that made what was happening in Kano look like a comedy. The passengers were attacked with gruesome ardour. Peter did not know the providence that saved him. When he jumped down from the lorry, he started running back towards Kano, probably, that was why he survived. Other people who escaped from the lorry and attempted to get to Eastern Nigeria were mercilessly slaughtered on the way.

Peter continued to run until he noticed that nobody was after him. He sat down along the road to rest. He did not know when he fell into a deep slumber. As if it were in a dream, he heard some people speaking in Igbo language. The voices were close and loud. He opened his eyes, and saw a man clutching the hands of two small boys, probably his children.

'Where are you going?' Peter asked the man in Igbo language, just to let the man know that he was of Igbo origin too.

'What are you doing here,' the man asked in return.

'I escaped from Kano, but they attacked us again at Zaria. I don't know where else to go.'

'Follow us,' the man told him, 'I heard that there is a church around here where a white priest is protecting some people.' Peter, unflagging, got up and followed the man. They stumbled on dead bodies as they walked. Some corpses were already decomposing. Dogs and vultures feasted on lifeless bodies. From the level of the decomposition, it seemed the pogrom started in Zaria before it got to Kano.

Peter was following the man, but kept glancing back at intervals to make sure that nobody was after them. They walked for two hours before they saw the church. The white priest was standing with some natives at the gate, admitting and consoling anyone that came to take refuge inside the church.

Some natives had some weapons with which they had been warding off attackers that wanted to kill those taking refuge inside the church. But the number of refugees was augmenting tremendously. With such number of refugees, Peter knew intuitively that the church would be invaded before the end of that day. Some killers had started gathering in the vicinity.

Peter was intensely hungry. He came out of the church, walked up to one of the natives, and begged him in Hausa language to take give him something to eat. He did not know why he took that decision. The man looked at him and said tearfully, 'come my son, you did not commit any offence, and should not die.' He led Peter into a nearby house, which Peter later understood was the man's house. A woman was sitting in front of the house, crying and supporting her chin with her right hand. 'Stop crying', the man told her, 'take this boy and give him something to eat.'

'Come my son,' the woman told Peter, 'we must fulfil our Christian duties. Ignorant people are killing their brothers because of politics. Very soon they will understand their error.' She was still talking when the noise in front of the church grew in intensity. The killers who had been fighting to invade the church had outnumbered the guards. Peter saw his benefactor running to lend force to other guards.

The fight did not last long. The killers defeated the guards and invaded the church. The man came back some minutes later, snivelling. 'What is happening?' his wife asked.

'They have invaded the church, and are about to set it on fire with all the refugees still inside it.'

'Burn our church? Now you believe what I told you?' the woman asked him.

'Yes, you were right. We should have known that,' the man replied, and disconsolately broke into tears.'

'Why is he crying?' Peter asked the woman, surprised that a person who was not in any danger was crying, while he, the hunted person, remained calm.

'I told him that it was a wicked political killing, but he did not believe me, and joined them to kill his brothers. Before he discovered the truth, it was too late. He made effort to protect those who ran into the church. But now, they are going to burn our church. When they finish with Igbos, they will turn their attention to us, their fellow northerners. Soon, our people will understand their stupidity.' She wanted to say something more, but the smoke rising from the church took her mind away. Peter heard the screams of agony. The man and his wife watched tearfully as about two thousand refugees were burnt to death inside the church.

Peter did not set his foot outside the man's house for three years. When the Civil War started, he heard it as a story, and never knew that his people were the Biafrans.

When he returned to Eastern Nigeria after the Civil War, he was already fifteen years old. Everybody in his family was sick and gaunt. His three sisters and their children had returned to his father's house after their husbands were captured and executed by Nigerian soldiers. His father too had been dismissed from the Coal Corporation because of illness. Some of his sisters' children had died of malnutrition during the war, and those still alive, as Peter noticed from their appearances, were still under the threat of the malnutrition.

Peter had no option than to join his elder brother in his carpentry business. Soon after they started working together, many people sought their talents to renovate their houses the invading Nigerian soldiers destroyed during the Civil War. Peter and his brother worked diligently to satisfy their numerous clients, and made a lot of money from their assiduity. But proceeds from carpentry were not the type that turned poverty into affluence. It only ended the malnutrition and other associated illnesses that threatened their family, and still surfeited for Peter to indulge in licentiousness.

The Civil War had left everybody in Biafra impoverished. The Government of Nigeria confiscated the little money the Biafrans left in Nigerian banks, and left the population with death as an option. Many people continued to die of hunger, malnutrition, and other diseases. Mothers who could not bear the sight of their children suffering from malnutrition started whoring to feed their families. Contemptible and derogatory as it appeared, fathers turned their houses into brothels, where they forced their wives and daughters into prostitution. Whorehouses suffused the whole region of Biafra. Only men whose wives were still young, or men with young daughters, had food to eat. Imponderable as it seemed, yet factual, were the scenes in homes where mothers and their daughters were involved in prostitution at the same time, inside the same room of their makeshift houses. Their husbands and fathers stood at the door, collecting money from clients, and pleading with those queuing up to be patient. A scene humiliating and poignant when one understood that the majority of these clients were Nigerian soldiers who had come to Biafra on a duty of extermination.

Apart from people like Peter and his brother whose skills were indispensable at that time, only Nigerian soldiers had the money to spend and pay for the services of prostitutes. And they paid only when they wanted to pay. Most of the time, they took the women by force, and paid with threats, while their fathers and husbands watched helplessly.

It was some of these debased houses that Peter started visiting. Before long, he got hooked to a prostitute, Nkiruka, who was nine years older than him. His family despised the woman, and attempted to break the relationship by force. His elder brother and his father spanked him many times. But Peter continued to meet her secretly, and his family did not relent. They did everything they could to disentangle him from the grip of the prostitute. At a time, it seemed Peter was going to bow to the pressure from his family. But Nkiruka was not ready to lose her esteemed client. She stepped up her wiles and begged Peter to marry her. Beyond belief, to the consternation of his family, Peter married her.

She continued to whore even as she was married. Peter and his brother made some attempts to stop her weird way of life. They were thorny and futile attempts. When they threatened to throw her out of the house, she brought home her clients, Nigerian soldiers, to beat them up. No day passed without a fight between her and somebody in the family. Those who could avoid her avoided her, and those unable to avoid her always got into conflict with her.

After eight months of their marriage, she gave birth to a male child. Everybody knew that the child was a fruit of prostitution. Peter was not the father of the child. Yet, odd as it might seem, Peter's family still accepted the baby with joy. It seemed bastards were no longer illegitimate in Biafra at that time.

With the passing of days, condition of life in Biafra ameliorated. A knew construction company came to renovate some of the public buildings in Biafra, and to build camps for Nigerian soldiers. Peter's brother applied to work as a carpenter in the company. The company employed him. He left his workshop for Peter.

What the Construction Company paid Peter's brother was very little when compared to what he earned in his own workshop, but he continued to work there, with the hope that things would change with the passing of time.

Peter worked alone at the workshop, and earned all the money that came his way. He almost sustained the family alone. His wife was not happy with this arrangement. With the knowledge that what her husband earned was bigger than what the construction company paid her brother-in-law, she sought the separation of her own family from the rest of the family. Peter objected. But when his wife threatened him with a visit by the soldiers, he accepted. His brother was highly embittered. He resigned from the Construction Company and went back to his workshop. To punish Peter for taking his wife's counsel, he sent him away from the workshop.

Peter had no money to establish his own workshop. He tried to sustain his family by doing other menial jobs, but was unable to make any progress. His condition worsened daily.

Gradually, he returned into misery and penury. In his poverty, his wife saw no more need of him. She abandoned him and her son, and went back into full time prostitution.

Forsaken and forlorn, without fortune, yet with a lot of fortitude, Peter fortunately forced his son on his mother to foster. Then he left Enugu for Abakaliki, the only area with fertile land in Biafra, and started rice farming. His farm was not mechanised. He was unable to produce the quantity of products that could liberate him from the grips of poverty. However, he saved enough money to build a house at his hometown, Nsukka.

He lived at Abakaliki for fifteen years. When he finally came back to Nsukka, he looked twenty years older than his age. He was miserable, dejected, and sick. His body was infested with guinea worms. He could no longer indulge in any rigorous activity. His parents, brother, sisters, and their families returned to Nsukka too. Peter went back to his brother's workshop, which his brother had re-established at Nsukka, and ate from the stipend his brother paid him. Nobody had seen his wife, and nobody asked after her.

The location of the University of Nigeria at Nsukka gave the town a metropolitan status. So when the transportation with motor cycles started, the university campus became the most fertile ground for it. Peter, with the support of his brother, bought an old motor cycle, and joined in the rush. He progressed. Before the end of the year, he accumulated a lot of money, the type he could not make in all his years of farming and carpentry. But it seemed he was destined for grief.

His wife, Nkiruka, returned with five children of unknown ancestry. She was old and haggard. Rough life of prostitution and rigours of childbirth had taken the shine off her body. Wizened and unable to maintain parity with younger girls in her trade, starvation threatened her. Left with no option but to look for her erstwhile husband, she came back to Peter's house. It was a bizarre sight. Peter rejected her, and refused every entreaty to allow her into his house. His old father intervened, and told him that Igbo culture forbade the rejection of children, legitimate or illegitimate. His only son she abandoned many years ago was very happy to see his mother too. He tearfully begged his father to forgive her. For the sake of his son, Peter took his wife back, together with the five children she got from prostitution.

With another big family, Peter's affluence waned as rapidly as it came. He worked harder and longer to feed his wife and her children to the detriment of his fragile health.

With the passage of time, with good alimentation and calmness of mind, Nkiruka's body, though jaded, started exhibiting little attraction. And to show her gratitude for what her husband had done for her, she went back into prostitution. This time, her husband's house became her base. Peter could not bear this. Her sixteen years old son was embarrassed. He fought with all his might to stop his mother from going back into prostitution, but to no avail. Peter's house became known all over the town as a whorehouse, and a haven for armed robbers. What worried Peter most was that she started initiating young girls of the neighbourhood into the trade. Every night Peter squirmed on his bed as he listened to the moans and groans of young girls in sexual orgy. He threatened to send his wife away again with her illegitimate children, and nearly did it. She became afraid of the consequences of such action. To hinder it, she sent her clients after Peter. They beat Peter mercilessly that he spent three months in the hospital. When he recuperated, he made no other effort to stop her.

Bambam discovered the house and sent his most ruthless boys to kill Peter. They did not have his picture. All they knew was that he was a cyclist, and that he lived in the house opposite the church. They arrived there at 2 a.m., and waited for two hours in front of Peter's gate.

Peter's wife had slept with one of her clients, who was also a cyclist. Her client woke up very early after a night of licentiousness, and started his motor cycle to go home and prepare for the day's work. Bambam's boys heard the sound of the motor cycle, and drew their guns. Peter's wife opened the gate and held it for her client to move out. The boys waited. The cyclist appeared through the gate. Sounds of gun rumbled over the whole neighbourhood. They shot him twice on the head and three times in the stomach, and left the scene immediately they certified him dead.

Peter did not know who killed the cyclist or why they killed him until the cyclist who gave his address to Nneka told him that Nneka had asked for his address, and only then did he infer that the bullets his wife's lover received were meant for him. He became afraid that they would still come for him whenever they discovered the error. He abandoned his house and ran away from the town.

Professor Ngadi was at the Senior Staff Club on a Saturday night. The club was a place where lecturers met to chat and gossip. Those who were enmeshed in marital disharmony, fugitives of nagging wives, went to the club to drink away their sorrows. It was also at the club that every politics in the university started. Important decisions in the university were taken at the club. What happened during the senate sessions were mere formalities. Some people were of the opinion that the Staff Club was a place for people whose life depended on alcohol. But this opinion was repudiated by a bronze image of a man's head inside a cup of wine with an inscription: BEST BRAINS ARE PRESERVED IN ALCOHOL, clearly written under it.

Going to the Staff Club had been Ngadi's routine since he joined the staff of the university. He had no wife to bother about, though he never lacked female companies to warm his bed. Female students who needed academic favours were always willing to keep him company at night. And knowing full well that he was a bachelor, some made extra effort to lure him into marriage.

Of all the faces of the women he had seen in his life, none had ever taunted him the way Nneka's face taunted him any time he saw her in his class. He had been sitting at the club for an hour, waiting idly for his friend, another professor of identical libidinal propensity, a lewd man whose mind also dwelt in women's pants. He was the first person Ngadi told about Nneka, and he had given Ngadi the stratagem he could use to manipulate her. Unfortunately, no stratagem worked on Nneka. They were determined to devise another stratagem to trap her. While Ngadi waited for him, Bambam and some members of the Red Scorpions visited his house.

Besides his friend at the Staff Club, Ngadi also had a date that night with Uchenwa, a final year female student. She had been failing Ngadi's examinations since her first year in the university. She was pretty and glamorous, but not in the class of Nneka. She could not bind Ngadi with the same spell like Nneka. But like Nneka, she had rebuffed and scorned Ngadi's overtures, and quite unlike Nneka, she had no immunity against Ngadi's wiles by virtue of academic brilliancy. Nobody knew if she had been failing Ngadi's examinations because she had been performing badly or because Ngadi wanted her to fail. Whatever it was, she was determined to graduate with her mates. The only way to achieve such feat was to submit her will to Ngadi's wiles, and her wits to his whims. She did not want to claim irregularity or vindictiveness in the marking of her papers. It was unnecessary. She had no assurance of justice from the University Senate. To take the matter to the University Senate would also take an indefinite time before her case would be settled. She was already in her final year, and would not like to stay a day longer than her mates. If a night of sex with Ngadi would solve her problem, why complicate her life? she thought. After all she was no longer a virgin.

For Ngadi, Uchenwa was one of his most difficult conquests. She had once insulted him verbally. That was the first day he made overtures to her. Tonight, she would be the person begging for his attention, and he would be dictating the pace. He expected her to be in his house before midnight. But to sit down in the house, and wait with expectation and excitement for a lover, was like waiting for eternity. Each minute would have the duration of an hour. He did not like the torment of waiting, rising up from the seat and running to peep through the window at every rustle of leaves by the wind. He continued to chat with his friend at the club, just to reduce the anxiety.

Bambam and other five members of the Red Scorpions saw him from their concealment when he left for the club. They stealthily went into his compound. They had no difficulty with the door. The only door Bambam could not unlock was a door yet to be constructed. Ngadi had no children, wife, or dog in the house to announce the entrance of the Red Scorpions. His house was exactly how they expected a bachelor's house to be; bachelors like Ngadi whose time was divided only between academics and women. There were unwashed plates in the sink. There was a pot of hot rice on the stove, probably the last duty Ngadi performed before he went to the club. His refrigerator contained eight bottles of beer, some ripe tomatoes, and a loaf of bread.

Bambam and his boys drank the eight bottles of beer quickly, refilled the bottles with water, re-corked them, and put them back into the refrigerator. Bambam had warned his boys not to steal or destroy the Professor's property. They were there strictly to disorganise his house, upturn his chairs and tables, and frighten him. But on entering the house, they discovered that the house was already disorganised.

There was a tin of coffee on his table with an evidence of recent usage. They emptied the content into the trashcan. One of them urinated into the tin, covered it, and placed it back on the table. They moved to the kitchen and noticed the pot of rice. They sat down and started eating from the pot. Just in a matter of seconds, the pot became empty. 'Let's go!' Bambam said.

'I want to shit,' one of them said, and started going to the toilet.

'No, don't do it there. Come here,' Bambam ordered.

'What?' the boy asked.

'Defecate into the pot,' Bambam instructed. The boy grinned, squatted over the pot from which they had just eaten, filled it with excrement, and replaced it on the stove. 'We have warned him. Let's move,' Bambam ordered. They moved out of the house and locked the door again.

Professor Ngadi drove into his compound. He had inserted the key into the keyhole of his front door before he saw

Uchenwa coming into his compound. He smiled and waited for her to get closer. She did not smile back at him, but he still embraced and kissed her.

There was no immediate visible evidence of any intrusion into the house. Ngadi sat down on the sofa and pulled Uchenwa to sit on his legs. Slowly, he started kissing and caressing her. After a while, she had an urge to urinate, and went to the toilet.

Ngadi was not hungry, but he felt that Uchenwa would be intensely hungry. He went to the kitchen, put fire to the stove. Without opening the pot, he put the shit on top of the stove. Once hot, the pot started releasing a nasty odour. Uchenwa was the first to perceive the unpleasant odour. But out of politeness, she endured it in silence, thinking that Ngadi had farted. The Professor too thought that the stench was a result of the girl's visit to the toilet. Politely too, he opened all the windows in the house to let in fresh air. When the awful smell became so unbearable, Ngadi rushed to the toilet, thinking that Uchenwa did not flush her excrement. But the toilet was clean and empty. Uchenwa knew that she had only urinated, and that urine could not smell as horrible as what was reeking in the house.

'A rat must have died somewhere,' she suggested.

'No, there was no smell when we came in,' Ngadi objected. They started searching for the origin of the odour all over the house. When Ngadi remembered the pot he left on the fire, he told Uchenwa to go to the kitchen and put out the fire, while he searched for the origin of the odour. Uchenwa walked into the kitchen and ran out again with her fingers in her nostrils.

'It is from the kitchen,' she said. Ngadi ran into the kitchen, and noticed that the smell was actually coming from the pot of rice.

'What could have happened,' he asked and uncovered it. The vapour from the excrement invaded his nostrils. It was unmistakable, human faeces. Ngadi covered the pot quickly and ran out of the kitchen.

'Some people invaded my house,' he said demurely.

'Throw away the pot so that this stink would stop,' Uchenwa suggested. Ngadi got up, covered his nose with one hand, and with the other, took the pot outside the house and threw it inside the gutter. The stench subsided. Uchenwa was amused. She started laughing.

'Why did you laugh?' Ngadi asked. 'Is it a funny thing?'

'I am laughing because you cooked shit for me the first time I came to your house,' she replied. Ngadi smiled too, but was not amused. He knew his life was in danger. The pleasure he would have derived from whatever he had wanted to do with Uchenwa had been surpassed by anxiety over his life. He tried to remember whom he had offended, but was unable to recollect any incident. Weary and dejected, he went to the refrigerator and retrieved two bottles of beer.

'I hope you drink beer?' he asked Uchenwa.

'Yes I do,' she replied and took a bottle from him. Ngadi uncorked his own bottle and noticed that it did not release any gas. He poured the content into a glass and flinched at what he saw. Uchenwa opened her own bottle. It was water too.

'God, who could have done this to me?' Ngadi cried. Uchenwa looked at him and started laughing again. Ngadi was incensed this time by her behaviour. He sighed, bowed his head in distress, and supported his chin with his left hand. His condition was pitiable. Uchenwa stopped laughing, sat down beside him on the sofa, and threw her hand on his shoulder.

'Where do we go from here?' she asked him.

'I don't know. This is strange. I have not offended anyone, why are they after me?' Ngadi asked, exasperated. Uchenwa laughed at this assertion of innocence. If you are innocent as you think, what am I doing in your house? She mused within her.

'Whatever you think about it, your house is now a dangerous place for one to sleep. It would be better for us to go to a hotel, or do you still want it here?' she asked him tauntingly, enjoying his anguish and perplexity. For her, it would have been better if the intruders had killed Ngadi.

'Want what here?' Ngadi asked aggressively.

'Me, is it not why I came? I am prepared now, and I want it now,' Uchenwa said and started undressing.

'No, please don't, I am not in the mood now,' Ngadi protested.

'What do you want me to do? You have been punishing me for the past four years. And now, you want to run away. No, I won't take it,' she insisted.

'Come to my office on Monday morning. We shall settle your case once and for all. For now, I am worried, I cannot do anything with you,' Ngadi said dejectedly.

'If you say you don't want me, I will go, but always remember that I came to give you what you have been demanding, and you refused to take.' Ngadi did not make any other comment after her. Uchenwa picked the skirt she had removed and started dressing again, slowly and provocatively.

Ngadi would have sworn that Uchenwa knew something about what happened in his house if it were not for the note he saw on the table in his office on Monday morning. He had gone to a hotel the moment Uchenwa left his house, and had been sleeping at the hotel, hoping to discover why he was being threatened before he went back to his house.

That Monday morning, he got into his office and discovered that somebody had been there too, although there was no other sign of intrusion apart from the note on the table. It read:

Dear noble Professor,

I know you like beautiful things. There is a beautiful first year girl in your class. She has not seen the result of the examination she took last semester. I would be very grateful if you do something about it. She would be in your office any time. I hope you will recognise and help her.

Did you enjoy your meal on Saturday night? Please let's avoid another visit. It may not be a friendly affair again. I hope you will comply. God bless you.

Ngadi read the note six times. 'So it is her,' he murmured. That was the first time he received threats from anybody since he became a professor. It piqued him that the threat came from a first year girl. He went to the bookshelf and started rummaging hastily for Nneka's papers. Fear and impotent rage benumbed his senses. He had been in the university long enough to know that this threat to his life was serious. However, he was grateful to God that it was only a warning. He would have been dead if they had wanted to kill him.

Sadly, he retrieved Nneka's papers from the bunch on the shelf. 'Imagine what a first year student is doing to me,' he murmured. On a second thought, he smiled and murmured, 'nothing is impossible for a woman, first year or final year.'

In spite of Ezenwa's assurances that Ngadi would never molest her again, Nneka was still afraid to go to his office alone. She lingered in front of the office, waiting for anybody that could give her protection. Somehow, she saw Bully going out of the Department. She could not believe her luck. She ran after him, calling him and beckoning at the same time. Bully heard his name and turned. When he saw her, he stopped and smiled.

'What did you come here to do this early morning?' Nneka asked him.

'My room mate forgot his key, and I brought it for him,' Bully replied.

'Is he in this department?' Nneka asked.

'Yes, he is in final year.'

'You have not visited me for a long time, is that how you show your love?' Nneka teased. Bully smiled.

'I will visit you tonight,' Bully promised, very happy that he received attention from the most beautiful girl on the campus.

'Please do me a favour,' Nneka pleaded immediately.

'What do you want? Bully asked, ready to donate his life if she needed it.

'A professor in my department has been chasing me, and I need to see him. I don't want to go to him alone. Could you please accompany me?'

'Yes, why not?' Bully replied, took her hand, and they started walking to Ngadi's office.

Nneka knocked gently on the Professor's door. A coarse weary voice responded from within. She opened the door and moved in fearfully. The usual lusty eyes of Ngadi wore a look of tragedy. He was so jittery that words refused to come out fluently from his mouth. He could not tell Nneka to shut the door when she entered, as he usually told every female student. The door remained ajar, and Bully lurked outside the office.

'What do you want?' Ngadi asked her, visibly trembling. Nneka too was jolted by his comportment.

'Still on my result sir,' she said feebly.

'Is that the reason for all these threats?' he asked angrily.

'What threat? I don't understand,' Nneka protested, and immediately remembered Ezenwa. Who knows what he had done to Ngadi, she thought.

'I know you won't accept. Nobody would ever accept. But I have to tell you that you exaggerated things. I just told you that I love you. We could have resolved our differences without going to extremes. Bully heard the word love and peeped through the door. Ngadi saw his ugly face and winced. Completely softened, Ngadi's amorous arrogance disappeared. Nneka wondered again what Ezenwa did to instil such fear into him.

'Here is your answer sheet,' Ngadi said and threw the papers at Nneka. She saw her grade and smiled.

'Thanks,' she said, and left the office in jubilation. The grade she saw on the paper was the highest anybody had ever made in Ngadi's examinations. She did not know if she actually merited the grade, or if Ngadi gave her the grade to pacify those threatening him. Whatever was the reason, she was very grateful to Ezenwa.

When the second semester examination started, the anxiety and fear of sexual exploitation by anybody did not worry Nneka again. If it were not for Ezenwa, the fear would have hindered her diligence towards the preparation for the second semester examination. But thanks to Ezenwa. Now, as the examination progressed, she could predict without error the result of her performance in the examinations she had taken.

When the examination came to an end, she packed her belongings with hilarity, and took a taxi to the motor park, where Ezenwa and Nyadiba were already waiting for her. Whenever she thought about home, she remembered Ezenwa's grandfather. She had been compiling lists of questions she would ask him, and prayed constantly that Ezenwa would not be immersed in the flurry of Christmas celebration, and neglect her interests.

Ezenwa was glad that they were going home for the Christmas break. He wanted to stay with his family too, especially his mother, whose dishes he missed dearly. Yet a little gloom skulked around his enthusiasm. If he were to choose, he would have preferred to stay back on the campus. He had been thinking about the Christmas break in two minds because of a nagging fear that had kept him in insomnia many nights.

Nneka was the most beautiful girl in the town. The little time she had spent in the university had endowed her with a flamboyant deportment that completely obscured her timidity. The last time she went home for holiday, her house recorded the highest number of suitors ever known in the history of the town. Although she rejected all the suitors, a lingering fear of them had not stopped tormenting Ezenwa. 'One never knows with women', he had often said. He was afraid that she could become whimsical any time and jilt him. And it was the Christmas season, a time when almost everybody came home to celebrate the festival in the village among his kith and kin. It was also the time when young men mostly came to their villages to look for wives among the girls of the village.

There was a tortuous feeling within Ezenwa that some wealthy people would come home too, especially those who lived in Europe and America, and would try to influence Nneka's decision with their wealth. He had wanted to urge her to stay back with him on the campus, but he was afraid she would refuse. Besides refusal, Ezenwa did not want her to feel that his existence completely depended on her caprices. He would be demonstrating his unselfishness too by allowing her to go and stay with her parents, being their only child. So he decided to go home with her for the Christmas break. With this decision, his bane remained.

Nneka alighted from the taxi at the motor park and saw Ezenwa and Nyadiba where they were waiting for her across the road. She paid the driver and crossed over to them.

'You wasted time,' Ezenwa told her.

'Don't you know that I am a woman. I have to get everything I would need at home,' she replied.

'I hate to hear that you are a woman. You always hide your inefficiency behind womanhood,' Ezenwa grumbled. Nneka shuddered and stared at him. She had observed that he had been nervous, flustered, and hostile for the past two days. She hoped that she was not the cause of what was bothering him.

'Why did you snap at me like that?' Nneka asked, perturbed. Ezenwa glanced at her and mumbled incoherently. Nneka hated to be a cause of grief to him. Consequently, she sought an opportunity to be with him alone, to discover the cause of his sadness.

'I am thirsty. Where can I buy water?' she asked him.

'Go to that shop there,' Ezenwa said and pointed at a shop opposite the motor park.

'Accompany me please,' Nneka pleaded. Ezenwa could not refuse her anything, but still ruminating on what might be his fate if she jilted him, he followed her across the road. Once they were alone, Nneka asked him why he was behaving strangely.

'Strange? Now you know I am strange? You now think my behaviour is strange? When cult boys and your lecturers were threatening you, you did not think I was strange?' he asked sarcastically.

'God!' Nneka exclaimed, 'that's not what I meant. I was worried by your countenance. And for the past two days, you have been snapping and flaring up at every speech I make. I just want to beg you to forgive me if I have done anything wrong. You know that I would never in my life attempt to offend you deliberately. I....' She could not finish her apology before sorrow and tears overwhelmed her. A crying beautiful face was not a good sight to behold. Ezenwa took her hand and started walking towards the shop.

'I did not mean to be harsh on you,' he apologised. 'I was only afraid of what would be my fate when we get home. And the fear took over my actions.'

'Your fate? Like what?' she asked, perplexed.

'You remember that the last time we were home for holidays, a lot of suitors came for you,' Ezenwa said shamefully.

'Oh shit!' she shouted. 'Is that why you are worried? I am disappointed by your behaviour Ezenwa. So you have been with me all these years and could not trust me. How could you ever think that I would look at another man while you are alive? No, it would never happen. Even if you are dead, it would still be difficult for me to look at another man, or are you planning to jilt me?' she asked.

'Jilt you? How?' Ezenwa asked in return.

'If you are not thinking of jilting me, why do you think I would do it to you?' Her question caught him unawares. He attempted to explain why the thought got hold of him, but every explanation he made sounded awkward. Embarrassed, he apologised again, bought the water, and led her back to the motor park.

Chapter 31

After two days at home, Ezenwa's desire to see Nneka became intense. He had expected her to visit him the previous day, but she did not come. He wanted to obliterate the thoughts of her from his mind, but the nostalgia was so intense that he could not stop thinking about her. It seemed the plot of his life was woven around her. Every property he owned had her mark. Everything he touched exuded her whiff. The cloth he wore at that moment was a gift from her on his last birthday anniversary. Her framed picture on the table smiled at him like a sun goddess. He sighed, wore his trousers and went to Nyadiba's house. Perhaps a chat with Nyadiba would alleviate the unbearable desire to see her.

Ezenwa met Nyadiba's father just in front of the house and greeted him. 'Good afternoon Corporal,' Ezenwa said.

'Good afternoon my son. How are you?' Mr Igwe asked.

'I am all right Corporal,' Ezenwa replied.

'How was your last session at the university? Did your teachers tell you why Hitler lost the war?'

'No, Corporal, but....' Ezenwa attempted to explain. But the initial negation had given Nyadiba's father the incentive he needed to start his own lectures.

'Then your education is worthless,' Nyadiba's father cut in. 'I told my son that any education without the history of the World War is worthless. Now tell me, what course of study are you pursuing?' he asked.

'Political science sir,' Ezenwa answered.

'I am not "sir", I am a corporal. You must give me my title, so don't make the mistake again!' Nyadiba's father warned.

'I am sorry Corporal. I am studying political science.'

'Very good. If you are studying political science, and you don't know why Hitler lost the war, then your study is worthless.'

'I know about Hitler sir,' Ezenwa said.

'I have told you that I am not "sir". I am Corporal Stephen Igwe.'

'I am sorry Corporal,' Ezenwa apologised, 'I know about him sir... I mean Corporal.'

'What do you know about him? Do you know his connection with Mussolini? Do you know the part I played in the war?' Igwe asked.

'Yes, Mussolini was the Italian leader....'

'That's not my question,' Igwe interrupted again. 'I want to know if you know the Nazi philosophy, and the role I played in the defeat of Hitler.'

Nyadiba heard his father's voice, and did not guess twice to know the subject. He was only displeased that his father had been scaring away his friends with his World War stories. He ran out of the house to rescue the person that had fallen into his father's net.

'Is it you?' Nyadiba asked Ezenwa, smiling. 'I should not have bothered myself after all,' he said and turned to go back into the house.

'Wait Nyadiba!' his father shouted. Nyadiba stopped and turned again. 'I asked your friend if he knows the Nazi's philosophy, but he does not know. I am sure you do not know it too. Now listen and learn it now. Hitler was....' Nyadiba sighed and started walking back into the house. Ezenwa followed him immediately. Corporal Igwe was not discouraged by their apparent rudeness. He followed them into the house, shouting at the top of his voice, telling them what he thought they ought to know about Hitler. He only stopped when Nyadiba invited Ezenwa into his room and shut his door. But sooner had this happened than they heard him talking to somebody again outside the house on the same subject.

Nneka had heard a lot of stories about Nyadiba's father and his obsession with the World War, but never had the opportunity of meeting him, or had been adroitly prevented by Nyadiba from meeting him. Nyadiba thought that such contacts, with the accompanying embarrassment, would always diminish his worth in the eyes of his friends.

Nneka had arrived at Ezenwa's house immediately Ezenwa left the house. Ezenwa's brother told her where Ezenwa had gone. She went after him immediately. Unfortunately for Nyadiba, his father was outside the house again when Nneka arrived. So he was the first person to meet her.

'Good afternoon sir,' Nneka greeted Nyadiba's father.

'You are wrong,' he replied sternly. Nneka shuddered and stared at him to know her fault. 'I am not "sir". I was a corporal in the Royal British Army, so you must address me as Corporal Igwe,' he explained. She smiled and greeted him again. 'Good afternoon Corporal Igwe.'

'Good afternoon beautiful girl. How are you?' Igwe asked with smiles. Nneka was amused by the sudden change of countenance.

'I am fine sir,' she replied. He frowned. 'I mean Corporal,' she added. The smile returned to his face immediately. Nneka was amused. She laughed boisterously. Ezenwa heard her voice.

'That's Nneka. Your father is teaching her history,' he told Nyadiba.

'Let's go to your house. I know he would never allow us to rest unless we are ready to listen to his trash,' Nyadiba suggested and walked furiously out of the house.

Nneka had relaxed and continued to listen to the stories of Hitler when Nyadiba and Ezenwa came out of the house.

'Let's go,' Ezenwa said and attempted to drag her along.

'It is good you came out too,' Nyadiba's father said happily when he saw Ezenwa and Nyadiba. 'I was about to tell her that she resembled Hitler's wife, and that if she is not careful, she would get married to a man of Hitler's character.' Ezenwa roared with laughter. Nyadiba, in spite of the embarrassment, laughed too. Nneka was unaware of the agony her interaction with Igwe was producing in Nyadiba. She tried to extricate her hand from Ezenwa's grip and continue to amuse herself.

'Let's go, Uyanna had been waiting for you,' Ezenwa coaxed her.

'Let's go, Uyanna has been waiting for you,' she mimicked, sticking out her tongue. 'It's now you know that I exist,' she fumed.

'I was wondering why you have not come,' Ezenwa said.

'And when you did not see me why didn't you come to know if all is well with me?' she asked.

'I did not come because I was expecting you,' Ezenwa replied. Nneka knew why he did not come. The excuse that he was expecting her was so flimsy that it annoyed her.

'I have told you to get rid of that complex,' she said angrily. 'I have told you that I love you. Whatever kind of phobia that prevented you from visiting me is your problem alone, it has nothing to do with me.'

'Don't be angry please,' Ezenwa pleaded. 'I am sorry. I am wrong. You are right. I don't like to see your suitors. That is why I did not come,' Ezenwa confessed. Nneka smiled.

'They have been coming even when I was in the university, and my mother has been counting them. As I was preparing to come out now, two more people came,' she explained.

'And what did you tell them?' Ezenwa asked jealously.

'Of course I accepted. I will marry one of them before the end of the month,' Nneka replied teasingly.

'I hope I would be invited,' Nyadiba chipped in.

'Why not?' she asked.

They had just arrived at Ezenwa's house. Ezenwa walked into the house, and held the gate for Nyadiba and Nneka to enter. Nyadiba came in first. Nneka wanted to come in, but saw the distress her taunts had produced on Ezenwa's face. Baffled, she stopped at the gate.

'Come in please!' Ezenwa told her, a bit angrily. 'You know that sometimes madness starts like this. You say things you don't want to say and think that you are still with your senses, you will not know that everything you say has a mark of acute madness.'

'If anybody is mad, it is you,' Nneka retorted. 'I did not visit you because my mother was sick, and you refused to visit me, because you are afraid of meeting my suitors.'

'That's enough please. I don't want my grandfather to hear that,' Ezenwa said quietly.

'I will tell him now,' she threatened. Uyanna heard their voices and came out from the house.

'Good afternoon sir, or are you a corporal too,' Nneka joked. Nyadiba sighed. Ezenwa stared angrily at her. Her eyes caught Ezenwa's angry stare. She looked askance for a while before she saw the agony on Nyadiba's face. She squirmed and wanted to apologise. Ezenwa winked at her three times. She got the signal and did not apologise. An apology would have embarrassed Nyadiba more than the comment. It had never occurred to Nneka that such jokes could be an embarrassment to Nyadiba. Uyanna wisely read the misdemeanour and effaced the embarrassment with a question.

'Were you here some minutes ago?' Uyanna asked Nneka.

'Yes,' she replied. 'Ezenwa's brother told me where he has gone, so I went there and brought him back.'

'Thank you for bringing him back,' Uyanna joked.

'No, I won't accept only your verbal expression of gratitude. You must pay me for bringing him back by answering some of the questions I want to ask you.'

'Feel free. I have always told you to ask me anything you want me to explain to you any time you like.'

'Ok, I want to know how....'

'Sit down first!' Ezenwa interrupted her and pointed at a chair. She sat down and brought out a list of questions she had compiled.

'What is that?' Ezenwa asked.

'Questions I compiled,' Nneka replied. Ezenwa and Nyadiba roared with laughter.

'You compiled questions as if he is about to undergo a test,' Ezenwa commented.

'Whatever it is, I am ready,' Uyanna said.

'Please let me ask my questions. I don't have much time. My mother is sick, and I have to prepare our lunch,' Nneka said.

'Go ahead,' Uyanna said.

'I want to know how one can be whatever one wants to be in life.'

'You want to be the queen of the world,' Ezenwa teased.

'It depends on what you want to be and why you want to be what you want to be,' Uyanna answered. 'For example, if you want to be something because you want to help humanity, that is an act of love. And the moment you start nursing that thought, the thought will take form and become a reality.'

'How would it happen?' Nneka asked.

'Thoughts have elective affinity, just like love attracts love and hatred attracts hatred, thoughts are attracted to their likes. When you emit thoughts of love, the thoughts will go directly to the fountain of love, the Almighty God. As long as you keep the thoughts of love alive in you, the force from the Almighty God will continue to be with you, and will be nourishing your thoughts with vigour and force. It is this force from the Almighty God that will overpower every obstacle in your way to success. When the time comes, you will be surprised how your dream will turn into reality. It happens like magic. You won't even know how it happened, but the events of your life will lead to it.'

'I don't understand,' Nneka said, befuddled.

'But do you believe that God is Almighty?' Uyanna asked.

'Yes I do,' she replied.

'Just that connection of love you made with your thoughts is enough to make you whatever you want to be in your life. But I will like to know what you want to be, so that I can explain how it works.'

'I will like to be a health worker, I want to take care of orphans,' Nneka replied.

'That is a wonderful ambition,' Uyanna said. 'Now, what you have to do is to keep nursing the thought. Don't worry about whatever will be happening in your life. You will finally get to your ambition. When difficulties come, don't be afraid, because every difficulty is meant to put you in the way of your ambition. There would be hardships too, sometimes unsavoury and inevitable events, but don't panic. Keep your thoughts alive and pure. Every difficulty is an agent from the Almighty God to guide you to success.'

'What happens when it is so obvious that something is going to hinder the realisation of her ambition?' Ezenwa asked.

'That is what I said. As long as her ambition is from an authentic love for orphans, evil forces opposed to love must fight to prevent it. But they would only be pushing her to success. Everything they do would ironically lead her to her ambition. Nothing conquers love. And when it is love for children, it becomes indomitable. Children are innocent, their bodies and their spirits are pure and innocent. Pride and selfishness have not severed their link with God. Their spirits fight for the protection of their interests without relenting. And now that your love belongs to them, their Angels are all around you, protecting and supplicating before God on your behalf.'

'I don't understand anything,' Nyadiba interrupted. 'Does it mean that we should not work for our own needs, that we must do everything for the good of others, when we know that nobody else is doing anything for our own good?'

'No, that's not it,' Uyanna explained. 'You must work for your own good too, but the underlying intention should be for the benefit of others. You don't have to do anything for your own glory. You must not go after your dreams with selfishness. That is the only way to be in constant contact with God, and the only way to share in his almighty power.'

'What about me?' Ezenwa asked.

'What do you want to be?' Uyanna asked.

'I want to be a politician.'

'To liberate Biafra?' Uyanna asked. Ezenwa was astounded by the question. Uyanna knew exactly what was going on in Ezenwa's mind.

'How do you know that?' Ezenwa asked, surprised.

'It is all over you,' Uyanna replied.

'How?' Ezenwa asked, amazed.

'I saw it in you when you where growing up. I remembered your interests and the questions you have often asked whenever you heard stories of Biafra. I have watched your actions too. I saw the hatred you have for injustice, and knew that the love for Biafra and the hatred for injustice, all in you, must unite one day.'

'Do you mean to say that there is nothing like destiny, and that we could always be what we want to be?' Nyadiba asked.

'No, what we call destiny first of all comes from the circumstances of our birth. These circumstances influence everything we do. Our ambition is always the direct influence of these circumstances. The fact that you were born to Igwe's house is in line with your destiny. Whatever you chose to do with your life must be influenced by the circumstances of your birth. That is your destiny. Ezenwa came into my family because his destiny had been decided before his birth. Now you heard his ambition. All these started because his father was in the Biafran Army. He had been telling him stories of Biafra, thereby planted the love for Biafra and hatred for Nigeria in him. If he were born into a family where nobody speaks about Biafra, he could not have known anything about Biafra. His ambition would be different. He is strictly in my family to learn things that would guide him towards his destiny.'

'So this is why I was born into your family,' Ezenwa said happily.

'Don't allow what I said to start guiding your actions. Remember that I am a human being, and not God. So I could be wrong. You have the ambition you have chosen for yourself. Go after it, it is when you are after it that you will know why you were born into my family.'

'Does it mean that before somebody dies, he must have fulfilled his destiny on earth?' Nneka asked.

'Yes, you cannot die unless your have fulfilled your mission on earth,' Uyanna replied.

'What about children who died immediately after they were born? What mission could they have completed?' Nneka asked. Uyanna laughed, and cleared his throat.

'You know that nobody lives independent of others. A child who died at birth came only to live in pregnancy. His mission was to help his mother to carry out her own mission. Perhaps while she was pregnant, she avoided doing, or did certain things, which unknown to her, had influenced the life of another person towards the person's destiny.'

'Does it mean that we are all in the world to help other people?' Nyadiba asked again.

'Exactly,' Uyanna concurred.

'Please tell me,' Nneka pleaded, 'what about abortion? What do you think about it?'

'It is an exhibition of selfishness and wickedness. It is the conglomeration of all the evils in man.' Only selfish people participate in abortion. People who think only about their well being, and do not bother about the pains they give to others. Don't you know that the spirit of an aborted baby always bore the mark of the mother's wickedness? With that mark as evidence, he accuses her day and night before God, asking for justice. To tell you the truth, a curse would be placed on any woman that commits abortion and her accomplices until they make a sincere confession, and ask for God's mercy.

'Is it not the destiny of the baby to die by abortion?' Nyadiba asked.

'It cannot be. The journey of destiny starts at birth. When an aborted baby was stopped from coming into the world by selfishness and wickedness of the mother, how could he have completed his mission on earth? He has to complete the nine months of pregnancy, come into the world through birth, anything that happens after that is part of his destiny.'

'I understand,' Nneka said, and glanced at the paper in her hand to ask another question. They heard somebody wailing outside the house.

'Who is that?' Uyanna asked.

'I don't know,' Ezenwa said and ran outside to verify. Nneka and Nyadiba followed him. Uyanna was slow in rising, so he was the last to come out. They saw their neighbour's daughter wailing, while her mother consoled her.

'What happened to her?' Uyanna asked.

'A snake bit her,' her mother replied.

'A snake!' Ezenwa, Nneka, and Nyadiba exclaimed simultaneously. Uyanna smiled mirthlessly.

'And where are you going?' Uyanna asked his neighbour.

'We are going to the hospital. I don't know what else to do,' her mother answered. The pain was so unbearable that the girl could not walk.

'Don't you think she could die before you get to the hospital?' Uyanna asked the woman.

'What else could I have done?' she asked in return. 'She cannot die unless God wants her to die. And if it is her time to die, nobody on earth can save her,' the woman answered.

'Did you hear that?' Uyanna asked Nneka. 'Bring her into the house,' he told the woman.

'For what?' Ezenwa asked, distrustful of his grandfather, thinking that the girl would die in their house. The woman made no objection and carried her daughter into Uyanna's house. Uyanna went into his room and came out with some dried leaves. He threw a handful of the leaves into his mouth and started chewing.

'Show me the exact spot where the snake bit you,' he told the girl. She pointed at her left heel. Blood was trickling out from the wound. Uyanna spat the chewed leaves on the girl's heel, and started rubbing it gently. After about five minutes, he removed his hand and stared at the spot. Pus started coming out from the wound. The girl stopped wailing. Six minutes later, she got up and started walking. Do you still feel any pain?' Uyanna asked.

'No, she replied. Uyanna smiled.

'What did you do? Magic?' Ezenwa asked his grandfather.

'No, not magic. I did what God told me to do,' Uyanna told them. Confused, the woman asked how much she would pay Uyanna for curing her daughter. Uyanna became incensed.

'How dare you tempt me with money for doing what I was sent to do?' he asked the woman angrily.

'No, it is not temptation, I....'

'Take your daughter and get out,' Uyanna shouted with rage. The woman was taken aback. She took her daughter's hand and hurried out of the house.

'Why didn't you take money from her?' Nneka asked.

'That would be an abuse of privilege. I received the knowledge without payment, and I must use it to help humanity free of charge too. Is it not what Jesus told his apostles when he sent them out on a mission.'

'So you know about that too?' Nneka asked. Uyanna smiled.

'I have told you that I am a friend of Jesus, because I try to do everything he said that we should do. That is why he answers me any time I call him. But the problem of the churchgoers is that they talk a lot about things in the bible, but do not put them into practice, yet they call me a devil.'

'Who gave you the knowledge?' Nneka asked.

'This is the question I thought you would have asked instead of asking why I didn't take her money.'

'I am sorry,' Nneka said, abashed.

'That's all right,' Uyanna accepted. 'There are things one should never play with in one's life,' he explained. 'One of them is exploiting the needy. It is an ignoble show of selfishness. It cuts one off from the source all knowledge, the Almighty God. Do you understand what I mean?'

'Yes,' Nneka answered. Tell us how you came about the knowledge of the herb,' she pleaded.

'As you all know,' Uyanna said, 'I always go inside the bush for one thing or the other, but most importantly to be with nature. I like to listen to the songs of birds. I have learnt to interpret what they say. Do you know that animals talk?'

'No!' they chorused.

'Know it now. Animals talk, but you can't understand what they say unless you are someone who respects nature and longs to learn what it has to impart. But to answer your question, I went into the bush one day to get some herbs for malaria. Along the path I tread everyday, I saw two black dangerous snakes fighting. I thought they would run away at my approach, but they did not. I stood still and watched them. They continued to fight until they were tired.

As if something unseen interfered, they stopped biting themselves and moved away from the path in opposite directions, one to the left, and the other to the right. I knew that something was about to happen. I followed the one that moved to the right. Just about six yards away from where they fought, it stopped and started biting a tree. I was baffled, but continued to watch it. White sticky liquid started coming out from the wound it gave to the tree. It started rubbing its body on the white substance. It made sure the liquid got into the wound it sustained in the fight. After that, it went away. I remarked the tree and went in search of the second snake, and saw it about six yards away from the scene of the fight, dead. Then I went back and took some leafs of that tree, dried them and kept them.'

'This is strange,' Nneka commented.

'Very strange,' Nyadiba concurred.

'How do you know that the leaf would work? Have you used it before?' Ezenwa asked.

'No, I have not used it. But I got the message and accepted it. That is why it worked for me.'

'Do you think the message came from God?' Nneka asked.

'Of course, from whom could it have come?'

'But why should God show things to some people and would not show to others?' Nyadiba asked indignantly.

'I have told you earlier that God is never partial in distribution of his gifts. Only those disposed to receive them received them. If pride and selfishness do not fill your mind, with a little trust in his infinite power, you would receive his gifts too.'

'Can you show us the tree?' Nneka asked.

'Nneka, how can he show you the tree. It is not possible. If he does that, a lot of people would have the knowledge and his own importance would diminish,' Nyadiba said. Uyanna looked at him and laughed.

'That's where you are wrong my friend,' Uyanna said. 'I have no importance. To think that I am more important than anybody is the thought that comes out of pride, and pride would cut me off from the power of the Almighty God. Pride belongs to the fallen angels, while humility is an attribute of the Almighty God. Christ affirmed this when he told his apostles that he is meek and humble of heart.' He turned to Nneka and said, 'I will show you the tree.'

'Why do you want to show her the tree?' Ezenwa asked.

'To create a gap in my soul. Don't you know that if I refuse to teach her what I did not pay to learn, it would be selfishness on my part? And I have told you how selfishness, like a stone without openings, repels the flow of power and knowledge. But if I teach her, it would be charity on my part, and as I have said many times, the best way to exhibit love is through charity. By doing it, my link with God would be firmer, and I will make myself disposed to receive more knowledge and power. If I do not divulge this knowledge, it would block the space through which others would come in. Do you understand?' They nodded, but continued to stare at him. 'Come and see the tree,' Uyanna said and stood up.

'No, not now. I still have some questions to ask. Show me the tree later,' Nneka protested.

'All right, any time you want,' Uyanna accepted.

'Can I ask another question?' she asked.

'Yes, go ahead,' Uyanna replied.

'Do you have enemies?' Nneka asked. Uyanna stared at her. It seemed he did not know what to say.

'What do you mean by enemies?' he asked.

'Those who don't like you, and those you hate.'

'Well, I know there are people who do not like me, but I like everybody. I may not like their behaviours, especially when they are opposed to love.'

'You mean you don't hate anybody?' Nyadiba asked.

'Yes I don't.'

'Are you saying that if somebody meets you on the way, and for no reason insulted you, or attempted to kill you, you would still love the person?'

'To start with,' Uyanna commented, 'insult, just like pain, exists only in the mind.'

'I don't understand. What do you mean by existing only in the mind?' Nneka asked.

'Insult would never be insult unless you, the receiver, think it is an insult. For example, if Ezenwa calls you a fool playfully, you will laugh over it. But if somebody you don't know calls you a fool, you will frown and say that the person insulted you. The reason for the difference in reaction is because of what you think. Why should the same word from different people produce different sentiments? You took one as a joke, and took the other as an insult. The truth is that if you took both as jokes, and laugh over them, you would not see anything insulting in the word. It is like pain. Something is painful because we think it is painful. If we refuse to think that something is painful, immediately, the pain ceases to exist. That is why I said that what we think is the base of what we are.'

'For you nothing is painful?' Nneka asked.

'Yes, for me nothing is painful.'

'How can we eliminate pain? I would like to do it, please teach me,' Nyadiba pleaded.

'It is very easy, easier than you imagined,' Uyanna replied. They stared at him with rapt attention.

'How?' Ezenwa asked.

'It is very simple. Whenever you have the urge to cry, laugh. That's all.'

'It is not easy,' Nneka argued.

'Well I accept, it is not easy, but with constant practice, you will succeed.'

'I don't understand what you mean. Does it mean that if somebody wants to kill me, I should laugh and ignore him?' Ezenwa asked, agitated, perhaps to justify the things he did to protect Nneka from cult boys. Nneka understood why he was agitated. She threw a glance at him and sighed sadly.

'No, you must protect yourself,' Uyanna explained. 'Anybody who comes with an intention to hurt you must have rejected your love before he made the decision. But to maintain your link with the Almighty God, whenever you have the opportunity to defeat your foes ruthlessly, always show mercy. With that, your link to God will get stronger, because the mercy you have shown is his attribute and attracts him.'

They were engrossed in the explanation Uyanna was making, and did not know when Iroegbu came into the compound. He listened to Uyanna too and made a comment. 'It will be difficult to understand why you should show mercy to your enemy when you know you have got him where you wanted him, but I tell you, it is the best thing to do. I have told you this story many times,' he told Ezenwa, 'but for the benefit of your friends, I will repeat it.' He sat down. 'In the heat of the Civil War,' Iroegbu said, 'Nigerian soldiers surrounded my platoon. There was no way for us to come out of the predicament. We were running out of food and ammunition. Without food and ammunition, how could we fight? I cannot say if our enemies knew that we were in their midst. It seemed they did not know. If they knew, they did not make any effort to crush us. We had only two rounds of ammunition each to withstand any serious attack. If they had attacked us, they would have finished us just in a matter of minutes.

We remained in our position for many weeks, because we did not know what to do. But when we ran out of food completely, we decided to trust our fate into God's hand and make a move. We decided to move westwards and attack the Nigerian Brigade that isolated us from another Biafran platoon. We took the decision not only to save our lives, but also because we knew that if we could defeat the Brigade, we could open a space through which our soldiers on the Brigade's left flank could move in and attack our enemies on their south. It was a difficult situation. We were hungry, our weapons were inferior to theirs, but our life depended on the success of that attack.

I was the commander. So I told my men to pray and be ready to accept whatever might be the outcome of the encounter, and they obeyed promptly. Everybody knew that what we were about to do was suicidal. Imagine a situation where two hundred men, with less than two rounds of ammunition each, were about to confront a battalion with machine guns and armoured tanks. To tell you the truth, I thought we would never succeed. It was like madness, but we could not wait to die of hunger. We took the decision to invade their camp and open fire on them very early in the morning. It seemed God heard our prayers. It started drizzling that night. The rain was nothing to us. We have been living inside the bush like wild animals from the inception of the war.

At about 2 am, we started walking slowly and cautiously towards the enemy's location. The rain had not reduced in intensity, yet we were not discouraged. Along the way, just close to there camp, there was a flash of lightening. It lasted long enough for us to see a figure lurking in the darkness some metres ahead of us. We thought it was a monkey, and prayed that it would not make a noise that would give us away. Somebody wanted to shoot it, but I saw the gesture early enough, and wrenched the rifle out of the soldier's hand. If he had done that, he would have woken our enemies, and that would have been our end. We continued walking towards the creature, expecting it to run away as we approached. It did not move. Some of my men became afraid, and I would have been afraid too if my father had not warned me never to be afraid of anything if I want to survive the war. I told my men to stay back, took my bayonet, and walked boldly towards it. When I got close enough, I was shocked. He was a human being suffering from malnutrition. He was so sick that his head was twice bigger than the rest of his body. His skin clung to his bones. It was a pathetic sight. It seemed he had been inside the bush for a long time. There was another long flash of lightening. I saw his face clearly. He was smiling. For a brief moment I thought I saw death smiling. Indeed he looked like death. I wondered where he got the will to smile in spite his condition. I dipped my hand inside my bag, brought out a loaf of dry bread and gave him. He smiled again, and made an effort to take the bread from me. But he lacked the energy to raise his hand. I threw the bread at him, and took my men away. I knew he would be dead before the next day, so there was no point in trying to rescue him. Lives of many people depended on the operation we had at hand. We continued moving.

After about thirty minutes of walking, we got to the enemy's camp. Twenty minutes later, we have penetrated deep into the camp unobserved and....'

'How did you do that? Were they asleep?' Nyadiba interrupted.

'Yes, some people were asleep, but the sentries were all awake, but we were able to get close to them and strangle all of them without exposing ourselves. Then we hid inside their camp and waited for the day to break, so that we could see our targets. We had very little ammunition and did not want to waste it.

It seemed God was on our side that morning. We did not wait for a long time. Our enemies assembled very early for breakfast, and we opened fire. It was as if the heaven would fall. They started running helter-skelter. We did not stop until we have destroyed the camp completely. Some of my men wanted to continue chasing them and killing them, but I restrained them. I remembered that my father told me to always show mercy whenever I have the opportunity to defeat my enemies ruthlessly. I repeated these words to my men. Some of them thought I was mad, but that single act of mercy saved our lives...'

'How?' Nneka interrupted.

'That's what I am telling you. We did not know that our enemies had planned to attack a Biafran Brigade that morning. They wanted to surround the Brigade from the east, north and south flanks. When we attacked and scattered them, they thought it was the Brigade they had planned to wipe out that attacked them. And when we stopped shooting, they started regrouping to come after us. If we had continued chasing and killing them, we would have ran out of ammunition, and they would have picked us up like rats. But when we allowed them to escape, we hurried out of their camp. On our way out of the camp, we met some lorries bringing in the ammunition to be used in their operation that morning. The drivers and their escorts did not know what was happening. We ambushed them, shot all of them, and went away with their supplies. If we had continued slaughtering the soldiers in the camp, those lorries would have got into the camp behind us and discharged their wares. That supplies we took from them lasted until the end of the Civil War. I never lacked ammunition again to fight my enemies. Perhaps that is why I am still live.' Iroegbu ended his story and searched their faces to see the impression he made. They were all quiet and thoughtful. After a while, Nneka glanced at her wristwatch and stood up.

'I have to go,' she said, 'my mother is sick, and I have to prepare our lunch. But I still have some questions,' she told Uyanna.

'Feel free and ask me anything you like whenever you like,' Uyanna replied. Nneka took Ezenwa's hand, and they started walking out of the house.

'What happened later? Did you win the battle? What happened to the monkey-like man you saw in the bush?' Nyadiba asked.

'As a commander, I did not lose any battle. The most interesting thing is that we defeated them with the supplies we took from them. Yes, I went back with my men to that bush after the Civil War, and saw only the skeleton of the monkey-like man.'

Nneka did not return to ask more questions. Her mother was very sick that she had to stay at home always, cooking and doing other household chores. It was Ezenwa who visited her regularly, going immodestly very early and returning shamelessly very late. Her parents did not show any sign of resentment for his constant presence in their house. On the contrary, his own parents sulked and spoke to him with displeasure. His father was particularly worried about the great influence Nneka wielded over him. In the words of his mother, 'he has lost his mind to her.' They wanted to forbid Ezenwa from visiting Nneka, but Uyanna intervened.

'Who could be with that beautiful girl and not lose his mind,' Uyanna had asked. 'I am surprised that he still has the intelligence to come home at the end of the day. Leave him, he would get tired and retrace his steps. Interference would make things worse.' Thus the romance continued unbroken. Their holiday would have ended without any incident if not for the annual Harmattan Carnival in the town.

It was a fascinating annual event, which took place in the town on the night of every 26th day of December. It was more of a disco dancing festival, without any cultural or religious attachment, than a parade as in carnivals, as the title suggested. It attracted many people from surrounding towns.

Ezenwa had been looking forward to that night. A night that would put Nneka once again into his hands, far away from her mother's censuring eyes. He was well aware too that the suitors whose overtures Nneka had rebuffed would be at the carnival too. But he was no longer bothered. Nneka had given him, without mincing words, the assurance of fidelity he needed. He always consoled himself with the assumption that if she had rejected them before, she would reject them again. He was not bothered about those who might be uncivil to her. He had Nyadiba and Aghadi as back up forces to overwhelm anybody who would come with violence. That was the spirit with which he went to the festival.

Nneka had acquired the sophistication and flamboyance of a university undergraduate. She was no longer that naive and timid girl who looked away to avert the gaze of men. Her style of movement now was elaborately calculated to provoke and tantalise anybody who might care to stare. She had a suave, but deliberate and provocative swinging of hips that kept men's eyes glued to her back whenever she walked. Her exquisite figure and the way she carried herself that night at the carnival was gracefully prepossessing. She wore tight blue jean trousers and a blue T-shirt that accentuated every contour of her body. Whenever she moved, men stared with ecstasy and admiration. When she danced, they put their heads together and spoke in whispers. As she anticipated, some of her suitors were there. Courageous ones made effort to approach her again, while cowardly ones grieved from a distance.

She had just danced with Ezenwa and sat down to rest when she noticed a man staring at her with rapacious lewdness. She stared back at him and tapped Ezenwa on the back to get his attention. 'Do you know that guy sitting at the table on our right?' she asked.

'Yes I do. Why do you ask?' Ezenwa asked.

'He had been staring at me and making facial gestures. Who is he?'

'He is Chief Nwabueze's son. His name is Patrick.'

'Nwabueze, the politician?' she asked.

'Yes,' Ezenwa answered with imperceptible uneasiness.

Every native of the town knew Chief Nwabueze. He was one of the wealthiest men in the country, an unscrupulous politician, who was extensively detested by the Igbos in Nigeria for his perfidious stance on Biafra. Everybody knew about his malicious article that defamed the Biafran leadership, which he published in a Nigerian daily journal immediately after the Civil War. For it alone, the Igbo's hated him with passion. Although they hated him, they wisely sought and revered his wealth. He was the first Igbo man to renounce Biafra, and thus, the Federal Government of Nigeria gave him a political appointment immediately after the war. Since then, his economic growth had been constant. He had two wives, eight children, and many concubines. Patrick was his first child. He was eight years older than Ezenwa. He was very tall and imposing. He studied Business Administration at the University of London.

When Patrick came back from London, he became the Managing Director of Vitron Petroleum Limited, a private oil firm his father established. A pampered child, he had everything he desired. People said he was incompetent in the management of the affairs of the company, and that his father had surrounded him with managerial experts whose brains wheeled the establishment.

Ezenwa was obviously worried after he threw some glances at Patrick's table and saw him actually staring at Nneka in an impious manner. Ezenwa made a gesture of disgust and grabbed Nneka's hand.

'What is the problem?' Nneka asked, worried by the look on his face.

'Let's get away from here. That guy is staring impolitely at you like a wild animal,' Ezenwa retorted.

'Don't tell me you want us to go home because of his impotent stares. It is only a stare, and that's the only thing he can do. Sit down, forget about him and enjoy yourself,' Nneka advised. Ezenwa was cowed by her words. He sat down again, but no longer comfortable. His eyes kept darting towards Patrick's table. He did not want Nneka to know that he was nettled by Patrick's interest in her. Besides cult boys' threats, Patrick's wealth was another threat Ezenwa thought that might sway Nneka's interest. He had fought successfully and warded off cult boys' interests, and was ready to keep fighting. But threats of cult boys were infinitesimal to the influence of Patrick's wealth. A wealthy man was the dream of every woman.

When Ezenwa told Nneka about Patrick, he detected a little excitement in her eyes. It was not flagrantly obvious, yet not hidden to escape his observation. That was the beginning of his presentiment. He agreed to sit down there with her again, just to pretend that he was not bothered.

A group of boys surrounded Patrick. They were sycophants who sang his praises in exchange for some bottles of beer. They saw his gaze at Nneka and inferred what he wanted, but because of a lady, who was sitting beside him, nobody offered any assistance. The lady's name was Atinuke. She was a daughter of another politician whose friendship Patrick's father ravenously sought to use in the consolidation of his political empire. She was of the *Yoruba* tribe of Western Nigeria.

When Patrick came back from London, his father took him to Atinuke's father, introduced him to the family, and encouraged him to go after Atinuke. Atinuke was presentable, but not beautiful, not the type Patrick would go for. But just to honour his father's whims and caprices, he started dating her. When his father noticed that they had started dating, he encouraged Patrick to make a marriage proposal to her. Patrick did. With eagerness and less sagacity, Atinuke accepted the proposal.

Both Patrick and Atinuke knew that the proposed marriage was a political marriage, just for their parents' interests. But besides their parents jumbled interests in the marriage, they had their veiled interests too. Atinuke wanted Patrick's wealth, while Patrick needed her father's political connection for the progress of his oil business. The incongruity of the union was obvious in the eyes of the public. But self-interests blinded the players of the game, or they saw, but pretended not to see.

Atinuke came to Patrick's village, just to know her future husband's village, and meet his people. It was her first visit to Eastern Nigeria. Only her presence at the carnival restrained Patrick from approaching Nneka.

As if fate was out to pummel Ezenwa with hard blows, Atinuke became tired of the festival and sought Patrick's permission to go home. Patrick had another interest, so he told her to go home alone. No sooner had she gone than Patrick sent one of his sycophants to bring Nneka to his table.

The boy came with a swagger, inflated vanity, and a nauseating self-importance. He pretended as if Ezenwa did not exist, and started speaking to Nneka.

'That guy wants you,' the boy said.

'Are you talking to me?' Nneka asked, outraged by his rudeness.

'Yes,' the boy replied.

'I didn't hear you. What did you say?'

'I said that Patrick wants you.'

'Who is Patrick?' Nneka asked, feigning ignorance. The boy, by the change of his countenance, appeared to be shocked by her question. He could not comprehend her ignorance. It seemed she was the only person who did not know Patrick.

'You mean you don't know Patrick Nwabueze, the Director of Vitron Petroleum Limited?' he asked.

'Yes I don't know him,' Nneka answered.

'That guy sitting over there,' the boy pointed at Patrick. 'He is rich, and he wants you.' Ezenwa heard him, and seethed with rage. If it were outside the town, Ezenwa would have reacted violently towards the boy. But he was in his town. They knew themselves. And for that too, nobody could use force on Nneka. Whatever she decided to do would be by her own volition. Ezenwa waited to see Nneka's reaction.

The impropriety of the errand boy's manner of approach and Patrick's hurtful haughtiness incensed her. The errand boy spoke as if her life, henceforth, would depend on Patrick's magnanimity.

'Tell him that I don't know him, and that I don't talk with strangers,' she replied. The boy looked aghast. Nneka was the first girl in the town to respond to Patrick's solicitude disdainfully. Being just an errand boy, he was more concerned about how to deliver the scorn to a person he almost worshipped than the implication of what the scorn would bring to Nneka. He opened his mouth to argue, but lacked the words. Nneka noticed his frustration, and added more humiliation. 'Go and deliver the message, are you not his errand boy?' she asked him. The boy frowned and went back.

Ezenwa observed the change of Patrick's countenance with immense joy. He wanted to know what his reaction would be. Now, he had seen that not every woman could be enslaved by the glamour of wealth. Patrick asked his errand boy some questions and decided to come to Nneka himself. Ezenwa saw the gesture and whispered to Nneka, 'he thinks you are a prostitute, now tell him you are not.' Ezenwa knew exactly what Nneka hated to hear about herself. It always piqued her whenever she felt that she was classified with women of little virtue. If she had thought in that direction when the errand boy came, she would have given him a bag of invectives for Patrick. But as Patrick had decided to come himself, she sharpened her tongue and waited for him.

Patrick sat down beside her, but unlike the errand boy, he extended his hand and greeted Ezenwa. This gesture reduced the intensity of impudence Nneka had prepared to display to him.

'I sent somebody to call you, and you refused to come, why?' Patrick asked Nneka.

'Why should I come? I don't know you,' she replied.

'Do you really mean that you don't know me?' he asked with smiles.

'Why should I know you?' Nneka asked disdainfully. 'You are not my father and you are not my brother. What have I got to do with you that would make me know you?'

'I am Patrick Nwabueze, the owner of Vitron Petroleum,' he boasted; exactly what Nneka hated to hear.

'And what about that? What do you want from me?' she asked. Patrick was disconcerted. Her response was exactly contrary to his expectation. When his errand boy brought back a report of scorn to him, he thought that the boy lied, or perhaps, did not vaunt about his wealth before Nneka. Now that he had done it himself, and still was scorned, he was at a loss on what to do next.

'I just want you to join me at my table over there, so that we can have fun together,' he blurted out.

'I am sorry. I don't play with strangers,' Nneka replied.

'I am not a stranger. I have introduced myself.'

'It doesn't make any difference. And please, if you would not mind going back to your table, I am busy with my boyfriend.' This response was more than what Patrick could take. He looked at Ezenwa. Ezenwa averted his gaze. Patrick would have gone back to his seat, pretend as if nothing had happened, and lie that Nneka had agreed to meet him the next day. But Ezenwa was present and heard everything that transpired between them, and would divulge them later.

'Is it because of your boyfriend?' Patrick asked her.

'For whatever reason, I am not going anywhere with you. You can go if you want, but if you don't want to go, sit down here and continue embarrassing yourself,' she replied. Naturally, Nneka was not a rude girl, but she hated to be tempted with wealth.

'You are a rude girl. Don't you know that I can take you by force, and nothing will happen,' Patrick threatened.

'You cannot do it!' Ezenwa interjected immediately.

'That I cannot do what? Do you know who I am?' Patrick asked.

'Yes I do,' Ezenwa replied.

'Who am I?' Patrick asked.

'You are a fool and a son of a fool,' Ezenwa shouted. Patrick was infuriated. He rushed back to his table and gave orders to the boys whom he believed worshipped his wealth, and would do anything to please him.

'I want you to inflict some injuries on that guy, and drag that girl to my car. I want him to have something to remind him of the day he stepped on my toes.' That same errand boy behaved like a stranger in the town. It seemed he lacked information about Ezenwa's family, or he knew but was blinded by Patrick's wealth. He was the first person to jump up, picked an empty bottle, and charged towards Ezenwa.

'Beat who?' another boy asked Patrick immediately.

'Beat that boy!' Patrick shouted furiously and pointed at Ezenwa. His voice had risen, and had attracted the attention of everybody at the square. They gathered around him. 'I want to teach him a lesson he would never forget in his life,' he raged on.

'That's because you don't know him too,' one of the boys chipped in.

'Who is he?' Patrick asked angrily, seeing that nobody, except his errand boy had gone after Ezenwa.

'When you get home, ask your father if he knows anybody called Uyanna. Do that before you do anything to that boy, else you regret the day you set your eyes on that girl,' one of the boys told him and left the arena. Like that they abandoned him one after the other.

Ezenwa was more concerned about what would happen to Nneka than what the boys would do to him. There would never be any retribution from Uyanna as far as Ezenwa was concerned. There was no doubt about that. Ezenwa knew it from the onset. Uyanna had never avenged any wrong people did to him. From the time Ezenwa knew him, his gospel had always been on love and forgiveness. Uyanna had sometimes threatened people with vengeance. But in the end, the threats would end only as threats, nothing potent. It was the misgivings people had about him as an evil man that protected Ezenwa. However, Ezenwa could not swear that Uyanna would forgive anybody who molested Nneka, especially when it concerned sexual assault, and to no other person but Nneka; now Uyanna's friend too. The consequences might be dire. But before the retribution would come, Nneka must have been assaulted and ruined, and that would be the pain. Ezenwa looked around for a weapon to defend Nneka, but none was available. He regretted ever leaving his revolver on the campus.

The errand boy glanced back, and saw that nobody was coming to fight Ezenwa with him. Even Patrick had started walking away. He dropped the weapon he had picked and left the arena. Ezenwa was relieved. Once again, Uyanna's name protected him.

Patrick fumed with rage as he went home. It was not because he was rejected, but the manner he was rejected. He saw only explicit recalcitrance and abusive impudence in Nneka's response to his overture. Even if these qualities were not inherent in her response, Patrick's bloated ego and pride generated them, and so urged him to seek a means to avenge himself and humiliate her. He ruminated on the best way to carry out his vengeance. He decided to decoy her out of her house to rape her, and later settle her with money. This decision lightened his mood, and he went to bed happily.

Very early the next morning, Patrick drove to Nneka's house in the company of that his errand boy. Nneka was shocked to see him, and so early too. Her father was indifferent to his presence, but her mother received him with high hopes. He was exactly the kind of suitor she had dreamt for her daughter. She paced about the house, offering them every entertainment at her disposal, to the immense displeasure of Nneka. It amused Patrick. In spite of all Nneka's effort to remain unconcerned, and shun his interest, her mother, by her attention, had unwittingly given him the inducements he needed. Nneka had wanted to show contentment and pretend that she did not care about his wealth. But her mother was doing the opposite. Nneka saw the contempt and the smile of triumph playing lightly on Patrick's lips. She would have reprimanded her mother but for Patrick's presence. She hated to see her mother demeaned, thought less of, or denigrated by anybody. She reserved her anger for the time she would be alone with her.

'What do you want from me?' Nneka asked Patrick, unenthusiastically.

'I still want what I wanted last night,' he replied.

'I thought you understood what I told you last night. I have a boyfriend and I don't intend to replace him with another person.'

'The boy is a poor boy, he has nothing to offer. Just a little time with me, and you would lack nothing again in your life,' Patrick replied. Inferring that Nneka's mother could be eavesdropping, he added, 'I honestly like you and would like to marry you.'

Nneka knew there was no truth in the marriage proposal, just a way to buy her mother's sympathy. It irked her that her mother should be made to seem a fool.

'Marry me?' she asked.

'Yes,' Patrick replied, thinking that he had hoodwinked her with the proposal.

'That would be the most stupid thing to do,' Nneka said.

'Why do you think it is a stupid thing to do?'

'Because I saw you with another woman last night. It was after she had gone that you sent your monkey to fetch me.'

'Sent my what?' Patrick asked.

'Your monkey,' Nneka said and pointed at the errand boy. Patrick laughed heartily. The boy frowned and fumed, but that was all he could do. The fear of offending Patrick kept him from responding abusively to the insult.

'My friend is not a monkey,' Patrick said, still grinning gleefully.

'Yes he is,' Nneka insisted. 'You told them to beat my friend, and he was foolish enough to obey. But let him thank his God that he did not hurt Ezenwa.'

'I am sorry about that. I was angry. Please forgive me, and try me again,' Patrick apologised. Nneka continued to stare at the errand boy. That the boy did not say anything in defence of himself augmented Nneka's disdain for him, and she did not regret using a pejorative word on him.

'I don't understand what you mean. What about the lady?' Nneka asked.

'I don't think I would continue with her. She is just a girlfriend,' Patrick replied.

'You went home last night, slept with her, woke up beside her, left her at home, and came here to make a proposal to me. What do you think I am?'

'You are the irresistible girl I saw last night and changed my mind. Just understand it this way. I love you.'

'Do you change your mind that easily, and love easily too?' Nneka asked.

'No, not that I change my mind easily, but nobody would look at you and remain indifferent.'

'Do you really give that to me?' she asked, grinning.

'Yes I do,' Patrick replied.

'Let's be serious. What do you want?' Nneka asked again. Patrick shifted. He felt like a person before a judge, about to be sent to jail if convicted.

'I am serious em... what is your name, I have forgotten?' he asked.

'This is serious,' Nneka replied. 'Let's start from there. You never even knew my name, so how could you have forgotten what you don't know?'

'But it does not matter. What is in a name?' he asked. Nneka knew that no power in hell or heaven would make her change her mind and walk out of her house with him, let alone marry him. She knew also that the inequality in their social status was an impediment to any kind of intimate relationship between them. He might make pretences now, but would later turn her into his slave. From the lewdness she had seen in his eyes, there was a strong indication that he would marry two or three more wives like his father.

'I am sorry,' she said, 'I won't marry you. You don't love me. You don't even know me. Your behaviour is ridiculous. You saw me barely sixteen hours ago, and you are here making marriage proposal to me. Perhaps you think that every girl would jump up and say yes because you are Chief Nwabueze's son. Well, some girls would, but not every girl. I know that you like my body and needed sexual gratification. That is all men care about women. Instead of coming openly, you started hiding behind marriage and love. You are not the first person, and I know you would not be the last. It happens every day.'

Her words stung Patrick like a wasp. He thought she was vulgar. And as her mother could be listening, her boldness baffled him. He wanted to say something, but was at a loss for words. He started stammering. Nneka saw his confusion and was amused.

'Ok, if... if... If you can...if you cannot be my wife, you can be my girlfriend. I will give you a car, and buy a house for you. When you graduate from the university, I will employ you in my company.' This was his last and the biggest bait. He had been using it, and no woman had ever resisted it. He gazed at her face to see the effect. Nneka smiled.

'Now you are talking like a man,' she replied. 'It is better this way. You were hiding behind marriage and love, but now, I can give you my reply. Your proposal is exactly a proposal of a client to a prostitute, and I am not a prostitute.'

'No, I don't mean that,' Patrick protested.

'What do you mean, a person who receives material gifts in return for sexual gratification is a prostitute,' she maintained.

'I mean that I would give you everything to make you happy.'

'Happy? What do you know about happiness? Do you think that money and material things give happiness?' Nneka asked. 'Go ahead and tell me how your money would make me happy.'

'No, you don't understand,' Patrick argued, almost disgraced. He had hoped to find a greedy and gullible mind in her. Unfortunately he met an intelligence that was about to turn his wits into foolishness. 'I mean that I would give you everything you want,' he corrected.

'That's another wrong thing to say,' she replied, determined to humiliate him. 'I can never have everything I want. Nobody had ever had everything he wants. Even you, who want to give me everything I want, had never had everything you wanted, and would never have everything you want. For one, you will never have me.'

'But if you would...'

'I have finished with you,' she cut him off, got up, and left them. Patrick was shocked. He gaped at her as she walked away tauntingly. Her mother heard everything they discussed, yet thought that Nneka was rash in her refusal. It perturbed her that her daughter should lose such a wealthy suitor. In her own thinking, it would have been better if she had told him to give her time to think about the proposal. Her manner of refusal was not a good way to send away a suitor, moreover a rich one. Not many girls would have her luck to receive such proposal from one so rich. But Nneka had gone.

Nneka's mother watched in exasperation as Patrick and his sycophant drove away. She called Nneka. Nneka came out. But before her mother could say anything, Nneka tongue-lashed her with words filled with venom. Her father heard her harsh voice and came out too.

'I was surprised by her excitement,' he chipped in, 'I thought she was going to push you into the car and force you to go with him because he is rich.' What Nneka and her father gave to her mother that morning in the appearance of rebuke was more than what her mother bargained for. Nneka had never spoken to her uncharitably like that. What hurt her most was that Nneka accused her of trying to push her into prostitution. She tried to hold Nneka's hand and pacify her with explanations of her good intentions. Nneka evaded her grasp and went back into her room murmuring angrily. Her mother, beleaguered and dejected by her husband's criticism, burst into tears.

Chapter 32

Ezenwa got home after the carnival and slept peacefully. When he woke up, he woke up peacefully too. He had been afraid that Nneka could be infatuated by the glamour of Patrick's wealth, and she would make an imprudent decision, like many girls would do. But after he heard what she told Patrick last night, a new kind of pride and respect for her, which he had never accorded to any woman, grew in Ezenwa. If Nneka could, with such effrontery, affront and scorn the wealth of Patrick Nwabueze, then Ezenwa had no reason to be afraid. Nothing could wrench her away from his grip. He sat down on his bed and mused on all that happened the previous night. What could he have done if those boys had fought him and took Nneka away? Nothing than to rush back to the university, return with his revolver, and kill Patrick. Nothing else would have pacified him. However, he was grateful to God that it ended the way it did. He could not have matched the strength of Patrick and his sycophants. Nyadiba and Aghadi, on whom he always relied to back him up, had gone after some girls, and left him alone with Nneka. Joyfully, he got up from the bed, washed his face, and went to Nyadiba's house.

Nyadiba listened intently to the story, sighing intermittently, regretting ever having gone out of sight in pursuit of some elusive girls. 'If that was the case,' he said, ' Nneka is the best woman God has created.'

'I think likewise. I hope she would continue that way,' Ezenwa agreed.

After a brief discussion, they decided to go to Nneka's house and wake her up with a homage. If they had added haste in their movement, they would have encountered Patrick inside Nneka's house. But they walked languidly, and met Patrick when he had taken the first bend out of the house. This left them in doubt about his mission. They were unable to conclude if his presence in that area was in quest of Nneka. That moment, the fear Ezenwa thought he had suppressed and defeated rose up again, but its torments were postponed until Ezenwa ascertained that Patrick had actually visited Nneka.

When Ezenwa and Nyadiba got to Nneka's house, her mother greeted them with a sickly face. She lacked the usual enthusiasm with which she had always greeted them. Ezenwa inferred immediately that something had gone awry, and tactfully kept smiling to hide his nervousness.

Nneka heard his voice and came out to meet him. She had cried too, and made effort to cover her grief with levity and jollity. Ezenwa was not deceived. He had known Nneka too long to be deceived by a manipulative farce. He deduced immediately that Patrick's visit, and the diversity of interests it generated, must have brought the gloom in the family. He wondered, with palpitating heart, who was in favour and who was against Patrick's visit.

Nneka's father came out too. Ezenwa searched his face, and analysed the tone of his greeting to know on whose side he was, but discovered nothing.

'If you would not mind,' Nneka said, 'I would dress up and go to your house with you.'

'Why so early?' Ezenwa asked. 'You said that your mother is sick, and you have to help in the house.'

'Yes, but I am tired of this house. I can no longer rest here. I am tired of suitors,' she said angrily. Ezenwa's fear was confirmed. Patrick was here!

'You cannot run away from your house, and you cannot run away from your suitors. They will continue to come and go until they see you. You are lucky your parents are not like other parents that force or coax their daughters to marry against their wish,' Ezenwa said. Nneka's mother stiffened.

Ezenwa did not know what had transpired between Nneka and her mother over Patrick, so he did not observe the change in her mother's pose. He did not know the blow he had just delivered by his insinuation. But Nyadiba saw her, guessed the reason for the change in her countenance and added, 'especially when the suitor is a rich man, they would sell their daughters happiness.'

Truth, they said, is bitter. Nyadiba's comment was the truth, bitter and hot at the same time, too hot for Nneka's mother to swallow. She got up instantly from her seat and walked into her room. Her mind was filled with hatred for Ezenwa and his friend. If they knew how she felt about their comments, they would have hurried out of the house. She had always liked Ezenwa, but now that her daughter was rejecting a suitor of her dreams just because of him, she would look for a way to get rid of him, the nauseous nuisance. Anger gnawed persistently at her heart. She blamed herself for condoning the transgression of privilege that gave Ezenwa control over her daughter's whims. If it were not a transgression of privilege, she thought, why should miscreants invade her house early in the morning and make comments that not only tormented her, but also hardened her daughter's heart? A heart she intended to convince against all odds to give Patrick a chance. She decided to prohibit Ezenwa from coming to her house, but she waited for them to go before she would communicate her decision to Nneka.

Ezenwa, Nyadiba, and Nneka conversed for a while. Ezenwa noticed that the usual amiability for which he had known Nneka was lacking in her at the moment. He inferred her worries, and knew she would only divulge it to him alone, thus he sought an opportunity to be alone with her. 'I think I have to go now,' he said and stood up. Nyadiba stood up too. Nneka rushed into her room and dressed up to see them off. Her mother thought she was dressing to go home with Ezenwa. She came out to impede her.

'Where are you going?' she asked Nneka brashly.

'I want to see them off,' Nneka replied and ignored the brashness in the question. It was Nneka's way of life. She would never talk back to her mother or reply harshly to her questions in the presence of visitors. Even if her mother had ordered her back into the house, she would have obeyed and go back. But when she knew that her visitors would not hear her voice, she would give her mother hell. She guarded her response to the brashness, and waited for Ezenwa to get far from the house.

Well outside the house, Ezenwa reduced the velocity of his steps. Nyadiba understood his motive and walked away from them. Alone with Nneka, Ezenwa asked her what has been tormenting her. Nneka sighed.

'Patrick came to my house this morning with that his sycophant,' she replied.

'What happened?' Ezenwa asked, agitated.

'He made a marriage proposal to me.'

'And?'

'Of course I rejected it. How would I accept such proposal from somebody I met barely eighteen hours ago.'

'And your parents? What did they say?'

'My father doesn't like him too. I have not heard from my mother, perhaps we shall talk about it when I get back,' she lied. It was not only a lie to protect her mother's dignity before her boyfriend, but also an effort to prevent him from languishing in anguish and anxiety if he knew her mother's opinion of Patrick.

'I think your mother would want you to marry him,' Ezenwa said.

'Why did you say that?' Nneka asked, perturbed.

'She responded to my greetings aggressively this morning. Perhaps she thought that you are rejecting your suitors because of me.'

'No, that's not the reason. You know she is sick and was unhappy that I came back very late last night,' Nneka lied. Ezenwa believed her. She was happy that her lie convinced Ezenwa.

'That's all right. I am sure nobody would force you to marry anybody against your will. But if you decide to marry him, tell me on time,' Ezenwa said. Nneka flinched, astonished by his insinuation.

'What do you mean by that?' she asked and started weeping immediately. Ezenwa gaped at her. He only made the comment to see her reaction, and perhaps derive succour from it. He never knew it would lead to tears.

'I am sorry please. I don't mean to hurt you. I was worried...'

'When would you ever learn to trust me?' she asked angrily, cutting him off from what he was about to say. 'Perhaps I was wrong. I should have accepted Patrick's proposal,' she said and started walking back to her house.

'Nneka wait! I am sorry! Wait!' Ezenwa shouted after her. She did not stop. She had never exhibited any kind of intransigence before him, let alone walk out on him. He gaped at her with a melancholic gaze that would have stirred her heart if she had turned to look at him again. Her anger was not in favour of Patrick's interest, but protest against Ezenwa's feeble confidence. She was miffed that after many years of friendship, Ezenwa could still not trust her. He continued to make inflammatory insinuations in spite of the efforts she was making to allay his fears. It was because of him that she spoke to Patrick rudely last night. As if that was not enough, she made every effort to be uncivil to him that morning, to scare him away and give Ezenwa the peace he needed and richly deserved. Perhaps after this he would learn to confide in me, she thought.

She got into her house, threw herself on her bed, and started weeping. Her heart was heavy with grief. Her mother came into the room to tell her to stay away from Ezenwa, but saw her dismal countenance, and wisely left her alone.

Ezenwa told Nyadiba what Nneka did. Nyadiba was astonished. 'I cannot believe that Nneka walked out on you,' he said.

'But she did. I am telling you the truth,' Ezenwa replied, bewildered.

'Do you think it is because of that guy?' Nyadiba asked.

'Of course yes. What else could have made her behave like that? And you know, I have said things worse than what I told her now, and she had never been angry. I think she is looking for a reason to break our relationship, and not finding any, she feigned anger.'

'She might not want the guy as she told you, but don't underestimate the influence of her mother. Girls always listen to their mothers as far as marriage is the issue. I am sure she had been trying to convince her that she would have no future with you.'

'I think you are right,' Ezenwa accepted.

'What shall I do now. I cannot sleep until I resolve everything with her. Imagine what I have gone true because of her, only to be dumped like this,' Ezenwa lamented.

'Don't say that you were dumped. Let's wait and see how it is going to end,' Nyadiba consoled him.

'Is it not better I go back to her and apologise?'

'Never! Don't do it that way. If you do it that way, she would start using such behaviours as a weapon to coerce you. Whenever you disagree with her, she would threaten to jilt you. We shall go back there tomorrow morning, not today,' Nyadiba advised. Ezenwa, perplexed, lost his sense of reason, and accepted the advice. Why not? His lacerated heart was open to the influence of any kind of counsel, though he was lucky to have Nyadiba, who had always been witty and calculating in all his endeavours.

Ezenwa got home, flustered and dejected. Everybody in his house knew that something was tormenting him, but nobody knew what it was. Uyanna guessed, and guessed correctly, but preferred not to interfere, with the reason that such gloom was a necessary experience, the lugubrious lot of lovers. So many times he had told Ezenwa that women were like burning flames, good and useful at a distance, hot and painful when too close, deadly and dangerous when leaned on. Now, after this, Ezenwa would understand why Uyanna had always told him that a woman's backside was not a playground. For a woman as pretty as Nneka, it was very dangerous.

At night, Ezenwa could not sleep. He rolled on his bed from one side to the other, and prayed for day to break. He had been trying recently to undermine Nneka's grip on him by hiding his agitation each time she told him stories of suitors. Now, he felt like kneeling down before her to kiss her feet and tell her that his life was in her hands. In his state of mind, he was ready to do anything that would restore him to her affection.

Unknown to him, Nneka had been crying and regretting her action, and prayed too for the day to break. She too was ready to abandon her pride and let him know that she could not live without him. She had rejected Patrick and was happy that she did. As proud as Patrick was, she knew that nothing would bring him back to her house.

Unknown to Ezenwa and Nneka, Patrick had left Nneka's house, cursing and swearing, determined not to see her again. But on his way out, he saw Ezenwa and Nyadiba, trekking and laughing along the dusty road. Their legs were dirty, heavily coated with red dust. He inferred that they were going to Nneka's house. His ego revolted against his decision. He refused to accept that Nneka rejected him with all his influence and wealth in preference to poor Ezenwa. He took an inexpedient decision to continue making overtures to her. This decision was not just to satisfy his prurient interest, but also a kind of laborious and invidious machination to redeem his bruised ego, and probably clog the flow of love between Nneka and Ezenwa. If he could by such intensified effort, ensnare her in the intricacies of his web, satisfy his implacable passion, just once, he would dump her and forget her. Her beauty had nothing to add to his financial ambition.

The next day, as early as on the previous day, Patrick arrived at Nneka's house with a dismal maniacal enthusiasm. As a component part of the intrigue he was weaving, he asked to see Nneka's mother instead of Nneka. Nneka's mother went outside the house to meet him. After some minutes of intimate conversation, willingly and without wits, she was lured into the complexities of Patrick's plot, and promised Patrick to convince her daughter to accept his proposal.

Nneka was still on her bed, sadly mulling over the events of the previous day. She was afraid that she had offended Ezenwa. Her eyes were still red. She had cried all night, and was still sobbing hysterically. She was very tired. In that state of mind, her mother came into her room and told her that Patrick wanted to see her. She raised up her head, stared coldly at her mother, and told her to go and tell Patrick to eat shit. Her mother was astounded, and sat down on her bed to coax her. Her attitude infuriated Nneka. Nneka scolded her again, and told her to get out of her room. Her mother frowned, deeply offended by Nneka's comments, but was determined to accomplish the promise she made to Patrick. She started pleading with Nneka to give Patrick a chance. Nneka became furious and told her mother to get away from her side. Her mother stood before her, smiling mischievously. 'If you don't get away from my side I would go out there and give him the message myself. If you like him why not marry him. I am sure my father would allow you to go,' she chided her mother.

'Don't insult me. I am your mother?' her mother protested.

'I have lost confidence in your motherhood,' Nneka blurted out. Her mother gaped at her, and went back to Patrick. But instead of giving Patrick Nneka's message, she lied and told him to wait, that Nneka was preparing to come out and meet him. Patrick waited. But after what seemed like eternity, and Nneka did not appear, he became restless.

Nneka's mother did not know how else to convince her daughter to accept Patrick, yet she was determined not to lose a suitor as wealthy as Patrick. She went back to Nneka and attempted assiduously once more to compel her to come out. 'He said that he wouldn't go unless you come out and talk with him, or do you want me to bring him to your room?' Nneka's mother threatened.

'Do that and bid me farewell from this house,' Nneka retorted. Her mother was about to speak again when she heard voices outside her house. Nneka heard them too and leaped up from her bed.

Ezenwa and Nyadiba got into the house and saw Nneka's mother coming out hastily from the direction of her daughter's room. Her countenance was hostile, worse than what they saw the previous day. They greeted her, but she replied with scornful murmurs. Ezenwa was not deterred. He was not ready to concede his interest to the whims of any greedy mother, after all, where was Patrick when he was risking his life in fights with cult boys to protect Nneka. He felt that he had had enough anguish, and was prepared to chastise Nneka's mother effusively and abusively without mincing words. His words, as pejorative and denigrating as they would be, would teach her that somebody had risked his neck to keep her daughter healthy and alive. Perhaps she did not know yet that her daughter's happiness should be above any avaricious interest.

'Where is Nneka?' Ezenwa asked Nneka's mother insolently. His imperial tone surprised her. Baffled, she did not know what to answer. She knew that Nneka had gone to wash her face to come out and meet Ezenwa, having rejected all her entreaties to see Patrick. She also knew that Nneka would not hide her preference for Ezenwa and her resentment for Patrick. And she had earlier promised Patrick that Nneka was coming out to meet him. She became confused. That moment, in her sight, Ezenwa was the most loathsome encumbrance she had ever had, and should be dispelled.

'Nneka said that she doesn't want to see you again,' she lied.

'Nneka said this?' Ezenwa asked, astounded.

'Yes. And please go before she insults you,' she advised.

'What did I tell you?' Ezenwa asked Nyadiba. 'Any woman who did not succumb to the whiff of money must be an angel.' Nyadiba, in his usual witty and cautious reasoning, deciphered something unconvincing in the woman's statement.

'Where is Nneka?' Nyadiba asked, 'I would like her to tell Ezenwa to go away with her own mouth.'

'No, let's go,' Ezenwa insisted. 'Very soon, we shall go back to the university, then she would know that there are things money cannot provide.' Patrick heard him and laughed. Whatever would happen to Nneka later was not Patrick's concern. All he wanted was to take her to bed and push her away.

Nneka had wanted to dress properly, use make up on her face to hide the marks of stress. But when she heard the high pitch of Ezenwa's voice, she knew that something was wrong. She left everything she was doing and came out.

She wore very tight shorts and a tiny transparent shirt. The cloth showed her physical attributes clearly. In her imprudence and hastiness, she did not wear her bra to hold and obscure her breast. It jutted out, and was dangling inside the tiny transparent shirt. It was not a new sight to Ezenwa, and elicited no desire from him. Nyadiba looked away in embarrassment. Patrick had never seen such beauty in his life. He gaped unblinkingly at her, to the disadvantage of his hormones, whose reactions were embarrassingly manifested in a turgid element jutting out of his groin. He brought his legs together to hide it, but Nyadiba and Nneka's mother had observed it. Nneka's mother was scandalised by her daughter's unrestrained exhibition, and lashed out at her. 'Go back and dress properly,' she ordered.

Nneka threw a glance at her mother, took Ezenwa's hand, and started dragging him towards her room. 'Let's go to my room,' she said as she pulled him along. Ezenwa followed her.

Patrick continued to muse on what he had seen. He had wanted to copulate with Nneka and dump her, but now, he was not sure he could do that. Nobody could dump such beauty. That moment, his assiduity to get her acquired supplementary impetus.

Her mother loitered about the house, confused on how to retain Patrick. Her last trick had been discovered. Patrick had been rebuffed the second time, and he would have gone if not for his enraged sexual urge. He sat down calmly, and waited for his turgid manhood to subside before he could stand up.

Some minutes later, he told Nneka's mother that he wanted to go.

'No, not yet. Allow her to dismiss the boy,' she advised. Patrick was confused. He had seen Nneka smiling and pulling Ezenwa into her room, and who knew what they were doing there? The thought of her naked body returned to torment him. He wanted to tell her mother to go and bring her out, but decided against it. Perhaps there a trick to get rid of Ezenwa, the fool. He sat down again and waited. But when Nneka did not appear, he discovered that Nneka's mother had lied to him. He sighed, whispered to Nneka's mother, and went away.

Nneka told Ezenwa everything that happened the previous day, including her mother's interest, which, hitherto, she had been unwilling to divulge. They could have been inside the room for eternity. When they finally came out, Patrick had gone, but left a message that he would be back. From that day, a kind of rivalry started between Ezenwa and Patrick. Patrick relied on Nneka's mother's influence to deliver her daughter into his hands, while Ezenwa was sustained by Nneka's unflappable display of desire for him. The whole thing became a knotty scheme when her mother convinced her father that Nneka had been unruly and rude to her suitors. With that conviction, Nneka's mother compelled her husband to force her daughter to give all her suitors commensurate attention. So when Nneka received Patrick the next morning with a smiling face, Patrick thought that he had broken her obstinacy, and was about to capture the elusive treasure.

The share of Nneka's attention did not pique Ezenwa. His only concern was that Patrick had a car, and with the assistance of Nneka's mother, visited Nneka more than him. With the monotony of Patrick's visit, Ezenwa's monopoly of Nneka's affection was threatened. This rivalry continued until the end of the Christmas season, the time for Patrick to leave the village, and the time for Ezenwa to go back to the university with Nneka. Ezenwa was happy, because their holiday was about to come to an end, and with that, the scramble with Patrick for the possession of Nneka would end. Patrick saw that he had lost the game, and to no other person but the less privileged Ezenwa. He decided to make a last effort.

One morning, instead of going to Nneka's house as he usually did, he went to Ezenwa's house, and demanded to see him. Ezenwa saw him through his window, and thought that he had come to harm him. He hid under his bed and sent Ilodinuno, his younger brother to alert his grandfather. Uyanna came out and interrogated Patrick. He only sent for Ezenwa when he was convinced that Patrick's visit was without peril. Ezenwa came out to meet Patrick.

'What do you want with me?' he asked Patrick.

'I need to talk to you about your girlfriend,' Patrick told Ezenwa when they were already out of the house.

'My girlfriend?'

'Yes.'

'What about her?' Ezenwa asked cautiously, thinking that Patrick was about to make a threat. If it got to threats, he would seek Bambam's help. Bambam must have a way to hit Patrick tactfully and still remain invisible.

'I am sorry for the way I intruded into your affair, but I want you to understand that I meant no harm. You know we are men, and that the girl is too beautiful for any man to overlook,' Patrick said.

'That's true,' Ezenwa agreed. 'But what exactly do you want from me?' he asked.

'The truth is that I saw you with the *babe* at the carnival, and since that day, my body is yet to return to normal, so I need your help.'

'How do I come in?' Ezenwa asked.

'You see, the truth is that I am not going to marry her. Forget about that crap I gave her mother. It was just a ploy to clinch her. All I need is just a *screw* and I would leave her for you.'

'You mean you just want to *bang* her and leave her?'

'That's all I want,' Patrick said. Ezenwa's brow began to thicken at such obscenity. 'But not for free,' Patrick added, almost immediately to expunge Ezenwa's fears. 'I am willing to pay any price you want. I will pay you and not her.'

Ezenwa became wary and smiled tactfully. 'You should have told me this all the while,' Ezenwa said, 'I need money as the Sahara Desert needs rain.'

'Name your price,' Patrick challenged.

'Twenty thousand Naira,' Ezenwa said, just to scare Patrick away.

'No, this ridiculous,' Patrick objected. Nobody would pay such price just to *screw* a girl.'

'Some girls worth it, especially the one I would later marry. Or do you expect me to give my future wife to you for less than that?' Ezenwa asked. Patrick remained thoughtful for a while. Twenty thousand Naira was nothing to him, but he was determined to get Nneka with little amount of money, just to humiliate her. He continued to bargain with Ezenwa. When

Ezenwa refused to accept less, he went to his car and came back with ten thousand Naira.

'Here is half, I will give you the rest when you bring her to this hotel tomorrow,' Patrick said and gave Ezenwa the money and the address of a hotel. Ezenwa counted the money quickly.

'It is complete,' he said and smiled.

'The deal is sealed. I am waiting for you. Don't fail. If you fail you will pay dearly for it. Nobody takes my money without delivering the goods,' Patrick threatened.

'No, trust me. As long as you will give me the rest, I must bring her,' Ezenwa replied.

'I am waiting,' Patrick said and drove away. Ezenwa was astounded. He laughed at Patrick's vanity. He had never seen such absurdity in his life. As far as he was concerned, no woman was worth a thousand Naira just for a *bang*, even if her genitals were made of gold. To pay ten thousand Naira was outrageous, let alone with a promise to pay more. And after all said and done, who would give him Nneka? Patrick must be a fool indeed to think that money could tempt Ezenwa to deliver Nneka to him. However, instinct warned Ezenwa that Patrick wanted more than sex, and that whatever he had in mind that compelled him to pay such exorbitant amount must be dangerous. But intuition told him that ego could induce such absurdity. He rejected the suggestion of his intuition. Perhaps Patrick had planned with Nneka's mother to kidnap her and keep her captive against her wish. Nneka too would only cry and protest for some days, and calm down later to enjoy whatever Patrick had to offer. In such circumstance, twenty thousand Naira was insignificant. Immediately, the premonition of such an unpleasant possibility started tormenting him. He ran into the house, kept the money, and hurried to Nyadiba's house. Nyadiba always had a cool head, and Ezenwa knew that he must have a solution.

'You should have asked for more money,' Nyadiba said and laughed.

'I am not worried about the money, but about the consequences of it on Nneka. Right now, I don't know what her mother has planned. She was determined to give Nneka to Patrick at all cost. This might be a plot between them. And you know, the time for him to go back to his base has come. If he goes with her, I would never see her again. Who knows what he has promised her mother.'

'No, her mother would not do a thing like that. What about her education? Won't she get her degree?' Nyadiba asked.

'Damn degree! You don't know the mentality of women when wealth is the issue. They reason without intellect.'

'In that case, the best thing to do is to warn her not to go to any place with her mother or anybody, but don't tell her about the money, unless you want to risk her anger,' Nyadiba advised.

'Am I a fool? If she hears about the money, she would insult me, and force me to return it,' Ezenwa agreed.

'What shall we do with Patrick, I don't want him to come to my house again and make threats. Though I am not afraid of his threats, but the subject is too dirty for people to hear.'

'Do you think he too would make a threat another person would hear?' Nyadiba asked. 'If the story gets out, people would call him a fool. Can you imagine him telling somebody something as repugnant as that? And you know he has a bride. Do you think he would like her to know what he has done?'

'That is true. Oh, why haven't I thought in that direction? All these nonsense would have ended,' Ezenwa said regrettably.

'It is not yet late. We can go to his house tomorrow morning with the money and break the news to her. I am sure Patrick would deny and would not touch the money,' Nyadiba suggested. Ezenwa accepted. But before Ezenwa did anything, he went to Nneka's house and warned her not to go anywhere with anybody. It was a puzzling instruction shrouded in mystery, which Ezenwa refused to divulge. Yet Nneka obeyed. Her only fear was that Ezenwa might be planning to use the measure he used on cult boys on Patrick, which, without doubt, would generate unsavoury consequences. But as she had learnt not to question or interfere in such affairs, she remained calm. If Patrick was killed, he must have begged for his death. Nneka knew that Ezenwa would never opt for extreme measures unless there was a threat to her life or his own life. Now that he had warned her to stay indoors, she knew the threat existed.

Ezenwa and Nyadiba arrived at Patrick's house. The number of security men guarding the house surprised them. Before they would be permitted to enter inside the compound, they must say who they wanted to see, and give a cogent reason for their visit. They knew it would be difficult, yet they were not deterred. They approached the gate gently.

'What do you want?' one of the security men asked.

'We want to see Patrick's wife,' Nyadiba said.

'Patrick's wife? Patrick is not yet married,' the man replied.

'We mean the woman he intends to marry,' Ezenwa corrected.

'Does she know you? Did you have any appointment with her?' the man asked.

'No, but our mission here is very important,' Ezenwa answered.

'I don't understand,' the man said. 'The woman is not of your tribe, and this is her first visit to this village. How can you convince me that you know her?' he asked. As he was talking, another security man joined them.

'I think it is better we tell her. It is up to her to know if she wants to see them,' the second security man advised. The first man took the advice and wanted to go and inform Atinuke of their presence.

'But why do you want to see her?' the first security man asked again. Here was the problem. What would they say? If they said something flimsy, Atinuke would ignore them, and the security men would send them away.

'Tell her that we brought the money back for her,' Nyadiba said. The security man went to Atinuke and told her exactly what Nyadiba said.

'Which money?' she asked him.

'I don't know but I think it is better you see them,' the man advised. Money was a delicate issue. Nobody resisted its attraction. Atinuke, as rich as she was, knew that nobody owed her, and that she had not lost any money, yet she left the packing she was doing to attend to people she did not know.

'Bring them in,' she told the man, and waited for them in front of the house. Ezenwa saw her and moved quickly towards her before Patrick would see him and intervene, or tell the security men to beat him and send him away.

'What do you want?' Atinuke asked Ezenwa with a deep frown on her face.

'I am sorry to disturb you this early morning,' Ezenwa apologised. 'Actually, it is Patrick we want to see.'

'He is very busy now, he has some visitors. Why do you want to see him?'

'I brought back his money.'

'His money? Which money? The guard said that you want to meet me, and now you are talking about Patrick.'

'No, that wasn't what we told him. We asked for Patrick, and he told us that he was busy, then we told him that we needed somebody whom Patrick could trust, so he came and called you,' Nyadiba lied.

'What is the money for?' Atinuke asked impatiently.

'Actually, Patrick has been coming to my house every morning, and has been trying to convince my sister to marry him,' Ezenwa explained. 'Yesterday he came and my sister was not at home, so he gave my mother this money to keep for her. But when my sister came back, she told me to return the money. She said that she won't touch his money until they are legally married. You see, she is a very intelligent girl.'

'Who wanted to marry your sister?' Atinuke asked, confused.

'Patrick!' Ezenwa claimed.

'Which Patrick?'

'This Patrick Nwabueze.'

'Marry your sister? I don't understand. Tell me the story again,' Atinuke pleaded.

'It is simple,' Ezenwa said. 'Patrick wants to marry my sister. He has been coming to my house every morning. But he came yesterday and did not meet her, so he left this money for her. But when my sister came back, my mother gave her the money, she rejected it and told me to send it back to Patrick. What I said was very simple.' Atinuke started shivering hysterically. It looked as if she was going to faint. She wanted to ask more questions, but was lost for words. When she finally said something, everything she said was incomprehensible, but Ezenwa and Nyadiba understood that she wanted them to wait there. She moved away briskly, murmuring and gesticulating furiously.

From where they were standing, Ezenwa and Nyadiba heard her voice in something that sounded like a squabble, and another voice trying to calm her down. The second voice was a man's voice, which when it got closer, they understood was Patrick's.

'Where are they?' Patrick asked. Ezenwa and Nyadiba heard his voice and turned. Patrick's father and his bride were coming behind him. When Patrick saw Ezenwa, his rage subsided. Atinuke noticed the change instantly. Patrick winked repeatedly to Ezenwa to stop speaking. Ezenwa pretended not to understand, and as Patrick approached, he shouted,

'Nneka told me to bring back your money.' Patrick made another desperate sign to him to shut up, but he pretended not to understand and wanted to repeat his message.

'Who are you and who is Nneka?' Patrick asked, still making facial gestures.

Atinuke deduced that Patrick might attempt to give Ezenwa signs with facial gestures. She left her position behind him, came to his front, and stared unblinkingly at his face. Seeing that his game was over, Patrick did not allow Ezenwa to repeat his message before he called some security men.

'Who brought these boys into this compound?' he asked the security men.

'They said that they wanted to meet Atinuke,' one of the security men replied. It was then that Patrick understood their intention, and started trembling with fear. If they had convinced

Atinuke, her engagement to him would have been jeopardised, and his dream of her father's political connection would be aborted.

'Throw them out!' he shouted to the security men. The security men grabbed Ezenwa and Nyadiba and started pushing them out of the house. That was not how Atinuke wanted the matter to be settled. She would have liked to ask them some questions to clarify their intention. But since Patrick had thrown them out, she kept quiet, and kept her eyes wide open. That was the last time Ezenwa saw Patrick.

Chapter 33

Ezenwa, Nyadiba, and Nneka returned to the university after the holiday. Everywhere was calm and peaceful. It was their second year in the university, and Bambam's final year. A day after they arrived, Nneka went to the Department of Microbiology and saw some of the results already published on the notice board. Professor Ngadi had published his own results too. Nneka searched intently for her name and saw it. 'Ezenwa is indeed a wonder boy. See the ease with which he make things happen,' she muttered and smiled.

After her encounter with Ngadi over her first semester result, Nneka knew that he would never dare withhold her result again, and he did not. She smiled again and exclaimed, 'I love Ezenwa, I love my wonder boy. Wonder boy! Wonder boy!' She was very happy with what she saw on the notice board, and went in search of Ezenwa to thank him for all he had been doing for her.

Ezenwa had gone to her room with Nyadiba. Her room mates told them that she had gone to check her results. They started going to the Department of Microbiology, but saw her coming up the road. Nneka saw them too, stopped, and waited for them to come to her. As they were coming, she saw another girl coming behind them. She resembled somebody she knew very well. Her attention was diverted from them to the girl. When the girl got closer, it was Joy, Nneka recognised her, screamed with ecstasy, and started running towards her. Ezenwa thought that she was coming to him, but when she ignored him, and continued running, he was forced to turn and see the object of her joy. He saw Joy, sighed, and turned away his face. He had not forgiven her, and would not have spoken to her if Nneka had not expressed so much joy at seeing her. It was just like Nneka, always forgiving and loving again with ease. Nyadiba bought Ezenwa's sentiment too, but since Joy's presence elicited so much enthusiasm from Nneka, he extended his hand and gave Joy a lacklustre greeting too. What Ezenwa and Nyadiba did not know was the confession Joy made to Nneka, the only reason why Nneka forgave her.

After they maimed Solomon, Joy was afraid of what would happen to her. She quickly confessed the part she played in the failed attempt to rape Nneka. Nneka forgave her. For fear of Ezenwa's vengeance, Nneka hid the confession from him, and saved Joy the retribution that would have been her lot.

Ezenwa and Nyadiba did not want to get involved in women's discussions. Ezenwa in particular hated to see Joy, so they walked ahead of them, while Nneka conversed with her animatedly.

'What did you come here to do?' Nneka asked her.

'What else could I have come to a university to do?' Joy asked in return.

'That's good!' Nneka exclaimed. 'What course of study?'

'Microbiology,' Joy replied.

'That's my course. Where do you live?'

'Eyo Ita Hall, Joy answered'

'That's my hall. Which room?' Nneka asked.

'Room 223.'

'Directly opposite my room. Once again we are together,' Nneka said. From there, she led Joy to her room and introduced her to her room mates. That day, another incongruous friendship started between Nneka and Joy. Nobody else saw the incompatibility vividly as Ezenwa did. It was not because of Joy's old and treacherous misconduct. Ezenwa had always known that a heinous rivalry and a ruinous jealousy dominated Joy's sentiments about Nneka. His new discomfort was based on the information he got from Bambam about some wicked characters living with Joy in Room 223 of Eyo Ita Hall. It was a resident of that room, Berta, that took Nneka's nude pictures for Ben Jack, and Ezenwa was yet to settle that score.

Ezenwa was scared of Nneka's friendship with the occupants of that room. He wanted to warn Nneka, but Bambam restrained him. 'Leave her,' Bambam said, 'we still have that score to settle. I know that before long, if the story you told me about Joy is true, she would join forces with Berta against Nneka. They would try to betray her again, and then our moon would be full.' Ezenwa agreed and left Nneka to associate with Joy, but prayed that her wits would not be outwitted by obscure wickedness hiding behind smiling faces and flattering voices of treacherous friends. Flattery, he knew, was a weapon that could easily disarm intelligence. Bambam could have been a prophet. Some weeks later, his prediction manifested.

The Oak Theatre, a popular theatre group in the University of Nigeria Nsukka, wanted to make a drama presentation of one of the most popular plays written by of one of the university's professor. The drama was extensively publicised that every student wanted to watch it, except Nneka, who knew that she could not go out at night. She had tried to convince Ezenwa to go with her. Ezenwa refused, and argued that such places could easily be invaded by cult boys and that anybody who wanted to injure her could easily do it and escape unseen. 'Darkness offered cover for deeds of darkness,' Ezenwa had told her. She accepted.

On the night of the drama, Berta told Joy to bring Nneka to the theatre at all cost. Joy tried to convince Nneka to go with them. Nneka refused. But with effort and assurances of protection against cult boys, Joy doused her fears and convinced her to go to the theatre. Foolishly, against all reason, and in disobedience to Ezenwa's instruction, just to please Joy, Nneka accepted Joy's invitation and went to the theatre. Naturally, Nneka had never gone anywhere without attracting immense attention. The moment she got into the theatre, some students started making catcalls. It was more than any attention Nneka had ever received in her life. She sat down quietly, and neither smiled nor looked at anybody. Then Joy said, 'Nneka you are really blessed. See how everybody acknowledged your entrance.'

Bambam heard the furore, turned towards the entrance and saw Nneka, Joy, and Berta coming into the theatre. He murmured angrily, stood up immediately, looked around to make sure that nobody gave him any attention, and sneaked out of the theatre.

The drama started and ended two hours later. Nneka enjoyed every minute of it. She chattered on her way back to Eyo Ita Hall, praising the performers and lamenting sorrowfully about her life of seclusion that had been preventing her from participating in such social activities.

It was dark, and many people were going in the same direction with them. The darkness was so thick that it was difficult to differentiate between a man and a woman. Nneka glanced back repeatedly and continued talking. Joy threw in some comments once in a while, but Berta remained mysteriously mute.

The distance from Eyo Ita Hall to the Arts Theatre was not long, but was enough for any evil-minded person to perpetrate any nefarious act and disappear without a trace.

The moment the girls crossed the road, from the side of the Arts Theatre to the side of Eyo Ita Hall, Nneka saw somebody running towards them. She panicked, removed her shoes, and attempted to run. Joy was afraid too and moved before Nneka. Nneka wanted to follow her, but Berta grabbed her hand, restrained her, and asked why she wanted to run.

'Can't you see that guy coming here, he might be coming after me,' Nneka replied and tried to extricate her hand from Berta's grip. Berta held her firmly. Nneka struck her in the face and started struggling to free herself, yet Berta did not slack her hold. Bully saw what he thought was a fight and increased his pace. He was just on time to prevent Nneka from striking Berta again.

'What is the problem?' he asked and pushed Berta away.

'Oh it is you Bully,' Nneka said, relieved. 'Were you in the theatre?' she asked.

'Yes, and after the drama I started looking for you, but because of the darkness, it was difficult to locate anybody. It was when a car passed that I saw you with the car's light and started coming.' Berta sighed disappointedly and walked away.

'What is the problem?' Bully repeated.

'Nothing, I saw you running towards us and wanted to run away, but she held me back.'

'She held you back?'

'Yes.'

'Why? Assuming someone is coming to hurt you, she would hold you for him?'

'I don't know why she did it,' Nneka replied, breathing rapidly and regretting ever disobeying Ezenwa.

'This is strange. You were three, where is the third girl?'

'She ran away too,' Nneka said. Bully looked around and would not have seen them if it were not for the flash of light from another passing car. Four boys were hiding behind the water tank under a mango tree some metres away from them.

'Hold my hand and don't panic,' Bully told Nneka. She took his hand, and they started walking towards her hall.

'What is it?' Nneka asked, trembling.

'Nothing, just don't look back,' Bully replied. The boys started coming towards them. There was another figure standing in the middle of the road with his hand inside his jacket. The boys saw him, stopped, and withdrew into the darkness immediately. Bully looked back again, and did not see them.

'Now run! Run! I am right behind you,' he told Nneka. She started running. Bully ran behind her. Bambam, standing in the middle of the road, laughed, tucked his revolver back into his waistband and went away. Bully bade Nneka farewell in front of her hall.

It was still very early the next day. A girl told Nneka that a boy was waiting to see her outside the hall. She peeped through the window and saw Ezenwa standing in front of the hall. 'What is it this early morning?' she murmured fearfully and went down to meet him. She knew he would never visit her in the morning unless there was a problem. His face was murky too. It must be something serious.

'Why this early?' she asked him.

'Where did you go last night?' Ezenwa asked in return. Nneka flinched. She never thought that Ezenwa would know about the theatre. He was not there, and she knew that Bully was not his friend and could not have told him. How then did he know? She wanted to lie, but desisted.

'I went to the theatre,' she confessed.

'With whom?' Ezenwa asked.

'With Joy and Berta,' she replied.

Ezenwa stared at her, shook his head sadly and said, 'I don't have much to tell you, but listen. Joy plotted with Solomon to violate you. It seems you have forgotten that. Berta snapped you nude at the bathroom. It seems you don't know that. Now tell me, why are they the only people you want to associate with? Why are you senseless?' Nneka was astounded. She gaped at him, and made no response. He continued, 'Berta was paid last night to bring you to the theatre for the same person for whom she took your nude pictures, the same person who planned with Peter the cyclist to rape you.' Nneka was overwhelmed by the treacherous acts of those she thought were her friends. Tears started flowing down from her eyes. 'It is not yet time to weep. You can weep when I finish,' Ezenwa jeered. 'Do you know that you would have been kidnapped last night?' he asked. Nneka heard him, but did not reply. She felt it was better to cry than listen. At least, he would see her remorse and stop jeering at her. 'The same person made another attempt last night. But thank your God that Bully did what he did.'

Nneka shuddered and started trembling uncontrollably. Now that he mentioned Bully, she could not doubt the veracity of his story. She did not tell him what Bully did. How did he know? All these confounded her. She knew that Ezenwa had a solid and perhaps infallible intelligence network, but never knew it was as efficient as he had just made her to understand.

'From now on, stay away from Joy and Berta, if you don't, you would get yourself into a big problem, where I cannot help you out,' he said and went away.

Nneka went back to her room sobbing, not out of grief for having been betrayed by her friends, but for being seen as disobedient. And more, Ezenwa had called her "senseless". She had vowed never to give Ezenwa any cause to doubt her loyalty and commitment to his effort to protect her. She cried bitterly, and for the first time, regretted ever being a beautiful girl. Her room mates, especially Lucy tried to console her. But Nneka had lost confidence in the friendship of every girl. In her eyes, Lucy was another traitor who would have no compunction in handing her over to her enemies. The only person she knew, who still possessed the heart of a human being, was Ezenwa, and perhaps

Nyadiba. Ezenwa was the only person who could not harm her, and she had disobeyed him and made him angry. She wept for a while, and decided to go and apologise to him, and tell him about a thought that had been haunting her. She had told him about it once, but he did not believe her, now, she would prove to him that she was not wrong.

Ezenwa was baffled when he saw Nneka in his room. It was just some minutes after he had reprimanded her. 'I have something to discuss with you,' Nneka said. The tone of her voice startled him. Whenever she came with such tone and a mournful countenance, the topic was always serious.

'About what?' he asked.

'About Me,' she replied.

'I hope you are not going to cry about what I told you now?'

'No, I discovered something about myself,' she said. Ezenwa frowned.

'About you?' he asked, confounded.

'Yes,' she replied, 'I discovered that I am cursed.' Ezenwa sighed.

'So you left your room to come here and tell me such nonsense?' he asked.

'It is not nonsense,' she insisted. 'If I am not cursed, why am I not free? Why should I live in seclusion? Why should I always attract attentions wherever I go? How many people have you hurt because of me, and how many more would you hurt? Look at me. Whether you accept it or not, I am under a curse. That is why I am not free.'

'Is that all?' Ezenwa asked sarcastically.

'No, that is not all. Have you ever thought about what would happen to the man I would marry?'

'No! 'What do you think would happen to him?' he asked, smiling.

'He would never have peace, and would not have a long life,' she replied. 'He would be fighting daily to protect me. He would be killing his fellow men everyday, and one day he would be killed. And if he is too weak to fight, he would die of broken heart, because other men would exploit and abuse his wife before his eyes. I want you to accept the reality. I cannot be your wife, else you die before your time.' She forced the last sentence out of her mouth. Ezenwa's reaction to the reality, as she called it, was contrary to her expectation. She had expected him to jump up in a rage, and later calm down in tears. That was not to be. He started laughing, loudly and mirthlessly, as Uyanna always laughed whenever he was confronted with a problem.

'Nneka,' he began, 'what I want is your freedom and happiness. If you want to be a spinster all your life, go ahead if it would make you happy. But I do not know how you hope to do that. Are you going to be a prostitute, or live as someone's concubine?'

'God forbid!' she exclaimed. 'If a diviner told you that Nneka would be a prostitute, won't you spit on him and call him a charlatan?' she asked tearfully.

'Then what devil put such idiocy in your mind?' he asked. 'If you have decided to marry another person, why not be open and clear to be?' he insinuated.

'No please, not that,' she pleaded. 'I was only concerned about your safety.'

Ezenwa started laughing and said, 'you have told me once about this curse, I did not listen to you. Now you come up with it again. Stop worrying yourself about me. I am ready to take them as fast as they come. I have never been a coward.' Nneka gaped at him, and saw that irrepressible part of him, that which made him Ezenwa. She smiled and embraced him.

'Forgive me for disobeying you last night,' she said happily.

Bambam would have gone after Jack immediately Jack was discharged from the hospital. But Jack was a prominent member of the Red Scorpions. He had many people in the cult loyal to him too. They were the same people Bambam would send to eliminate him. Apart from their loyalty to Jack, Bambam would be risking revolt within the cult if they discovered that he wanted to kill Jack because of Ezenwa, who had no affiliation to any cult.

After the assassination of the wrong cyclist, Jack knew that Bambam had discovered his involvement in the rape attempt. He endeavoured to know Bambam's opinion about the incident. But Bambam was not a fool. He pretended as if he did not know that Jack was stabbed. After all, Jack did not bring any report about the incident to the Red Scorpions. Bambam neither reprimanded nor commended Jack for his cowardly act. After a long time of expectation, Jack relaxed his guard.

When Bambam noticed that Jack had relaxed his guard, it was already very late to go after him. The semester's examination was fast approaching, and Bambam needed to prepare very well for the examination. It was already late for him to attack Jack. He left him, but kept counting his indignities and waiting for the appointed time.

Since Bambam did not attack Jack as Jack had expected, Jack thought that Bambam's powers had started waning, or that Bambam was afraid of him after all. Jack had offended Bambam many times, ridiculed his orders, but nothing happened. He had made some provocative statements about Bambam in the presence of some Scorpions very loyal to Bambam. These were statements that challenged Bambam's leadership of the Red Scorpions and put his life at risk. Some Scorpions loyal to Bambam reported back to him, yet he did nothing. Thus they inferred from his protracted silence that Jack was getting more powerful, and some of them started drifting to Jack's camp. When Jack saw that he had more members of the Red Scorpions loyal to him than to Bambam, he decided to overthrow Bambam.

Bambam knew that Jack could never lead the Scorpions, because Jack had an insatiable desire for women. Anybody whose sexual urge had no reins, would, without doubt, lead the Red Scorpions to annihilation. He had no blame for those aligning with Jack. They did not know the truth. Perhaps they would have reacted differently if they knew. If they knew that Jack had, in an act of cowardice, covered his face to violate a girl whom Bambam had paid him to forget, they would have seen reasons with Bambam. If they had not allowed sentiments to becloud their reasoning, and made critical analysis of Jack and his flaws, they would have known that he was going to lead them to doom. Why were they so blind to see why Jack was fighting him? Bambam thought sorrowfully. Women would be the downfall of Jack, Bambam decided.

Two boys who were hiding with Jack behind the water tank that night of the drama presentation had gone to Bambam's room the next day to apologise. They knew that Bambam saw them, and that he knew them. Their intelligence warned them to go and swear their allegiance to him once again. Even if they had switched their loyalty to Jack, such visit would keep them safe from the line of fire in case of any clash between Bambam and Jack. Bambam knew their intention. He was not deceived. Nevertheless, he got every information he desired about Jack from them. Then he decided to pay Jack at exactly the time when the payment was due. He had seen the disunity in his cult, and could no longer trust anyone's loyalty. Without trust, he could not use them. Thus he sent for his friend, Barry, the leader of another cult, The Black Axe, of the University of Benin.

The Black Axe was a notorious cult that admitted anybody who cared to join them. Unlike Red Scorpions that used academic aptitude and natural intelligence as parameters for initiation, the Black Axe admitted laggards. For this, it had a numerical superiority over other cults. It was the worst organised cult. Their members often did not know themselves, and fought themselves regularly.

Barry was Bambam's childhood friend who grew up with him in the army barracks. When Bambam got the admission to study at the University of Nigeria Nsukka, Barry opted for the University of Benin. They often met at home during the holidays. Their cult affiliations had never interfered in their friendship.

In the letter Bambam sent to Barry, he made it glaringly clear that his life was at stake. To help Barry in the choice of weapons, he added: *bring a sexy girl along. My adversary has no resistance for women.*

Ben Jack sat silently in front of a bar behind the Department of Zoology, sipping his beer as he waited for some members of the Red Scorpions, those who were loyal to him. He had invited them for the last meeting where they would conclude the plan to overthrow and assassinate Bambam. Very eager to eliminate Bambam, Jack had been dreaming and planning what he would do with Nneka after the death of Bambam.

Hidden behind the wall separating the Department of Zoology and the Department of Botany, Bambam pointed at Jack.

'Do you see him?' he asked Oby, the Black Axe girl who came with Barry from the University of Benin.

'Yes I do,' she replied.

'Can you take him?'

'Why not?' she asked and looked askance at Bambam.

'Good luck! Do it as quick as you can. Anybody you see with him is my enemy and should be eliminated,' Bambam instructed. Oby got up and walked flirtatiously into the bar. The bar was a notorious joint for cult boys. It was located under a thick shade of tall cashew trees, which provided impenetrable insulation against the hot weather of Eastern Nigeria. However hot the weather was, it never penetrated the protection offered by the trees. This always left the bar cool and dry on hot afternoons. It was this uniqueness that attracted a lot of students to the joint until it became a rallying point for cult boys, and of course, a battlefield for rival cults. Wherever cult boys converged, there was always violence. And where there was violence, intelligent people stayed away.

Being a prerogative of cult boys, Jack was shocked to see a girl as attractive as Oby at the joint. He stared lustfully and silently at her for a while, thinking that she was waiting for another strong man. No female student had ever had the boldness to visit that bar alone without being under the shadow of somebody. When Oby bought a bottle of cold beer and started drinking, Jack felt that she was without scruples. Girls like this, very hot and sensual, he reasoned, could do anything with anybody, and still be discreet about it. Her strong man would never know. Oby stared at him and winked. Jack looked away. She got up and walked sensuously to the bartender, whispered something to him, and returned to her seat. Her movement was a calculated attempt to arouse Jack's sexual urge as Bambam had instructed. Jack glanced at his wristwatch, and saw that he still had an hour free before the arrival of his boys. He went closer to Oby. There was no harm in knowing her and conversing with her if he could not take her home, he thought.

'Hello,' Jack greeted.

'Hi,' Oby replied.

'Are you a new student? I have never seen you on this campus?' Jack asked.

'Do you know every girl on the campus?' Oby asked without any interest.

'No, but a pretty one like you could easily be known,' he replied. Oby smiled.

'You think I am pretty?' she asked gleefully.

'Extremely pretty. Are you waiting for someone?' Jack asked

'For whom?' she asked. 'No, my room mates told me about this place, and I decided to come and see for myself. But I want to go back to my room now. I am already tipsy,' she replied.

'Tipsy?' Jack asked, astonished. He believed that Oby must be a first year student, and does not know anything about the notoriety of the bar.

'Yes, this is my first time of drinking beer,' she replied. Jack's assumption was confirmed. She is an ignorant vulnerable first year girl.

'I want to go back to my room and sleep,' she muttered. Jack could not believe his luck. He had only wanted to chat with her, but it seemed he would do more than a chat. Oby looked at him and laughed.

'I am already ashamed of myself. Imagine a girl like me getting drunk in public,' she said gleefully. Jack continued to stare incredulously at her. She stood up, staggered, and sat down again.

'Where do you want to go?' Jack asked.

'Back to my room.'

'Which hall?'

'Okpala Hall.'

'Ah, that's too far. My house is just behind the Faculty of Engineering. If you won't mind, I can take you there to rest,' Jack offered.

'No, I am not going with you,' she replied. Jack continued to persuade her. She continued to refuse until she stood up the second time and staggered again. Jack thought she was actually under the intoxication of alcohol. He took her hand, a bit forcefully, and started dragging her to his house. She made feeble objections, then allowed him to coax her, and followed him grudgingly. His sexual urge was already out of control before they got to his house.

He unlocked his door hurriedly, pushed her into the room, and pushed her into the bed. She jumped out of the bed, looking aghast. Jack knew he had no time to waste. Very soon his loyal boys would arrive at the bar. How would he explain to them that he was late because of a woman? They would discard him immediately. That was the last thing he wanted.

He did not beg or coax Oby to have sex with him. He had never done that with any woman. It had to be with violence, against the girl's will, else he would not enjoy it. He pushed her into the bed again. Oby protested and wanted to get up. Jack jumped on top of her.

Raping was not a new game to him. He knew his techniques. He knew exactly what to do. Before Oby could get up the second time, he had torn her dress off and moved to tear her pants.

Blinded by his passion, he did not see when she retrieved the knife she strapped under her armpit with the cord of her bra. She deliberately allowed him to get on top of her before she stabbed him on the back. The dagger went deep into his ribs. He attempted to get up, but she was faster than him, too fast for a person under the grips of alcohol. She pulled out the dagger from his back. But he still succeeded to turn around. This time, lying on his back, ready to evade another strike. She stabbed him again. He attempted to evade the blow, but failed. The dagger caught him in the abdomen, just above the navel.

That instant, Jack noticed that she was an experienced killer, and not a drunken ignorant girl he thought she was. He started screaming. Afraid that Jack would attract people by his screams, she went to his throat. With two quick strokes, she cut open his windpipe. He lay on the bed, wriggling like a tail of a lizard severed from the trunk. She went into his bathroom, washed her hands, and left his house.

Barry followed his target into his room. The boy's name was Izu, but his friends called him Major. He was a ruthless Scorpion boy, second only to Bambam in ruthlessness. He was one of the most reliable hit men the Scorpions had ever had, an irreplaceable calibre. That he had joined forces with Jack had scared Bambam, and kept him unceasingly jittery. Bambam knew Major's reputation well enough to toy with his whims. That was why he told Barry to eliminate him too.

Major opened his door, and entered into his room. As he was about to shut the door, Barry came stealthily behind him, and pushed him deeper into the room. It happened so fast that Major threw up his hands in surprise.

'What do you want?' he asked and started looking around for a weapon. His gun was hidden inside a box under his bed. But the fastness Barry exhibited did not give him the time to get his gun. However, being a fearless fellow, he dived under the bed with an agility that astounded Barry, and started rummaging hastily inside the box. Barry bent down and froze when he saw the shinning pistol Major brought out from the box. Without wasting time, Barry fired two shots into his skull and ran away.

Major was a person of villainous reputation. When his neighbours heard the sounds of gun, everybody scampered away, thinking that it was another cult war. Twenty minutes later, Oby and Barry were among the fifty passengers of a bus going from Nsukka to Lagos.

The news of the assassinations spread on the campus immediately. Many people panicked. Nobody knew which group did the killings, or why it was done. Almost every cult member ran away from the campus.

Bambam was reclining on his bed when one of his loyal boys came with the information. 'That's how disloyal people die,' Bambam told the boy. The boy understood, and swore his allegiance again.

Ezenwa and Nyadiba heard the news but made no effort to ascertain the identities of the slain students. They knew it was a cult affair, and that Bambam must know what happened, or why they were killed, but they felt it was wiser to remain in the dark. This decision was a wise decision that protected them from anxiety. Ezenwa in particular would have told Nneka to leave the university if he knew the identity of the slain students. But he did not know, and did not panic like those who were involved. That same night, he strolled to Eyo Ita Hall with Nyadiba to give Nneka the story.

Nneka had heard the story. It was one of those things that reminded her of Ezenwa, and tormented her with the fear that he was vulnerable to that kind of death. Perhaps if she knew why those boys were killed, her fears would have been irrepressible. What saddened her heart most was the knowledge that if anything should happen to Ezenwa, it must be because of her. She lay quietly on her bed, thinking how best to avoid contacts with cult boys, so as to make Ezenwa less vulnerable. She remembered that she had often seen some girls, although beautiful, but were never worried by cult boys. Most of them went to church every day of the week, some were involved deeply in the affairs of the church that they became repellent to cult boys. They were never molested. She was deep in these thoughts when she heard the tap on her door.

'Yes, who is there?' she asked.

'It's me,' Ezenwa replied. Nneka almost ran to the door. It had been a long time since he came to her hall. She unlocked her door. Ezenwa and Nyadiba came in.

'Why are you alone?' Ezenwa asked.

'My room mates went out. Lucy has joined Pastor Jerry's congregation.'

'What? Lucy? Jerry? Oh shit!' he lamented.

'Why are you worried?' Nneka asked, overwhelmed by his agitation.

'I am worried because Jerry will now have a reason to be coming here.'

'Don't worry yourself, he has been coming and has never met me. Even if he meets me, he would not force me to follow him.' Ezenwa stared at her, wanted to make a comment, but remembered what happened the last time he made a comment about her and Patrick, and desisted.

Nyadiba glanced at his watch, the third time since they came into the room. The gesture attracted Ezenwa's attention.

'Do you have anywhere to go?' Ezenwa asked him.

'Yes, I want to visit that *babe* I told you about,' Nyadiba replied.

'Is she in this hall?'

'Yes, she is in room 305.'

'Go, before another guy grabs her,' Ezenwa said jokingly. Nyadiba ran out. That moment, two girls started screaming in the room opposite Nneka's. Ezenwa and Nneka could identify Joy's voice clearly. Many students started running to the scene. Nneka wanted to go, but Ezenwa held her back. She peeped through her keyhole and saw when five boys emerged from the room. Minutes later, Joy and Berta ran out of the room with bruises of flagellation all over their bodies. Nneka winced.

'That's the price of betrayal,' Ezenwa said.

'What do you know about that?' Nneka asked, trembling.

'I swear, I do not know anything about it, but I know that anybody who offended me must never go unpunished,' he replied. Nneka stared at him for a while, and refused to accept a nagging thought that he had joined one of the cults. She preferred to believe that such feats, as he has been displaying before her, could only be achieved through the powers of Uyanna.

Chapter 34

Nyadiba had noticed the girl in his class. She was always elegant and reticent. He noticed that she sat on a particular seat everyday. Therefore, he deduced that she must be a very diligent student. Only punctual students could sit on the same seat daily.

One early morning, he came to the class and saw her alone. He approached her and started a conversation. She responded pleasantly. Her amiability and wit baffled him. She was not impressively pretty, but had a kind of elegance that could pass for beauty. From that day, they continued to be friendly until the friendship started emitting the fires of passion and irrepressibly turned into a love affair. Her name was Anita. When Nyadiba introduced her to Ezenwa two days later, Ezenwa almost swore that he had seen the girl somewhere. She resembled somebody he knew very well.

Nneka had been faithful to her scheme to make herself less palatable to cult boys. She had started participating actively in the affairs of her church. When she was not in Ezenwa's room, the only place she could study without distractions, she would be at the church, singing or teaching catechisms. Ezenwa had introduced her to Anita and wanted them to be friends, but Nneka was deeply immersed in the activities of the church to care about anybody's friendship. Ezenwa was not worried, although the attention he received from her had diminished drastically. Whenever she visited him, it was only to study in the serenity of his room. He had observed too that she had started receiving compliments on her beauty with smiles, and never talked about curses again. Although he was not happy with the little attention he received from her; it seemed her love for him was getting cold, but he was very happy about her romance with the church. Perhaps the change was a divine scheme to save her from the hands of her enemies, he thought. To occupy his own time and allow Nneka to participate actively in the church, Ezenwa joined a tourist club together with Anita and Nyadiba.

Their membership of the club coincided with the clubs agenda to visit a war museum at Umuahia, six hundred kilometres away from Nsukka. Every member of the club had the right to come along with his friends, as long as they paid their transport fares. Nneka refused to go. She was in the heat of preparation for a concert to be held in the church. Without her, Ezenwa could not go too. He did not want to look forlorn among other boys and their girlfriends. Nyadiba and Anita had no impediment, so they decided to go.

Every student was aware of the dangers of such trips. Apart from the bad roads, which had made Nigeria a country with the highest number of road accidents, there existed also the dangers of highway robbers. The most frequent and violent robberies had been taking place along that road, which linked the eastern region of the country to the northern region. The ruthlessness and impunity of these robberies depicted a situation of a region characterised by inefficient law enforcement. Robbers killed and maimed without haste. A prominent politician was killed on that road some months ago. It was only when a prominent man became victim of such heinousness that the government reacted. From the police force headquarters, they posted David Ekundalo to the zone to restore normality. Not because the citizens of the zone needed tranquillity, but because these robbers had exceeded the limit allowed to them. They had abused their freedom by killing a prominent politician and a sycophant of the Federal Government of Nigeria. With that, a matter of necessity grew into a matter of urgency. David was intelligent, crude, and brutal. There was no doubt that he possessed the formulae to end the barbarity of these robbers.

Some students who were members of the tourist club were also members of some cults. They rarely moved out of the campus with their guns. But when they knew that they could come in contact with armed robbers, some of them decided to arm themselves and prepare for a gun battle. Nyadiba did not want to be overtaken by surprises. He went with his revolver too.

Scary stories were circulating about Kruba, the leader of one of the most brutal robbery gangs, whose penchant for killing was legendary. He had often killed without provocation. There were stories circulating among the members of his gang that he had once robbed a pregnant woman, and the woman in anger swore that the child in her womb would terrorise armed robbers. Kruba heard her, went back to her, and fired two shots into her protruding belly. Members of his gang were enraged by the act, and told him that it was a senseless killing, at which he replied, 'it is my duty to eliminate my potential enemies.'

On another occasion, his gang had invaded a man's house, and demanded for an amount of money the man had never had in his life. The man told them that he had never had such amount of money in his life and begged them to take everything in his house. Kruba told him to go and beg for the money from his neighbours.

'Nobody would give me that amount of money. They know that I cannot pay back,' the man argued.

'Don't argue with me!' Kruba shouted. His voice reverberated through the house, and woke the man's only child, a six months old baby, who was born after eight years of childlessness and its accompanying sadness. The baby wailed uncontrollably, and attracted Kruba to his cot. 'Such a beautiful thing!' Kruba exclaimed. The man and his wife started trembling. Kruba observed their tremor and decided to bargain with their baby.

'Are you ready to get the money or do you want me to kill this child?' he asked the man. The man knelt down and begged him to come back another day and take the money.

'No, I want it now,' Kruba replied and took the child's legs, lifted him precariously out of the cot. Perhaps it was a compulsion for the man to cede to his demand. Perhaps it was sheer wickedness. 'The money or I smash his head on this wall,' Kruba threatened. The man's wife started screaming, telling her neighbours to go and call the police. Kruba was infuriated, and before any member of his gang could stop him, he smashed the baby's head on the wall. The brain splashed all over the room. The baby's father rushed towards Kruba to fight him with bare hands. Kruba sprayed him with bullets before he got close to him. His wife fainted. Kruba ordered his gang out of the house and followed behind them.

Some members of the gang started grumbling, and were nearly out of the house when Kruba turned back. The woman was still lying unconscious in the pool of her husband's blood, with the remnant of what used to be her child lying beside her. Kruba stared at her and said, 'I better spare you the agony you will face when you regain consciousness.' He shot her twice on the head.

The cruelty and brutality by which he was known by his gang gave him an extraordinary diabolic character. Everybody winced at his heartlessness and the unreasoning impulse with which he killed. He was a wild animal in the structure of a man, devoid of sentiments and reason. He had once killed a man, his wife, and six children without stealing a thing from them. Most nauseating was the killing of two beautiful girls he met on the road one day. Without questions and answers, he murdered them in cold blood. One of his boys was infuriated and questioned the rationale behind the shooting.

'Nothing, I only denied their boyfriends the pleasure of their beautiful bodies,' Kruba answered and lit his cigarette. That gang member decried his cruelty and threatened to quit the gang. Kruba shot him that night too. 'For being too daring,' Kruba had said.

Kruba had been living a kind of life the members of his gang did not understand. Nobody had ever seen him with any woman. In all his speeches and acts, he always gave the impression of a person who had ineffaceable hatred for womanhood. He was not a homosexual. This was indisputably obvious. He had never made a move suggestive of such inclination. But of all the mysteries about him, none equalled the effort he made to conceal his nakedness. One of his boys had once made a ribald joke that he was only concealing his mal-formed genitals, and another argued that it could be because he had none at all. It was only a joke, but they did not know how close they were to solving the puzzle. In their two years of operation as a robbery gang, none of his boys had ever seen him naked. When he once bathed in their gaze, he did not remove his pants. This strangeness haunted them. But none of them dared question him. Apart from his gang, his other companions were whisky and Indian hemp.

Early in the morning of that Saturday, the members of the tourist club embarked on their journey in a school bus. The road was unnaturally deserted. In spite of the incessant robberies and other misfortunes witnessed on the road, it was never without heavy traffic, being the only link between the East and the North. The driver of the school bus was the first person to notice the deserted road. He alerted his passengers, and wanted to stop. Encouraged by the guns they tucked into their waistbands, some cult boys ordered him to continue. After about sixty kilometres, they drove into a roadblock mounted by a robbery gang. Then the driver saw the reason for the dryness of the road.

'It is Kruba's gang!' one of the students shouted.

'How do you know?' Nyadiba asked him, and pulled out his revolver.

'Look at those dead bodies,' the boy said, pointing at some dead bodies littering the scene. 'No other gang would perpetrate such heinousness.'

One of the robbers raised his rifle up, fired some shots, and the driver of the school bus stopped.

'This is Kruba and gang!' the robber shouted almost immediately. If he had expected the students to panic and scream, he was disappointed. None of the boys trembled. The girls were afraid, but were calmed down by their boyfriends. This must have been the first time Kruba and his gang encountered students while in operation. They did not show any kind of frenzy or preoccupation that the students could be armed. They ordered the driver out of the vehicle.

Nyadiba saw Kruba, and started trembling. He attempted to jump down through the window of the bus. But Kruba was on guard beside his window, and was ready to shoot anybody who would try to escape. Nyadiba withdrew his head from the window, and brought out his revolver to shoot Kruba.

It seemed someone else called Kruba's attention. He left his position at the side of the bus and went to the front, out of Nyadiba's line of fire. Nyadiba tucked his revolver back into his waistband, jumped down through the window, and wanted to dive into the bush, but was worried about Anita. He searched for her among the students that had started alighting from the bus, and did not see her. He decided to move alone. He had just made two steps before Kruba spoke again, this time, just behind him.

'I would not attempt that if I were you,' Kruba said. Nyadiba had no time again to retrieve his revolver and shoot Kruba. He started shivering. Kruba came to his front, stared at him, creased his brow, and smiled.

'God has answered my life long prayers,' he told Nyadiba. 'I will kill you, but before I do that, you must take me to others.' Nyadiba understood that he was talking about Ezenwa and Chima. Kruba did not search Nyadiba. It was not necessary. He did not care about his money. The fact that they were students had quenched the robbers' zeal. Students rarely had money. 'I bet you never guessed that this day would come,' Kruba told Nyadiba. His attention was diverted completely away from other passengers. Nyadiba knew better than to open his mouth to reply or beg Kruba for mercy. He kept mute. Anita heard everything Kruba said and wondered what Nyadiba had done to him.

David Ekundalo was inside his office at the police station when the distress report of the gangs operation came to him. The bearer of the report also warned him that it was Kruba and his gang. David had wanted to send some policemen to the scene. But somehow, an impetus he could not control propelled him to lead the policemen to the scene himself. So many times he had sent his men to quash the gang and they came back with tales of woe, either running away from the superior firepower of the robbers, or bearing dead bodies of their colleagues. And daily, he continued to hear the stories of horror and cruelty of this particular gang, whose mark of operation was always a heap of dead bodies.

The robbers were still in operation when the policemen arrived. They had been there for two hours and had no fear of police interference. Of course they knew that the police had always fled from them. The robbers had superior weapons. But now, with David, the police had superior tactics, and that was what David employed.

'We are going to take them from the bush,' he told his men. They left their vehicles far away and ran down to the scene through the bush, well hidden by trees and shrubs. 'Wait for my signal before you start shooting,' David instructed. Still hidden, they crawled closer to the road, close enough to hear what the robbers were saying. Groans of the wounded and the dying victims filled their ears.

'It would be difficult to shoot them without killing some innocent people. There are a lot of people there,' one of the policemen whispered to David.

'Let's tell them that they have been surrounded, and order them to drop their weapons,' another suggested.

'Let's try that first, but if they don't obey, don't start shooting immediately, let's wait until they get into their cars, then shoot them inside their cars,' David instructed his men. Some policemen, from their facial expressions, doubted if the robbers would obey such order. But before any of them could make any suggestion, David gave the order.

'You have been surrounded. It is better and wiser for you to drop your guns and surrender before we blow your heads off!' His warning rattled the robbers. They had never heard such warning from the police, and worse still, very close to them.

On instinct, they prostrated among the students, and Kruba shouted back.

'That would be a grievous error. We have students here, and if any bullet comes our way, we shall kill all of them!' The policemen knew he was not bluffing. He had shot some people already, and would not feel any compunction killing more.

Anita heard her father's voice and shouted back to the policemen, 'it is true, please don't shoot!' Her father heard her voice and recognised it.

'Don't do anything. Let them go,' David told his men, trembling.

David was not disposed to play with the life of his daughter.

'Get into the car,' Kruba, still lying down, ordered some students. They started moving hesitantly towards the car, darting glances into the bush, expecting to hear sounds of guns, but none came.

'You get into the car too. I will maim you before I kill you,' Kruba told Nyadiba. Nyadiba got up and started moving towards another car.

'What about some *babe*s boss?' one of the robbers asked Kruba.

'Do your wish, take any of them you like,' Kruba replied.

'Thank you boss,' the robber replied. It was not every time that Kruba allowed them to take women. He liked killing women than doing any other thing with them. But that day, their operation was very successful, and he did not see any reason to deny his boys the pleasure. The policemen inside the bush were of no consequence to him, and did not present any kind of threat to him now that he had threatened to kill all the students.

The robbers started pulling up some girls from the ground and pushing them into their cars.

'We left you because you have no money, but you have other things we like,' one of the robbers said and pulled up a girl who had been crying and clutching her boyfriend's hand. 'Get into that car,' the robber ordered and pointed at the second car on which Nyadiba leaned helplessly. 'You too,' the robber said and pulled up Anita.

David saw his daughter and knew what was about to happen. He started shaking with fear again. Now, it was no longer possible to attack Kruba and his gang. Many people were standing up, including Anita.

The boy whose girlfriend was about to be pushed inside the car heard her crying and calling him to save her. By impulse and without caution, he pulled out his gun and shot the robber who was forcing the girl into the car. Kruba shuddered and turned in the direction of the boy, but was too late. Other cult boys had taken the signal from the boy. They brought out their guns and started shooting the robbers.

Nyadiba shot Kruba on the shoulder. Kruba dropped his gun. David looked on without a shot from him and his men. When the students stopped shooting, five robbers were dead, and Kruba was incapacitated.

'Now drop your guns!' David ordered the students, pointing his rifle at them. Anita was standing behind Nyadiba. Still protected by the car from the view of the policemen, Nyadiba extended his hand backwards. Anita snatched the gun from him and hid it inside her handbag. Other students dropped their guns and waited to be commended by the police.

'You are all guilty of illegal possession of firearms,' David told them. 'We are going to take you to the police station where you will make statements, and remain in custody until the day of your judgement.' They gaped at him.

'What about this robber?' Nyadiba asked, and pointed at Kruba.

'What we do with him is no longer your business,' David replied and ordered his men to bring all the boys to the police station and leave the girls to go.

Some girls followed them to the police station, but Anita did not go with them. While they were at the robbery scene, she had exchanged glances with her father. David gave her an admonishing glance, and Anita returned a look of gratitude. Nobody else knew what went through the two minds.

Nyadiba and other boys were locked in a cell at the police station. Illegal possession of firearm was a crime of dire implications. Nyadiba was worried by what will be the outcome of their case, especially when the examination in the university was about to be taken. He knew he would never go to jail, because he was not arrested with any gun. Those who had guns had accepted their guilt, identified their guns, and made statements on how they got them. They were mostly sons of wealthy people, and Nyadiba knew that before the next day, their parents would come to the police station to seek their release. That was obvious. Never had he imagined that they would be prosecuted. Never! Bribery and corruption were still norms in Nigeria. The boys were only detained in dirty and inhuman cells so that when their parents would come, they would pay any amount of money the police would demand before their children would be released. As for Nyadiba, he knew that nobody would come to seek his release. Even if his father knew that he was in detention, where would he get the money to pay for such imprudence? It was better his father did not know, even if he was going to miss his examination. His parents' exertion to fulfil his academic obligations was exacting and already a load too big for them to carry. He did not know Anita well, but she seemed to be from a rich background. Either her or Ezenwa would come to seek his release; otherwise he would languish in the cell. He had been wondering why the girls were allowed to go, even when they were together with the boys when the shooting occurred. Naturally, the Nigerian police would have arrested everybody, and accuse the girls alongside their male counterparts. Their families would pay to secure their freedom too, and the police purse would swell.

Anita went back to her house, and was lucky that her father was not at home. She told her mother everything that happened, starting from her romance with Nyadiba, and begged her to use her influence to secure Nyadiba's release. Naturally, Nigerians avoided discussions of love affairs with their parents, because it was always portrayed as something indecent. But Anita took the shame and told her mother the whole story.

Her mother had refused to help, but when Anita told her that she was the person who hid Nyadiba's gun, and could be linked with the shooting, her mother understood the consequences, and replied her with vituperations. Anita took the reprimand and the shame too as long as it would influence the release of her boyfriend.

'Where is the gun?' her mother asked.

'It was among those my father took,' she lied.

'What do you want me to do?' her mother asked. Anita could not answer her question before her father came in.

'Good evening dad,' she greeted David. He ignored her greeting and started admonishing her.

'It is good that you are at home,' David said angrily. 'I sent you to the university to study, and not to join any cult. Imagine the mess you would have been in if I had not led the operation myself. By now you would either be dead or in a police cell and the whole town would be awash with the news that my daughter is a cult member.'

'Dad, we are not cult members. It is only a tourist club. The problem is that some cult boys are also members of the club. Assuming it was a religious affair, would you call the whole congregation a cult because of some bad eggs,' Anita argued.

'Besides the cult issue, don't you know that by now, you would have been dead if we had not crushed the gang?' David asked. 'The robbers had already picked you.'

'Hmm Dad,' Anita hummed. 'The police did not do anything. Why not give honour to whom it is due? Those boys had killed the robbers before the police appeared,' she told her mother. Her father did not speak again. It had been his habit to boast and exaggerate before his wife whenever there was an incident like this.

'You are talking about little problems while the big one is waiting for you,' his wife muttered.

'What problem?' David asked, alarmed.

'Anita tell him your story again,' her mother ordered. Anita shamefully told her father everything she had told her mother.

'You see, sometimes when I say that you are a fool, you think I am stupid,' David told her after listening to the story. That was his only remark. He had not taken the cult issue serious. He would release the boys, but first, he would make some money out of them. As far as he was concerned, they were mere delinquents that should be kept for a while in a stinking cell, and be punished by irate mosquitoes.

Nneka heard the story of the arrests from Pastor Jerry. A female member of his congregation was a member of the tourist club too. When she told Jerry the story, she described Nyadiba as the boy with HIV. Jerry understood, and brought the news to Nneka with haste.

Nneka knew that Nyadiba and Anita went for the excursion. There was no unlikelihood in Jerry's story. But she sought to know from Jerry if anything incriminating was found on Nyadiba. Jerry saw her desperation and decided to exploit it. He had been seeking, for a long time, an opportunity to do her a favour, and later, demand for gratification. He had inferred that if Nyadiba was involved, then Ezenwa must be involved too. As a pedestal to lunch his scheme, Jerry started chiding and reproaching Nneka for being a friend of cult boys, saying things so denigrating and malicious.

Nneka seemed to be listening, but did not hear a word. She was completely engrossed in her thoughts and remained mute. Jerry was deceived. He misunderstood her silence for remorse, and thought that he had penetrated her blockade

'But these things should not worry you, I can help to secure their freedom,' he offered, when his ridicules did not elicit any response from her. Nneka heard only the offer for help.

'How would you help?' she asked, unconvinced.

'The inspector of police in charge of the case is my friend. I can vouch for your friend's innocence and influence his release.'

'Then do it, or do you want them to miss their examination?' Nneka begged.

'I will do it only on one condition.'

'What condition?' Nneka asked, ready to flare up.

'The condition that you stop seeing that boy.'

'Which boy?' she asked.

'Your boyfriend,' Jerry replied. Nneka was enraged. Their discussion had nothing to do with Ezenwa. If not for Jerry's lewd intention, why should he include Ezenwa in the discussion?

Nneka stared angrily at him and asked, 'Jeremiah do you know you are insane? You think I am one of your girls.' Jerry frowned in anger, not for being referred to as insane, but for being addressed by his full name, *Jeremiah*. Though it was his name, it was a name he had grown to hate. His life of ostentation made him renounce the name as obsolescent, in favour of its short form, *Jerry*, which he thought was more glamorous. He could still remember how he fought his illiterate parents to adopt his preferred name. The last person he could remember, who called him Jeremiah, was his dead grandmother. And he did not answer her. Now, a girl he had been after for the past two years had addressed him with the hated name.

'My name is not Jeremiah,' he muttered. Nneka was astounded, and gaped at him.

'What is you name?' she asked, amused by the foibles she knew could only exist in the mind of infants.

'My name is Jerry!' he shouted. Nneka burst into laughter. It was then that she understood why he frowned.

'From today onwards,' she said, 'as far as I am concerned, your name is Jeremiah. You can hang yourself if it irks you.' Jerry wanted to say something, but was interrupted by a tap on the door.

'Who is there?' Nneka asked.

'Open the door,' Ezenwa replied. Jerry did not know who was at the door, so he was surprised when Ezenwa came in. To his greatest disappointment, he saw that Ezenwa was not in the excursion group.

Ezenwa did not hide his resentment at the sight of Jerry in Nneka's room. The fact that they were reeling with laughter, perhaps from a joke by Jerry, riled him. He stared coldly at Jerry and sat down on Nneka's bed. Nneka knew Ezenwa very well, and could, with accuracy, predict his next move. Even his next speech was already formed in her mind. As a way to put a restraint on him, she sat down with him on the bed and started kissing him, a thing she rarely did, except when there was a poacher to scare away.

Jerry was ruffled. He averted his gaze in envy and stood up immediately. To stand there and watch a girl he had been trying to ensnare as she kissed another man was something unbearable to him.

To add to his disgust, Nneka glanced at him and said, 'Jeremiah go away.' Jerry seethed with anger, made no comment, and walked out of the room. Ezenwa's resentment was assuaged.

'He said something about Nyadiba,' Nneka told Ezenwa.

'Who said?' Ezenwa asked, astounded.

'Jerry.'

'That what happened?'

'That they were arrested. That was what he came to tell me.'

'I have heard it too. Anita just left my room, but what is Jerry's interest in it?' Ezenwa asked angrily. That instant, he remembered Jerry's malicious manoeuvre that scared Kate away from Nyadiba. And now, again, he came for Nneka. The time to pay Jerry had come. Ezenwa decided to consult Bambam later. Jerry had enjoyed a lot of freedom.

'What shall we do?' Nneka asked, perturbed.

'We are not going to do anything. He would be released tomorrow,' Ezenwa said.

Nneka did not doubt his words. Ezenwa had never said that something would happen and that thing did not happen. She only gaped at him in admiration.

Nyadiba was released the next day. Anita, against her father's advice, waited for Nyadiba at a distance away from the police station. She saw him coming down the road, ran up to him, and embraced him. She had brought some food from her house, which, against her mother's instruction, she had taken from their breakfast that morning. It was after Nyadiba had eaten the food that Anita told him that she was the daughter of the policeman who led the operation. She also told him the part she played to get his freedom. Nyadiba thanked her and would have liked the issue to end like that. But she told Nyadiba to tell her why Kruba wanted to kill him. Nyadiba flinched.

The story was obnoxiously heinous and repulsive, not something he would tell anybody he loved. Anita was a bashful girl, such baleful tales would make her wince and shrink away from him. That was the last thing Nyadiba wanted now.

'May be because I know him very well,' he replied.

'It is not true. If it were because of that, he would not have made the threat. He would have killed you immediately. Tell me the truth, and please don't lie,' Anita insisted. Nyadiba smiled.

'Well, it is a long story,' he said.

'I would like to hear,' she insisted. Nyadiba fabricated a story and gave her. The story was filled with unreasonable and complex intrigues that lacked cohesion. She did not see any reason that necessitated such threat from an armed robber on Nyadiba alone. Nyadiba knew she did not believe a word of the story, yet was happy that it satisfied her curiosity and restrained her from making further enquiries.

David Ekundalo had not taken time to look at Kruba. When they brought him to the police station, they called a doctor to threat the bullet wound on his shoulder, and not to save his life. Nobody cared if he lived or died. The police would still have killed him prejudicially even if he survived the wound. They only treated him to keep him alive for some days, and ask him some questions. Perhaps they would discover where he hid his treasure, and steal it from him.

Kruba sat in front of David, and stared at him without blinking. David looked at him, and something within him told him that he knew Kruba's face. But he could not remember where he had seen it. 'What is your name?' he asked Kruba.

'My name is Kruba,' he replied scornfully.

'Listen,' David said angrily. 'I am not here to joke with you. If I ask you the question again, and you don't tell me your name, you will know why I was posted to this zone. I have no mercy for robbers. I would soon let you see for yourself. What is your name?' David asked again.

'My name is Kruba,' he repeated.

'Soften him,' David told one of the policemen sitting with him on the bench, and left the office. Some seconds later, he heard Kruba's screams, and hoped that he would not die before he got the information he needed from him. The pain could have been unbearable, because Kruba started pleading for mercy earlier than David had anticipated. 'Ruthless people are generally weak in the body and in the mind,' David muttered and returned to continue with the interrogation.

'What is your name?' he asked Kruba.

'My name is Solomon,' Kruba replied, still groaning.

'Solomon? What is your surname?' David asked, a little worried.

'Solomon Uzundu,' Kruba answered. David gaped at him. The whole mystery unravelled itself before him. His body became cold. He started shaking. When he opened his mouth to ask another question, no word came out. Other policemen gaped at him, amazed.

Solomon was his son, though an illegitimate one, but still his flesh and blood. Nobody else knew this. In the fraction of a minute, everything he did with Kate, Solomon's mother, came back to him vividly. He remembered when he was at Enugu, then a sergeant. He remembered too that he was Solomon's Godfather. In fact, he had chosen that name, Solomon, in allusion to the biblical Solomon, son of the adulterous king David. Among other things, he remembered the sad end of his mother and father. He had made efforts to adopt Solomon after the death of his parents, but his uncle refused. David had no son, and would have nurtured Solomon with a lot of love. Now, it was too late. There would be no consideration of a reprieve for Solomon. It was completely out of the question. He was a notorious bandit, the reason why David was posted to the zone. The people of the state had been in jubilation since the day Kruba was arrested. To release him again would generate anarchy in the state. The citizens would take to the streets.

The policemen with David guessed that something extraordinary had erupted in his mind. David's distress was clearly written on his face. He was too stupefied that his brain refused to think. He stared at his colleagues. They stared back at him in surprise.

'Leave me with him!' he ordered. Slowly, his colleagues moved out of the office.

David was a very tactical and fearless policeman. He had created and controlled so many complex situations. He had smashed a lot of invisible robbery gangs, the pedestal for the rapidity of his promotion in the police force. But he had never been entangled in such an extraordinary labyrinth as he was in now. Kruba was the most wanted robber in the zone. David had done everything he could, orthodox and unorthodox, to catch him. Now, he had him in his grip, and was looking for a way to set him free. Free as what? Innocent? What would Solomon do with his freedom? Form another robbery gang and be well protected by his obscure police father? Kill and brutalise society again? Nothing tormented David more than the fact that he was going to be the prosecutor of his son. Dazed in the maze, he called his men back, and ordered them to take Kruba back to the cell. With a heart filled with sorrow, he took his files and went home. In complex cases like this, he had often sought his wife's advice. But this time, he could not say what her reaction would be, yet he decided to confess and seek her advice.

Ezenwa imagined how close he had come to death and shuddered. He knew that Solomon would have killed him at all cost, even if it was the last thing he did on earth. Yet the thought of his death did not worry him as the thought of what would have happened to Nneka if Solomon had seen her. He pondered for a while on why Solomon had not come to his village to kill him. Solomon knew his house and where to get him. Perhaps he was afraid of his grandfather. At the remembrance of Uyanna, Ezenwa's mind relaxed. The fear of Uyanna had protected him immensely from the machinations of his enemies.

The police had caught Solomon, and another danger had been averted. Ezenwa gave thanks to God for such protections, and with tranquillity, started preparing for the coming examination. But this tranquillity lasted for only a week.

Anita had gone home on the weekend and came back with a disconcerting report. She had told only Nyadiba in confidence, and made him swear to tell no one else, not even Ezenwa. Nyadiba agreed and swore to keep her secret, yet told Ezenwa the story an hour later.

David had gone home with some of the police files, including the files on the arrest of the students. He had never done any of his works at home in secret, so he left the files on the table as usual. Anita saw the files, and fortunately, Nyadiba's file was on top. Curiosity drove her to examine the report, probably to know what her father wrote about her boyfriend. She opened Nyadiba's file and read, but found nothing incriminating. She closed it, then saw Solomon's file, and started reading it too. She frowned, sat down, and started reading with great concentration. What she saw astounded her. The police report on Kruba looked like a farce by the police in the defence of a bandit, almost as a lawyer would defend a client. 'This is no prosecution,' she murmured. What puzzled her most was the certainty that her father had written the report. Everybody knew Kruba and all the crimes he had committed. Why would the police write such delusive report about him? There was no mention of any murder, even when she knew that Kruba was most wanted for murder than for robbery. Without any accusation of murder, Kruba would only be sent to jail. With a good attorney, he might get leniency. This worried Anita immensely. Wasn't it before her eyes that Kruba shot three traders, and would have kidnapped her too? Her father was at the scene of the incident, and was a witness to it too. Why then did he make such flimsy accusations, devoid of incriminating substances on which justice would hinge to punish Kruba as he rightly deserved?

Anita was not accustomed to meddling in her father's office affairs. But in this case, she was directly involved; if not for the interest of her boyfriend, then for being a witness at one of the scenes of Kruba's massacres. She could not sleep that night, as she ruminated on what she saw and the implications of it. What baffled her most was the deliberate dereliction of the name "Kruba" in the report. Everybody would have shuddered if they heard that Kruba was not condemned to death. For this, the police tactfully substituted Kruba with Solomon. At judgement, he would face justice as Solomon, faceless and disguised, not as the notorious murderer, Kruba, the synonym of wickedness. The effect of prejudice would be completely eliminated.

Anita did not know if the attempt to save Kruba was her father's idea alone, or the decision of the entire police force. On the quest for this knowledge, she consulted her mother.

'Why do you worry yourself about things that do not concern you?' her mother asked.

'Who said it does not concern me?' Anita retorted. 'Before my eyes that animal killed three people. I did not count those he has killed before we arrived. Now tell me mother, do you think it is just to set him free?' she asked.

'My daughter allow the police to do their job,' her mother replied and sighed.

'Yes that's what I want to know. Is it the decision of the police, or is my father alone in this?' Her mother did not answer. 'If my father is alone in this,' Anita warned, 'other policemen would be against him. That criminal has killed a lot of policemen. And if someone bribed my father to write this kind of report, sooner or later, my father would be killed too.'

'Stop saying that,' her mother pleaded. 'Nobody bribed him.' Anita gaped at her mother in dismay. Something in her mother's voice told her that something strange had happened. She defended her husband, but only feebly, and she lacked her usual defiance comportment. Anita enquired further, but could not extract more explanations from her.

It was vividly discernible that her father was in it alone, else it would not have dampened her mother's spirit. Thus distress over her father's safety substituted the aberration and the travesty of justice the report would yield, things that distressed her.

How would David explain what he did to other policemen whose colleagues Kruba killed? They must find a way to eliminate Kruba, and if David interfered, they would eliminate him too.

Anita returned to the campus in a disconsolate and agitated spirit. Nyadiba saw her distress and stroked her to tell him the cause. She told him everything she knew. Nyadiba was neither surprised nor distressed. The serenity Anita saw on his face was contrary to what she had expected to see from a person who Kruba's freedom portended danger. She searched his face intensely for any sign of panic, but found nothing.

'Don't worry about that, everything would be fine,' Nyadiba consoled her and led her back to Eyo Ita Hall.

Ezenwa was scared by the story. 'But why should the police commit such error?' he asked Nyadiba.

'She does not know too. It seems her father had been bribed,' Nyadiba replied.

'Let me go and tell Bambam,' Ezenwa said and hurried away. His only concern that moment was what Solomon would do to Nneka.

Bambam was inside his room with a group of Scorpions. In such situation, he would not discuss anything with a non-member. Ezenwa knew this and lurked outside his room, waiting for the meeting to end. About an hour later, he saw them coming out of the room, and waited for some minutes before he moved in.

Bambam was in high spirits when Ezenwa came in, in contrast to the anguish on Ezenwa's face.

'What's the problem? It seems death is pursuing you,' Bambam joked.

'That is exactly the problem. Death is after me.'

'What happened,' Bambam asked, thinking that it was another cult affair. Ezenwa told him the story of Solomon, everything that happened between them.

'You have been fighting for this girl for a long time,' Bambam commented. Ezenwa shifted. 'What do you want me to do for you?' Bambam asked.

'I want to know if there is a way to help us,' Ezenwa said plaintively. Bambam remained thoughtful for a while.

'There would be a way if you know when he would be released from jail, because I am sure he would go to jail, even if he was accused of stealing only a pin. But the number of years he would spend in prison would depend on the police report about him. If he was accused of nothing serious, he might be out in a year, and would come after you and your *babe*. I might not be available that time,' Bambam said.

'Is there nothing we can do now?' Ezenwa asked, desperate for a solution.

'He is in the police custody, and we cannot invade a police station. But...' Bambam stopped and gazed at the wall for some minutes, smiled, and said, 'there are two ways out.' Ezenwa sat up and stared at him. 'The first way is to kidnap Anita, and force her father to kill Kruba. But it is a risky venture. He might refuse, and as we do not know why he wanted to set him free, that circumstance might compel him to refuse. When this happens, they would augment the security around Kruba, and the second plan would fail too.'

'What is the second plan?' Ezenwa asked, disappointed by the prospects of failure in the first plan. Nneka's life was involved. Solomon was a brute who could not be taken with smiles.

'The second one is more complicated. It is entirely between you, Nyadiba, and Anita.'

'How?' Ezenwa asked impatiently.

'Poison him,' Bambam blurted out. Ezenwa shuddered. Though his life, and most desperately, Nneka's were at stake. The thought of killing somebody made him shiver. Solomon was a killer who he knew would kill him anywhere he saw him. It was only the fear of Uyanna that kept Ezenwa out of his reach all these while. Ezenwa knew this, but to prevent such attack by poisoning looked too burdensome for him.

Bambam saw when he winced, saw the dilemma on his face, then frowned and asked, 'perhaps you want me to do it alone? It is your life that is at stake, not mine.' Ezenwa apologised and begged to hear the whole plan. Bambam made a sign to him to be silent and continued his explanation. 'You know he is detention and he is fed inadequately, so he must always be hungry. He would eat any food that comes his way. You can put poison in anything and give him.'

'That's not easy,' Ezenwa protested. 'You know that before anybody gives any food to a prisoner, the police would ask the person to eat the food first.'

'You don't have to offer the food to him as if he is your brother or your friend. He would not eat anything you give him too, and you know that. You have to get the food into the police station unobserved.

'How do I get into the police station without arousing suspicions?' Ezenwa asked, still not convinced by the plan.

'You don't have to go there,' Bambam explained. 'That is why I said that you need Anita. Give her the food. She would pretend as if she had come to see her father, then move to the cell and give Kruba the food. He would eat it because he doesn't know her.' Ezenwa sighed. The whole plan seemed bizarre and unfeasible.

'Anita is weak and lacks that kind of courage. She cannot poison the devil even if she sees him with his two horns. Tell her this, and the next thing she would do is scream and report back to her father.'

Bambam listened attentively, remained thoughtful for a while, raised his head and said, 'then Nyadiba should go with her.' Ezenwa sighed again. Exasperation had taken hold of him.

'Listen, it is very easy,' Bambam explained. 'Buy the food, something with good aroma that would attract a hungry thief. Give it to Nyadiba. When they get close to the police station, he would put it inside Anita's handbag. Nobody would search her. Nyadiba could coax her to go with him on the pretext that he wants to thank her father for setting him free. But he must make sure that they go there during the lunchtime when Anita's father would be at home, so that they would have time to loiter about. I know that Anita would protest and tell him to meet her father at home. But with persistence, she could be cajoled. Is she not his girlfriend? With some endearing words, some head swelling flatteries, he would break her resistance. Is she not a woman? Try it, it will work. Buy something like fried meat. When they get to Kruba's cell, Nyadiba would take the meat from Anita's bag, and keep it where Kruba would see it. Once Kruba sees it, he would steal it. Is he not a thief?'

'But what would happen if Anita eats the meat herself?' Ezenwa asked, worried.

'Of course she will die. Nyadiba had to be very careful. There is no other way out,' Bambam said. Ezenwa thanked him and left, but still wary about the failure of such attempt.

Nyadiba heard his name and turned. Ezenwa waved to him frantically from a restaurant opposite the police station.

'What is Ezenwa doing there?' Anita asked.

'I don't know, perhaps eating. I know he has nothing to do with the police,' Nyadiba said and nudged Anita to go to the restaurant with him. They crossed the road, came into the restaurant, and saw the meat. Ezenwa was still clutching a large piece, which he was actually eating.

'Where are you going?' he asked Nyadiba.

'I told you last night that I want to thank Anita's father for releasing me free of charge,' Nyadiba answered.

'Join me,' Ezenwa told him and pointed at the meat.

'Not now, perhaps later,' Nyadiba replied.

'Who told you that I would be waiting for you. If you don't eat it now, I would finish it before you come out.'

'Then I will go with it,' Nyadiba said, picked the large piece of meat, and started wrapping it with a paper. Anita looked on in embarrassment. The strangeness of such behaviour was incomprehensible to her. Is it not a piece of meat? Why so much interest in it. But she kept quiet and waited for the time she would be alone with Nyadiba. He merited to be reprimanded unreservedly.

'What are you doing here?' Anita asked Ezenwa.

'I came to the market with Nneka. So I am waiting for her here,' Ezenwa lied, and hoped that Anita had not seen Nneka on the campus before she came out, else his lie would be discovered. Anita did not make another comment. It seemed she had not seen Nneka.

'Let's go,' Nyadiba said and took Anita's hand. They crossed the road again, about to enter the police station.

'Why did you take that meat?' Anita asked Nyadiba.

'I want to eat it,' Nyadiba replied.

'You should have eaten it there.'

'I would have wasted a lot of time. I am nervous about meeting your father. I want to be through with him so that I can relax and enjoy the meat.'

'But taking it away looked like greed to me.'

'No, is it not from Ezenwa?' Nyadiba asked as they climbed the steps into the police station.

A policeman saw Anita and told her that her father had gone for lunch. 'You have to wait for him,' the policeman said.

'I warned you,' Anita told Nyadiba.

'It is not a problem,' Nyadiba said. 'Let's wait.'

Many policemen were at the police station. Besides smiles and greetings they showered on Anita, none of them asked the reason for her visit. They identified Nyadiba as one of the cult boys that was detained there some weeks ago, and deduced that their visit must not be unconnected with his case. Nyadiba and Anita loitered around for a while before Nyadiba adroitly manoeuvred her towards Kruba's cell. Some policemen saw them, but looked away.

Solomon saw him, came closer, and started laughing. Strong iron bars heavily impeded physical contact between him and them, so there was no fear of violence from him. Nyadiba was not afraid of him too. Besides being in captivity, the gun wound on his shoulder also incapacitated him. In any fight, Nyadiba would defeat him.

'I should have killed you before the police came,' he told Nyadiba.

'What made you think I would have given you the chance to kill me?' Nyadiba asked.

'What would you have done?' Kruba asked, astonished.

'What I did to your shoulder,' Nyadiba said and pointed at his shoulder. Kruba looked at his shoulder and sighed.

'I was surprised when you fired,' he commented. 'I used to think you were fragile, and that Ezenwa was the only one among you with guts. What about his girl? Kruba asked, *banging* her day and night? Tell him that I would soon pay them a visit,' he threatened.

Nyadiba shuddered, and asked him what made him think that he would come out of that cell alive.

'Don't worry, there is always a way. Robbers have been arrested before me, and robbers have been released before me,' Kruba boasted. Nyadiba and Anita exchanged glances. Her agitation started again.

'So this is the bitch you *bang*?' Kruba asked Nyadiba.

'Any problem with that?' Nyadiba retorted.

'No, not after you cut off my *thing*,' Kruba replied. Everything they said was like a puzzle to Anita. The reference to Ezenwa, Nneka, and *thing* were shrouded in mystery. She could not trace any allusion from the story Nyadiba told her to what they were saying now. Nyadiba saw the confusion on her face and reacted quickly before Solomon would say more.

'Give me my meat,' he told Anita. 'I want to eat it here so that he would see what freedom offers.' Anita wanted to protest, but Nyadiba outwitted her, dipped his hand inside the bag, brought out the piece of meat and started unwrapping it tauntingly. From the corner of his eyes, he saw Kruba approaching. Anita saw him too, shouted and pointed at him.

'What?' Nyadiba asked, pretending to be unaware of Kruba's intention.

As quick as lightening, Kruba stretched his hand and snatched the piece of meat. Nyadiba feigned surprise.

'I warned you, but you did not understand,' Anita said and started laughing. Kruba started munching the piece of meat hungrily.

'Once a thief, always a thief,' Nyadiba commented and led Anita away from the cell before any policeman would see Kruba eating something they did not give him. At the same time, he prayed that the poison would be a potent one; of course it must be. Bambam had never made mistakes.

David came back some minutes later, and was enraged to see Nyadiba and Anita together at the Police station. 'What are you doing here?' he asked angrily.

'Nothing serious sir, I only came to thank you,' Nyadiba answered as they followed him into his office.

'Is that why she came with you?' David asked, unconvinced.

'We want to go and see mummy too,' Anita lied, and her father's countenance relaxed.

Solomon died four days later in a hospital. The police said he died of bullet wounds. Nobody cared to do autopsy on him to ascertain the cause of his death. Anita's father mourned him like a son. Apart from Bambam, Nyadiba, and Ezenwa, nobody else knew what killed Kruba.

Chapter 35

Examinations in the University of Nigeria Nsukka were always a serious affair. Diligent students performed very well, while layabouts and playful ones performed dismally. More than anything else, issues of examination malpractice were seen as a reprehensible absurdity, and were punishable by outright expulsion. To prevent it, lecturers always searched the students before they sat for any examination. It worked for a while before students' protests followed these searches. They argued that searching students was a kind of dehumanisation that created the impression that students were criminals. As would be expected, searching before examinations stopped. Then lecturers relied on their wits and vigilance to catch cheating students.

It was the first day of the first semester examination of Ezenwa's second year and Bambam's final year in the university. Jerry had prepared for the examination with exceptional diligence. The lecturer whose examination they were about to take was Professor Fitz. He was an Irish man whose friendship Jerry had courted for a long time. There was no better way to get the desired attention from Fitz than to make a good grade in his examination. Jerry was not a dullard. In spite of his scandalous womanising, he still had time to study and pass all his examinations. To impress Fitz, he had made exceptional endeavour at research, and was determined to give Fitz more than he required. That day too, Bambam decided it was pay time.

Jerry had left his notebook on a table inside the library of the Department of English and went to the examination venue. His classmate, a Scorpion boy, who Bambam had instructed to ruin Jerry, was also in the library. He picked the notebook, tore out some pages from it, and ran after Jerry.

Professor Fitz told the students to search themselves, and remove any incriminating object from their pockets before going into the examination venue. Jerry found no reason to do so, he knew he was clean, yet he dipped his hands into his pockets and was satisfied.

'Search yourselves, I won't listen to your pleas if I catch you,' Fitz repeated. This time, Jerry ignored the warning and started conversing with a girl standing beside him.

'You can go in now and take your seats,' Fitz told them. There was a rush into the hall. Some students had planned to sit together, and to accomplish this, they had to get into the hall and chose the positions they liked before other people would occupy them. Jerry was caught in the midst of the jostle. The Scorpion boy, who had been following him like a shadow, adroitly inserted the pieces of papers from the notebook inside Jerry's pocket.

The examination started some minutes later. The Scorpion boy was one of the brightest students of the class, an attribute of the Scorpions. He was well ahead of Jerry in academics, so he finished writing earlier than Jerry and sought permission to go. Professor Fitz collected his papers and permitted him to go. The boy left the examination venue and went to the Head of the Department of English.

'What can I do for you?' the Head of the Department asked him.

'I have come to report a student who is cheating in the examination,' the boy replied.

'Why didn't you report to Professor Fitz?' the Head of the Department asked.

'I don't want other students to know that I reported him. They would say that I am callous,' the boy replied. The head of the Department called two security men and went to verify the report with them.

Jerry was sweating to write all he knew, in the way that would endear him to Professor Fitz. The Head of the Department came in, and after a brief conversation with Fitz, focused his attention on Jerry.

'Hello young man,' Fitz called. Other students looked up, including Jerry.

'Me?' Jerry asked and looked behind him, thinking it was another person that Fitz called.

'Yes you, come out!' Fitz insisted. Jerry came out to the front of the class, absolutely certain that he had not infringed any rule. He was not perturbed.

'Search him!' Fitz told one of the security men. The security man dipped his hand inside Jerry's pocket and came out with the pieces of paper. Jerry gaped in astonishment.

'But I did not put anything inside my pocket,' he protested.

'That's entirely your business. You should have searched yourself when I gave the instruction,' Fitz replied.

'But sir...'

'Tell that to the senate,' Fitz said curtly, confiscated Jerry's papers, and made a formal report to the university senate.

Two weeks later, Jerry appeared before the university senate, and would have wriggled out of the problem, but for the glaring evidence of the similarity between the handwriting on his answer papers and the one on the pieces of paper Fitz found in his pocket. He was expelled.

Two days later, his car caught fire in a mysterious circumstance and was burnt to ashes in front of Aja Nwachulwu Hall.

Jerry refused to accept the verdict of the university senate even when the evidence from Professor Fitz weighed heavily against him. He sought the help of a lawyer to challenge the verdict in a court. While he waited for the court judgement, he astutely sought other avenues to obtain a reprieve.

His most efficient plot, which rattled the Scorpions, was the almost successful influence of some female members of his congregation. Jerry had selected the most beautiful and guileful girls in his church and sent them, with wiles, to tempt and influence six members of the university senate, those who led the panel that recommended his expulsion. These men were among the most influential members of the university community whose words, Jerry knew, could sway the decision of the whole senate, and rescind their verdict. Besides the girls, nobody else knew about Jerry's scheme.

After two weeks, the girls were able to sway four men in Jerry's favour out of the six. Two refused to succumb. Yet reprobate and irrepressible, Jerry sent different set of girls to them. But the two men remained immutable.

Distressed and desperate, Jerry came to Nneka again, and tried to compel her with stories filled with pathos, to use her spell on the two impervious professors.

'You know you are the most beautiful girl on the campus,' he told her, 'nobody would refuse your advances or reject your solicitude. Do it for me and God will bless you, or do you want me to end like this? What will happen to the good work I am doing for God through my church, do you want it to end too? Please stand on my side and let's fight God's battle.' Nneka gaped at him, petrified. 'I am not begging you to be a whore,' Jerry continued, 'just some minutes with each of them, then you make the request. I know they must succumb, four have agreed, it remained only two. Yes I know that, who could resist you? Nobody!'

Nneka was numbed. She gaped at him, lost for words. When she finally recollected herself, she replied, 'Jeremiah, I can now conclude that you are mad. You want me to have sexual intercourse with men, to influence them to rescind the expulsion verdict, yet you claim to be a pastor. Shame on you!' She spat on his face and pushed him out of her room. Two hours later, Nneka told Ezenwa the story. Thirty minutes later, Bambam heard it too.

If Jerry had known who was after him, he would have known how to organise a defence. But he did not know who was throwing the blows. Red Scorpions attacked with invisibility, and they left no trace after their attacks. It was difficult for Jerry to look in their direction, especially in such frenzy. If he had remembered that they had once sent a red scorpion to him as a warning of a looming danger, perhaps he would have looked in that direction. But that was a long time ago, almost a year, and nothing had happened to him since then. Still unaware of his enemy, Jerry made another spirited effort.

His congregation, in spite of the Jerry's scandals, united impressively to save him. The most prominent effort came from a boy, son of a wealthy politician of the ruling political party in the state, a gullible and witless student, who decided to marry his girlfriend, and celebrate his wedding in Jerry's church, just to change Jerry's image in the university community.

He knew his father would come to the wedding with other prominent politicians in the state. It would give the church the publicity it desired tremendously, and bring Jerry in contact with moguls, from whom Jerry hoped to find a way to influence the vice chancellor and the University senate on his behalf. He took it on himself and made sure that the vice chancellor and other prominent lecturers of the university were invited to the wedding. Even if he was not re-admitted into the university, Jerry hoped to exploit every contact he would have with the politicians. Opportunities like that were rare, and more, the offering in the church that day would be enough for him to buy another car. For this, he prepared his sermon diligently and was ready to explode.

Two days before the wedding, he replaced the advertisement board that usually hung in front of his church with a new one so bold and catchy. The inscription on the board was THE HOPE OF HEAVEN, A CHURCH OF SALVATION, written in capital letters. It served its purpose. It attracted the attention of every passer-by, and attracted the Scorpions too.

On the wedding day, Jerry arrived with some girls to clean and keep the building tidy. They decorated the entrance with expensive balloons, and decorated the inside with ribbons. The church that day was painted with splendour. It really depicted a grandiloquent setting about to host a celebration of affluence. Jerry took extra care to select the most guileful, reprobate, but charming girls in his church to usher in the guests. He inspected everything with critical attention. The girls were there, tempting without scruples. The sign was glittering where it hung. He was satisfied, and waited for the arrival of his guests.

Nobody saw the boy. If anybody did, nobody gave him any attention. He was a member of the Red Scorpions Bambam had sent to Jerry's church to do a mischief. The boy removed the advertisement board skilfully where it hung in front of the church, and replaced it with another, which read: THE HOPE OF HELL, A CHURCH OF DAMNATION. It was done adroitly in the same colour that Jerry and his congregation did not notice any change.

The guests started arriving some minutes later. All the prominent members of the ruling political party were at the wedding. Very few people saw the misnomer, and those who saw it simply laughed and forgot it. But journalists who saw it exploited it. They filmed and took snapshots of it from different angles.

Citizens of the state were a superstitious people. They shuddered with consternation and dismay when they saw the politicians they knew embracing and greeting each other gleefully with the macabre inscription: HOPE OF HELL, A CHURCH OF DAMNATION clearly written above their heads. Worse still were the pictures of almost nude girls, who the citizens of the state called the agents of the devil, walking up and down the aisle of the church.

The wedding would not have generated any controversy, perhaps would have been forgotten too, and Jerry would have triumphed. But the opposition party in the state started a campaign of calumny, a propaganda filled with humour and rancour, accusing the ruling party of a malevolent intention to sell the state to the devil.

The citizens reacted and called for the resignation of the Governor and their leaders in the ruling political party. The State Government made efforts to debunk the assertion of the opposition, but the citizens could not be appeased. Perchance, if some television stations had not televised the wedding feast many times, the State Government would have succeeded in pacifying its citizens with a mendacious and divergent stand. But with numerous broadcasts, the citizens argued about what they saw, and not about what the opposition party told them.

With the passing of days, the opposition party augmented their offensive, exploiting the ignorance of the citizens. The ruling party, still trying to deflate the claims of the opposition party, invited Jerry for a television programme, hoping that an explanation from the pastor of the church could appease the citizens and put an end to the issue. They told him to offer explanations about the wedding in his church, a thing Jerry cherished even with all the oddities surrounding it. He started preparing how to lunch his influence in the state, and the Red Scorpions also started how to seal their offensive.

Since he returned that tin of scorpions to Bambam, Ezenwa had never bothered to ask him where he kept it, or what he did with it. He knew Bambam had kept it somewhere, from where they took the scorpions they sent to their enemies as a warning before any attack. It was when Bambam started planning what he would do with the scorpions that Ezenwa saw where he kept them, and recoiled in fear. He had never imagined that it would be on such a scale.

There were about eighty glass jars of thirty inches in length and width. Each jar contained about two hundred and fifty live scorpions. A glimpse inside one of the jars covered Ezenwa's body with goose pimples. It looked as if the scorpions were taken from a sea of scorpions, as one would fetch water from a stream. He gaped at Bambam and asked what he wanted to do with the scorpions.

'We wanted to keep some scorpions to use, you know how and why. But we were overwhelmed on how fast they multiplied. And as you know, our law prohibits any kind of aggression or violence against scorpions, so we kept them and continued to feed them. But now, I am happy they are going to be useful,' Bambam replied gleefully. Ezenwa did not understand how or of what use they would be. Time and time again, live scorpions painted with red dye and tied with black thread had been seen hanging on the doorknobs of the Red Scorpions' enemies. If the Red Scorpions meant to use all the scorpions Ezenwa had seen for that same purpose, then it meant that every student in the university would receive some scorpions. He imagined what would happen if any of the jars broke accidentally. The neighbourhood would relocate on a state of emergency. Just a look inside any of the jars sent cold all over his body. How many years did it take them to nurture these scorpions? Ezenwa pondered.

When Jerry advised his congregation to live with only their *brothers* and *sisters* in the hostels, he told them that it was to enhance spiritual interaction. In this way, it would be easy for him to visit them and give them spiritual guidance together. Nobody knew how he hoped to achieve that, but when he bribed the staff of the Student Affairs Department, and influenced the posting of all members of his church to selected halls and rooms, everybody knew that what Jerry could not influence in that university could be counted on the fingers. To facilitate his designs, he made sure that his followers occupied the best rooms on the last floors of the halls. With this, instead of visiting the sixteen female hostels every week, he visited only four. And instead of visiting four girls in four different rooms, he visited them just in a room. Sooner than he expected, students started making references to these rooms as "Jerry's harem".

No one had ever seen Jerry in any male hostel. When some students asked him why he did not visit boys, he told them that boys were spiritually stronger than girls, and needed no prodding to do the will of God. Gullible ones believed this assertion while sceptical ones doubted it.

Many people saw the expediency of criticism on Jerry's way of life, especially on his spurious Christianity, but they had been criticising it with feebleness. Only one person had been reproaching Jerry arduously and relentlessly. His name was Godrick Onuma.

He was a third year student of Music, an ardent member of the Rastafari Movement. He walked all over the campus on barefoot, always clutching a long walking stick he cut from a guava tree, like the biblical Moses. His hair was almost twenty inches long, dishevelled, entangled, dirty, and unpleasant to the sight. His long beard gave him the picture of one of the Prophets of the biblical era that he always tried to imitate. He always wore a long black robe that had strips of yellow, red and green, the colours of the Jamaican flag. He was an extremist whose doctrines were based mainly on the life and speeches of the late Ethiopian leader, Emperor Haile Selassie, and the late reggae musician, Bob Marley. He believed in them, and almost worshipped them. Never had it been heard that he made a speech devoid of a quotation or a reference to them. He would have drifted into the desert if there were universities in the desert, and would have been eating only locusts and wild honey if there were locusts in Nigeria. Godrick would do anything just to be like John the Baptist. In substitution to locusts and wild honey, he ate only dry meat and bitter-leaf, which he often cooked with a pot of earthenware. All these, he claimed, were instructions from God, who he called *Jah*.

Claiming to be a prophet, Godrick almost got prominence when he predicted accurately the result of a football match between Nigeria and Egypt. But when Nigeria lost woefully in subsequent matches contrary to his predictions, his truthfulness came into question. Many people lost faith in him.

From his name and surname, Godrick Onuma, he formed the nickname *Godman*, and was generally known and referred to on the campus as *Rasta Godman*.

He preached and prophesied all over the campus. As would be expected at a time when even a mad man would have followers once he could pronounce the word "God", some people believed in Rasta Godman, and went to him for spiritual guidance. The most outstanding attribute he claimed he had was the spiritual gift to interpret dreams, a gift which, from every indication, did not exist in him. His analysis of dreams, for those who were foolish enough to seek his counsel, were mainly intelligent deductions from the questions he asked his clients. Those who were wise in their thinking could easily discover that Godman had no spiritual alliance with any god. But those who believed in him went to him. Those who did not believe in him scorned him.

When Bambam sent Ezenwa, Nyadiba, and Amaka, one of the Scorpions girls, to Godman with an imaginary story from a false dream, they did not know what Bambam wanted, or what Godman would do with the story. Ezenwa went first. When he arrived, he saw Godrick engrossed in his bible, neither raising his head nor questioning the identity of the intruder. Ezenwa went closer and peeped into the book, and saw that he was reading the book of Prophet Isaiah. Ezenwa stood still for a while before he greeted him, 'Good morning Godman.'

'Good morning Jah son,' Godman replied. He always called every male being *Jah son*, and every female, *daughter of Eve*.

'I have a terrible dream last night,' Ezenwa told him. Godman grinned.

'How was the dream?' he asked.

'I cannot remember how it started, but I remembered that scorpions were chasing me. I took refuge on top of a hill. The Scorpions came to the hill, a mysterious fire erupted from the foot of the hill and devoured them. But while I was on the hill, I heard cries of lamentation all over the campus. I was worried, because I thought it was the end of the world. Then I started praying. Suddenly an Angel appeared and told me to stay calm, that what I saw was what was about to happen to people who use the name of God in vain, especially members of an evil church on this campus whose members glorify nakedness. I wanted to ask the Angle to explain what he meant, but he disappeared, and I woke up.' Ezenwa stopped and looked askance at him. Godman was enthralled by the tale.

'Yeah, Jah son,' he said, 'your dream was a vision from Jah about what would happen to those who take the name of Jah in vain. As for you, go and rejoice that you have been saved from the coming retribution.' Ezenwa smiled, thanked him, and went away.

Four hours later, Nyadiba came with his own story, a distorted version of Ezenwa's dream. The only difference was that he told Godman that he saw Pastor Jerry devoured by scorpions.

That day would have ended like any other day for Rasta Godman, but when Amaka came with her own dream, slightly different from the previous two, Rasta Godman confirmed that it was a true message from Jah. Amaka had told him that the scorpions fell like rain, that she also saw Godman himself preaching and telling people to repent. That was all Godman needed. Before Amaka got back to her hostel, she heard

Godman preaching and prophesying, telling the community of The Hope of Heaven Church that doom awaited them, and that God was about to chastise them with scorpions. He took his prophecy to all the hostels on the campus. Very late, almost at midnight, he voice was heard as he shouted, 'Prepare for the coming retribution! Prepare for the coming retribution! Those who have ears let them hear!' Some students made fun of him, mimicked him and told him to "prepare for the coming examination". Some fanatical members of the Jerry's church threatened to attack him physically. He got the worst of the insults at Akpabio hall, where a student poured dirty water on him, and told him to wash his hair. Yet not discouraged, Godman continued preaching and prophesying until the early hours of the morning. Satisfied that he had given them the message, he went back to his room and slept.

Jerry was in the room of one of his girls with some members of his congregation. The topic of their discussion was about the coming television interview. Jerry was about to exonerate the ruling party from any link to his church, and to tell the world too that the name of the church was not Hope of Hell. Without doubt, he had turned into a celebrity after the wedding in his church. Each time there was a reference to the wedding in the news media, his name was always mentioned. He was discussing the coming television interview with his followers. That was the night the Red Scorpions decided to seal their offensive against him. Armed with more than two thousand live scorpions and a copy of the bible each, members of the Red Scorpions invaded all the hostels of the University, visiting only the rooms of Jerry's followers. The Red Scorpions had never lacked the expertise to carry out any attack on their enemies. They had carefully surveyed the rooms, and gave flawless attention to the rooms with the most ardent followers of Jerry. They visited every room in pairs, preaching and making citations from the bible. When one person preached and occupied the attention of the room mates of the room, his companion would dextrously open a can of scorpions and threw them under the bed. One of the first rooms they visited was the room where Jerry was conversing with some members of his congregation. He had removed his shoes, and his legs were resting on a stool in the room. The boy with the tin of scorpion saw his shoes. While the other boy preached, he skilfully allowed two scorpions to crawl into one of the shoes, then he threw the rest under the bed.

Ezenwa was in Nneka's room when they heard the cry of the first victim of the Scorpions. Many people ran to her room, and were surprised to see a live scorpion. It had no red dye on it. Nobody suspected the Red Scorpions, because their scorpions were always red. The victim's room mates were still arguing and wondering about the origin of the scorpion when they heard another painful cry from another room, followed by two simultaneous screams on the second floor. Jerry got up from the bed, put his leg into his shoe, and cried too. His cry shocked his hosts. He cried like a woman. Everybody remembered the prophecy of Rasta Godman.

The whole campus was thrown into panic. Nobody outside Jerry's church was attacked by the scorpions, except those who wandered to the rooms of his followers. The puzzle was that it was happening at the same time in all the hostels of the university, and some people were attacked twice. Male hostels had few members of the Hope of Heaven, those who went there only to poach Jerry's girls. For this, they recorded few incidents.

Some girls who had not been chastised by the scorpions abandoned their rooms and were seen loitering about the corridors. Those who had nothing to do with Jerry and his church locked their doors in shrewd dissociation from Jerry and his followers. The victims were taken to the hospital, and that night alone, the hospital recorded six hundred and fifteen cases of scorpion attack.

Jerry went back to his house that night a defeated man. His foot was still swollen, but the pain had abated. He had never believed in any prophecy, not even in the prophecies of the bible, let alone the prophecy of Rasta Godman, a semi-lunatic who called himself a prophet. But after the scorpions attack, he started pondering on the prophecy of Godman, and accepted that God was actually chastising him. He had been expelled from the university. The only thing left for him was his church, and he would not leave it in panic because of any prophecy.

More scorpion attacks were recorded the following days. The medical centre of the university was not disposed for that kind of epidemic, and soon ran out of drugs. The incident got to the news media again. Some journalists visited the university, conversed with many students, especially those who were attacked by the scorpions, and were amazed that only the members of the controversial demonic church were attacked.

The opposition party got the story of the scorpions too, and added it to their maligning propaganda, accusing the ruling party of an irrefutable alliance with the devil. From this, together with the economic woes of the country, the popularity of the ruling party waned.

Two weeks later, the university senate banned Jerry's church on the campus, and the fame of Rasta Godman spread across the country. When he started parading himself as a prophet, he knew he was only putting up appearances, seeking recognition. But after the incidence of the scorpions, he believed in himself. From then, nobody doubted the veracity of his prophecies again. Nobody jeered at hi. Nobody threw stones at him, or mimicked him. Everybody received his exhortations with fear and trembling. Eminent men, especially politicians, consulted him before undertaking any venture, and his fortune grew daily.

Chapter 36

Nneka continued without respite in her religious activities in the church, which had become a sort of solace to her. After her first public performance, the day she sang during a church service and was applauded with a resounding ovation, she discovered that there was a way to avoid living in seclusion, that beside a pretty face, she was as well blessed with a sweet voice. Out of joy, she wanted to give more.

She had made many new and trustworthy female friends too, and no longer contended with the whips of envy and scourges of jealousy, as was the case in her friendship with Joy. She still met and conversed with Joy, but always on unimportant things. One of her new friends was a nun, Camilla, a member of the Catholic Students' Choir. She lived alone in one of the rooms at Aja Nwachukwu Hall extension. Nneka visited her daily.

From the day Nneka became Camilla's friend, she stopped going to Ezenwa's room every day to study. This alienated her a little from Ezenwa, gave him the space to evaluate their friendship, and offered him the respite he needed. Fears and premonitions of betrayal by her female friends no longer worried him, because he thought that friendship with a nun was irreproachable. He still visited Nneka whenever he wanted, sometimes in Camilla's room, and continued to get undivided affection from her.

Camilla had never displayed any kind of hostility towards Ezenwa, but from her eyes, Ezenwa could read a tacit censure of any kind of immodesty. He diligently respected this censure, and no longer spoke about love, or made gestures that would embarrass Camilla whenever he was in her room with Nneka. He had often imagined the scandal he would create if a passer-by threw a glance at Camilla's window and saw him kissing Nneka. Without verification, the passer-by would conclude that Camilla was kissing a man in her room, and the scandal would spread like Harmattan fire. To avoid such scandals, he always stayed far away from Nneka whenever they were in Camilla's room.

The Catholic Students' Choir had been preparing for a concert for the last week of the semester, a week after the examination. Nneka was the major attraction in the concert. She was deeply engrossed in the preparation that she sometimes missed her lectures. Ezenwa was not bothered about this, he knew that she could always make up for the lost times. But when Bambam sent for him, and told him that there was a likelihood of a disastrous conflict on the day of the concert, Ezenwa was bothered as he had never been bothered in his life.

The date of the concert coincided with the date of the anniversary of the Zotus Club, a social club dominated by cult members. They claimed to be anti-colonialists, and rejected every kind of social heritage from Europe and America. They had started the preparation of the ten years anniversary of the club a year ago, and had invested a lot of money in it. They had invited artists from different parts of the country. Although most of the artists were unpopular artists, the club still hoped to make a fortune from their performances, contrary to the choir's concert, which was a free show. The members of the club wanted the concert in the church to be postponed, so that the students would attend their own show, and they would make some profit from the money they had invested. The choir refused to accede to the demand of the club, and violence started brewing.

There would not have been any conflict if the Catholic Choir had not used Nneka's pictures in the advertisement of the concert. Her joyful and spell bounding face was on all the posters the choir posted all over the campus. For this, the students started making mockery of the Zotus Club show, saying that they preferred a free glance of that beautiful face to the mediocrity of unknown artists. Consequently, Nneka became the prime target of the violence. This was why Bambam got involved.

'What are we going to do about it?' Ezenwa asked Bambam.

'I don't know. I have tried to incite my boys against the club, but many of them are also members of the club. I cannot interfere personally in their freedom of association. I wanted the conflict to be a Scorpions affair, but many of them did not like it. Moreover, there is a strong disaffection against me among the Scorpions. Many of them were embittered against me, especially for the times I took sides with you against them. This time, they might refuse to back me. If they refuse, then my power would be weakened. And when this happens, my life, yours, and hers, would be in serious danger,' Bambam told Ezenwa.

'But there must be a way out,' Ezenwa argued.

'Yes, only if you would join us,' Bambam proposed.

'Join you? Be a Scorpion?' Ezenwa asked nervously.

'Yes,' Bambam replied. Ezenwa winced. It was lamentably an undesirable proposal. Ezenwa had always known that a day like this would come. Haunted by his indebtedness to Bambam, he restrained himself from making any offensive gesture, or out of eagerness to please him, make a deleterious acceptance. He wanted to play for time, and somehow cajole Bambam into another option, which he knew Bambam must have. He was never without options. 'There must be another way,' Ezenwa suggested.

'I don't know of any other way,' Bambam replied brusquely. 'Are you willing to join or not?' he asked coldly.

'I have to think about it,' Ezenwa replied.

'That's all right. But while you think about it, I have to tell you that they planned to bath her with acid a day before the concert. One of her friends, whose name I am not willing to divulge, had been paid to take her nude pictures again. They planned to print these pictures on posters, and post them beside every bill the choir posted for the publicity of the concert. You know the scandal it would create. Do not think of telling her to abandon the concert, because her fate had been sealed. Even if she does not perform, they would still punish her.'

Ezenwa listened poignantly. Bambam's voice had developed a coldness that distressed him. His old inveterate geniality was completely obfuscated by a stern and scary disposition. He seemed to be in distress too, and needed

Ezenwa's membership to pacify his boys. He needed to retain his sphere of influence in the university. But being a cult member was a horrendous iniquity. Ezenwa knew that this iniquity would haunt him for the rest of his life.

'Are you going to join or not?' Bambam asked again. This was a complete volte-face to his promise to protect Ezenwa without commitments. Ezenwa remained silent. Perhaps if he knew the number of fights Bambam had fought for him and his girlfriend, he would have offered to join the cult without coercion. If he knew the number of people Bambam had killed, and was still willing to kill to guard Nneka's liberty, he would have accepted to join the Scorpions with smiles. In as much as he was not willing to give a hurried response to Bambam's importunity, dissociation from the cult was completely unthinkable. The consequences were glaringly obvious; Bambam would lead the onslaught against him and Nneka. For a fleeting moment, Ezenwa saw in his mind Nneka's beautiful face corroded by acid, and shuddered. He had wanted to play for time, but Bambam's voice and facial gestures had scared him. Ezenwa was not going to bargain with Nneka's life.

Against all wariness and warnings of intuition, he abruptly accepted to join the Red Scorpions. Bambam smiled, embraced him and said, 'we are now brothers, and I swear, I would defend her with my life.'

'How would the initiation be?' Ezenwa asked with emotion laden voice.

'Don't worry about that. You will be initiated this night. I will use my influence to waive and protect you from torture and the test of secrecy. You will only go through the prescribed rituals. It is nothing elaborate.'

'I want to know the process so that I can prepare very well,' Ezenwa insisted.

'No, I cannot tell you everything now. You will know when the time comes. But I promise, you are not going to be subjected to any kind of humiliation, except that which is inevitable. You can go now and start preparing. I will come with some members to take you to the shrine this night,' Bambam dismissed him.

'That's all right,' Ezenwa said demurely, stood up and started walking back to his room sorrowfully. His conscience chided him persistently, and imbued him with feebleness. The decision he had taken was, without doubt, devoid of sagacity. From the sequences of ruinous incidents on the campus, he knew his turn would come one day. One day he would be killed like others. Now, he agreed with Nneka. She was cursed indeed, and nobody could be her husband and remain unhurt.

Bambam arrived with two members of the Red Scorpions very late at night and took Ezenwa to the venue of the initiation. It was a shrine of the Scorpions. Before then, Ezenwa had always thought that the rituals of university cults were devoid of substance, just impotent ceremonies to inculcate fear and foster cohesion among the members. But that night, he saw an elaborate ritual that would make his grandfather look like a novice.

It was a very dark night. All the members of the cult wore black robes, with a carved image of a red scorpion hanging on their chests. Apart from the clothes they wore, each member had a charm that Ezenwa later understood was used during fights with rival cults. It was these charms, they claimed, that made them invisible, especially during fights with rival cults. Ezenwa was the only person to be initiated, because Bambam wanted to spare him the pain and trauma of a general initiation, which was always accompanied by bodily tortures.

The first step was the swearing of an oath of allegiance and secrecy in the name of the god of the Red Scorpions. A boy, the priest, painted his face with granulated red chalk, and told Ezenwa to kneel down in front of the shrine. Ezenwa knelt down. The priest made a sign to one of the boys standing behind him. The boy went inside the shrine and came out with a live vulture. Ezenwa winced. Another boy came from behind and blindfolded Ezenwa with a red scarf.

The priest took the vulture, chanted some incantations, and cut of the vultures head. All the boys at the shrine bowed down.

'Open your mouth,' the priest ordered Ezenwa. Ezenwa did not know what the priest wanted to do, yet he opened his mouth. The priest thrust the vulture's neck into his mouth and told him to lick the blood. Ezenwa licked it, and spat it out immediately he discovered what it was. 'No, you must swallow it,' the priest insisted, and put the vulture's neck into Ezenwa's mouth again. Ezenwa wanted to argue. Somebody tapped him on the shoulder from behind.

'It's an order,' the person said. Ezenwa knew they were very serious and could even use him as a sacrifice there. He swallowed the vulture's blood grudgingly. The boy who brought the vulture took it from the priest, licked the blood too, and handed it over to the next person. Like that all the boys at the shrine licked the vulture's blood. When they finished, the boy took the vulture inside the shrine and started cooking it.

As the vulture was still on fire, the priest told Ezenwa to repeat some words after him. Ezenwa did not understand the language, but he obeyed the priest. He knew that every word he uttered compromised his liberty. It was only after the last word that he understood that he had given over his soul to the devil.

The boy who was cooking the vulture came out with it in parts, but still with the feathers. The priest told Ezenwa that they had prepared the meat of one of the most blessed creatures on earth, that he would let him pick any part of the meat blindly from the tray he would present to him. All these did not bother Ezenwa as long as the cult would protect his girlfriend for whose sake he was selling his soul to the devil.

The priest tapped him on the shoulder and told him to pick. Ezenwa dipped his hand inside the tray, touched something, and raised it up. The priest took it from him, examined it closely with the light from a red candle, and announced that he picked the head. Some people clapped. Bambam embraced Ezenwa. The priest removed the blindfold from his eyes. Then Ezenwa saw that he had picked the head of a vulture. He did not know why there was jubilation, and nobody would tell him the significance of anything they did until after the initiation.

'Eat it,' the priest ordered.

'Yes, you swore to be obedient, and to abide by laws of the Red Scorpions,' the priest reminded him. Ezenwa looked around for Bambam to rescue him; hadn't he promised to waive humiliating rituals for him? Bambam stared back at him with impassivity. Reluctantly, Ezenwa picked the vulture's head and started munching. Everybody applauded. Bambam came to congratulate him.

'Eat it, it doesn't kill,' Bambam said, and went back to the line. The priest stared at him as he ate the vulture. The taste was horrible, but Ezenwa shut his eyes and swallowed it. Then came the part where he nearly absconded.

'Undress and prepare for your birth,' the priest said, still with that solemn voice with which he started the ritual. Ezenwa undressed and stood before them, stark naked.

He heard voices behind him, turned, and saw stark naked girls coming to the shrine, each bearing a burning red candle. That was the first time he saw completely naked woman in his life. Naturally, his genitals reacted, and everybody applauded again. He became confused, and stared back at them. 'You are alive,' the priest said.

'What?' Ezenwa asked, afraid that they were about to force him to have sexual intercourse with the girls.

'You are about to be born fully into the scorpions world,' the priest told him while the girls were lining up in front of the shrine, with their legs wide apart.

'You are going to crawl through their open legs into our world, the world of the Scorpions,' the priest informed him, and led him by the hand to the first girl. 'Each of them has something to tell you, and you must wait until she finishes before you move over to another person. They are all mothers. Each of them gave birth to a scorpion. The last girl will be your own mother. She would raise you up as a mother raises her son, with a lot of affection and love. She would do everything you want her to do for you, but would never interfere in your love life, unless you permit her.' Ezenwa flinched.

Crawling through the legs of the girls was a symbol of a new birth, a birth into the world of the Scorpions. But the thought of a vicious girl replacing his cherished mother was highly repugnant to him. He bent down to crawl through the legs of the first girl. She started chanting something he did not understand. He waited. After the incantation, she dipped her thumb into her vagina, and drew three lines with it on Ezenwa's forehead. Ezenwa protested and wanted to discontinue. The priest compelled him to crawl through all the legs. All the girls made the same gesture, and mumbled some words. When Ezenwa got to the last girl, she did the same thing, pulled him up, and led him into the shrine. Ezenwa waited to see what she wanted to do. She knelt down, picked up a cup, and gave him. 'Drink it!' she commanded.

'But what is it?' he asked.

'You have no right to know until you have taken it, and you must take it,' the girl warned. Ezenwa took the cup and peeped into it. Everywhere was covered by darkness. The only light available was of the flickering red candle the girl held very close to her face. He did not see the content of the cup, and could not guess what it was. 'Drink it if you want me to be your mother,' she said again. Ezenwa stared at her scornfully and drank the liquid. It was whisky. He licked his lips, and wanted to ask for more. It completely wiped out the taste and odour of that repulsive vulture he ate. 'Now I can tell you what you drank,' the girl said gleefully.

'It is whisky,' Ezenwa said.

'Yes, whisky, but mixed with the fluid from my vagina,' she said happily.

'What!' Ezenwa shouted, and inserted his two fingers into his throat to puke, but was unable to vomit.

The girl smiled ruefully and told him that she was at his disposal from then onwards. 'I will do for you anything a mother can do for her son,' she said.

'Go to hell, you and your motherhood,' Ezenwa replied, still grieving for doing the most odious and absurd thing he had ever done in his life. The girl walked out of the shrine. Other jubilant girls embraced her. Ezenwa came out of the shrine too. Bambam came to congratulate him. He started complaining about the thing he drank.

'Forget about what you drank, it doesn't kill,' Bambam said.

'But why should I drink the vaginal fluid of somebody I don't know,' Ezenwa protested.

'Whether you know her or not, she is now your mother,' Bambam said.

The priest grabbed Ezenwa's arm and made a deep incision on it with a sharp blade. He screamed. Blood started coming out. His Scorpion mother came with a jar. The priest took the jar from her and put it under Ezenwa's arm. Blood started trickling into the jar. Ezenwa sighed and started crying.

When the priest felt that he had collected the quantity of blood he needed, he went into the shrine with the jar, accompanied by Bambam and Ezenwa's Scorpion mother. Ezenwa heard the priest's voice as he sacrificed his blood to the god, but did not understand the language he was speaking. The ritual was diabolic indeed, more than what he had expected. Instantly, his conscience taunted him, and told him that he had willingly sold his soul to the devil. He shook his head sadly. If he had seen the wooden image of the devil with a cup in his hands into which the priest poured his blood, he would have wept bitterly. He underestimated the consequences of the initiation.

Bambam roused him from his deep thought, and told him that the initiation was successful. The priest came out from the shrine with the girl and told him that they would take him down to the stream to bath him, and the initiation would be complete. His scorpion mother came with other girls, and took Ezenwa's arm gently. Silently, they led him to the back of the shrine.

There was a stream behind the shrine, just like the stream in his village. The girls started bathing him, without doing anything erotic or vulgar. Ezenwa hated every touch of their hands, but could not make any objection. Some minutes later, Bambam and two other boys came down to the stream with his clothes. The initiation was over.

It was a week to the examination. Neither Nyadiba nor Nneka knew about the initiation. Ezenwa was too ashamed of it to tell anybody. He had been having nightmares, where demons with horns and tails were singing a reception song for him in hell. If he became afraid and cried, one of them would say, with the voice of Bambam, 'relax, it doesn't kill.'

Ezenwa had visited Nneka in her room with a pang of guilt, and bruises of profanity tormenting his conscience. Nneka had embraced him as she used to do. But the sensation of her touch was no longer felt. Every contact Ezenwa had with her seemed to be sacrilegious, like the embrace of vice and virtue. He kept unclasping Nneka's hands from his waist as if they were serpents. But later, he tried to dominate his conscience by thinking only about her beautiful face, and consoling himself that it was worth the initiation. He prayed that her spiritual fervidity would sanctify his despicable iniquity.

Bambam vowed to protect the concert with every might at his disposal, and threatened to fight the Zotus Club to extinction if they refused to accept his terms. The Zotus Club cancelled their anniversary celebration a week before the date of the concert. Ezenwa knew how the concession was obtained. His spirit was enfeebled when he saw Nneka rejoicing and preparing for the concert animatedly. In her words, 'the concert would go on without troubles.' Perhaps if she knew how that peace was obtained, she would be shedding tears instead of joy.

Although a truce had been reached between the choir and the club, and there was no sign of any danger again, no alert from Bambam, Ezenwa did not confide in the ability of anybody to protect Nneka. Nobody would be willing to stand in the way of bullets for the sake of a girl he did not know. Ezenwa had been initiated into the world of the Red Scorpions, but that was not enough. His latent enemies were of The Black Axe and The Yellow Lizards. The Scorpions would only offer their help when the deed must have been done, so Ezenwa conferred with Nyadiba, the only person he still trusted, and they decided to arm themselves and protect Nneka and Camilla as the concert drew nearer.

Ezenwa was a fellow with an inflexible will. He had never shot anybody with a gun, and did not intend to shoot anybody, but would not hesitate to shoot if the occasion called for it, like in the arrogant and unreasonable plan of the Zotus Club.

Nneka did not want to disappoint her fans. She was at the centre of the concert, and made elaborate efforts to learn all her songs, especially the songs in foreign languages. She had hitherto abandoned singing to give attention to her studies and the examination, but when the examination came to an end, she started spending her nights in the church, singing and dancing.

Some days to the date of the concert, Ezenwa met her at the church. She expected him to lament and accuse her of negligence, and was prepared to offer her apologies with a promise to make it up to him after the concert. But Ezenwa said what she did not expect to hear.

'Tell me what you plan to do at the concert,' Ezenwa told her. She smiled, and with enthusiasm and tenderness, explained everything to him. 'That's good,' he said, 'if you ever need my help, let me know. I want you to have a good performance.' Nneka was moved by this show of concern. He had been very critical of the time she spent at the church to the detriment of her studies. So it now gladdened her heart to hear him promise to help her if she needed his help. She embraced him tightly again and kissed him. He inhaled her breath and blessed the day she was created.

The concert came exactly the way it was scheduled. The theatre was filled to the capacity. Those who came late stood at the back. Others who were unable to come inside the theatre were seen hanging on the doors and the windows, peeping through any available hole to catch a glimpse of that beautiful face they saw on the billboards.

The first presentation was a traditional dance, an exquisite performance. The crowd applauded with frenzy. The second performance, a folk song that evoked emotion, was done by a group of girls in the choir. Nneka was not among them, yet the crowd cheered loudly. It was Nneka's turn to perform. The song was a folk song too, which she sang and danced alone, accompanied by rhythmic beats of drums and gongs. Her appearance was greeted by a protracted ovation. The auditorium shook with noise. So many people stood up to have a clear view of the beauty on the stage. Every movement of her body was provocative. Her waist held the spectators like a spell, and elicited a resounding applause. Her performance from the beginning to the end was accompanied by undulating ecstasy of admiration. Plaudits from spectators drowned her voice.

After Nneka, other groups continued to sing. Every performance had a touch of splendour and excellence. The most emotive was a dirge Nneka and Camilla sang together. Some people clapped cheerfully, others shed tears of emotion. Ezenwa watched from his seat. He neither clapped nor cheered. He did not want Nneka to see him, else she would be distracted. Moreover, the hysteria from the crowd had imbued him with jealousy. Most resentful were the distressing comments two boys sitting behind him were making about Nneka's waist.

After the concert, Ezenwa went behind the stage to congratulate Nneka. 'How was my performance?' she asked, ready to accept any comment he would make. She knew it would be devoid of falsehood.

'You were marvellous. I almost died of jealousy,' he replied. She giggled and accepted his compliment.

Chapter 37

Ezenwa and Nneka went home for the holiday three days after the concert. Nyadiba did not travel with them as usual. He opted to spend two more days on the campus with Anita.

Uyanna was sitting in front of his house as usual when Ezenwa came in. He saw his grandson, stood up to embrace him with the usual hilarity, as he always did whenever Ezenwa came home for holidays. Ezenwa extended his hands for the embrace. Uyanna stared at his face, frowned, withdrew his outstretched arms, sat down immediately, and turned away his face. Ezenwa was astonished by such quick change of mood. He looked at himself to see if there was anything on his body that repelled Uyanna, but saw nothing. 'Good afternoon grandfather,' Ezenwa greeted.

'Good afternoon,' Uyanna replied coldly. Ezenwa was confused, but did not want to worry himself because of an old man's sentiments. He left Uyanna and went inside his father's house. There would be time to redress whatever he had done wrong. He greeted his mother, and sat down to converse with his brother.

Some minutes later, Uyanna sent for him. Then Ezenwa knew that the issue must be grave. He was afraid that Uyanna would start talking about premonitions. The old man's face had a gloomy look. Ezenwa gaped at him, askance.

'Why did you give yourself and your destiny over to demons?' Uyanna asked gravely. Ezenwa shuddered. He should have known that Uyanna must know.

'I don't understand what you mean,' he lied.

'Yes you understood everything,' Uyanna told him sadly. 'They followed you into my compound. When I wanted to embrace you, they warned me to stay away, that you gave yourself willingly. Look at the mark of the covenant. Look at it! Look at the mark! Three lines on your forehead, and that on your arm. Even as I am talking now, they are behind you, covering your mouth with their hands, trying to prevent you from making a confession. Listen to that! That I should mind my own business.'

'I am sorry grandfather, I did it for protection. They wanted to kill me and kill Nneka,' Ezenwa lamented.

'Who wanted to kill you?'

'Cult boys.'

'It is not true. Nobody would have hurt you or her. It was only a threat from these demons to get hold of your soul and control your destiny. You allowed fear to dominate you. Why did you forget everything I taught you? Didn't I tell you that nothing would happen to you unless you allowed fear to get hold of you?'

'You did.'

'And what happened?' Uyanna asked. Ezenwa remained silent. 'I would not have worried myself if you were not my flesh and blood,' Uyanna said.

'But grandfather you know about these cult problems and did not do anything to protect me,' Ezenwa complained.

'What protection do you want me to give you? Did I not tell you that any interference I make in your life would affect your destiny? My son, I have taught you the merits of good and evil. It is left for you to choose which one you want. Evil has a price, and good has a price too. Every decision you make, good or bad, determines what your destiny would be. Why should I interfere when I have told you that by good acts you would link yourself to God, who is almighty, in whose protection no evil can reach you? You forgot everything I taught you and fell to the wiles of Satan.' Ezenwa continued shivering with fear. He had underestimated the implications of the initiation.

'If I had not joined, they would have bathed Nneka with acid,' he complained.

'That was what I told you my son. I told you that whenever the devil wants to get you, he would come through her. Now you see it. Nothing would have happened to her. And if she has not been sexually defiled, either in thoughts or in deed, her purity has an immense power that protects her.'

'I know what I am saying grandfather, they have tried many times to violate her.'

'And what happened?' Uyanna asked sarcastically.

'I always get the information and rescued her,' Ezenwa replied.

'No, you did not rescue her. It was the Almighty God, but these demons made you think you did it. That was a grand plan to buy your soul and your destiny. Now, they can control you, give you what they want, and take from you what they like. You may die a poor man, because they would take the wealth God reserved for you, and give it to their most faithful servants.' Ezenwa winced and started weeping.

'What shall I do? Is there no way out?' he asked tearfully.

'For confessing and asking for a way out, you have started walking towards freedom again,' Uyanna said. 'But the price is great. They were faithful to the covenant, and justice demands that you be faithful too. Your quest for freedom requires an immense sacrifice, something you must give to reclaim what you lost. The sacrifice you will make is only a show of penitence. As you make the sacrifice, beg Jesus Christ to extend his mercy on you because you are a Christian and have a share in his victory. It is the only way to get back your freedom.'

'You can do the sacrifice for me, can't you?' Ezenwa asked Uyanna.

'No, I cannot. It must be from you. You have to sacrifice something most valuable to you.' Ezenwa sighed again. What is more valuable to him than Nneka? Uyanna conjectured his thoughts. 'Even if it is her,' he added. Ezenwa continued to cry. How could he give up Nneka for whom he sold his soul to Satan? The very thing he wanted to protect was about to be lost. He bowed his head in agony.

'Is there no other way out?' he asked again.

'No my son, you have to suffer the pain so that the sacrifice will have value. If the demons want to interfere in your destiny, God's angels would see a base to stand and defend you. When Satan makes a claim on you, Angels of God would tell him that you have paid willingly with tears. No sacrifice, however little, will ever be in vain.'

'Grandfather, this is difficult for me. I cannot live without her.'

'You can my son. The earlier you made the decision, the better for you. And when you have made the sacrifice, you must keep to it, so that these demons would not see any means of getting close to you again.' Ezenwa remained silent, quivering and pondering over what he had brought on himself. For a brief moment, he felt like deriding his grandfather and damning the consequences. But Uyanna spoke again.

'You must know too that these demons can determine what will happen between you and her as long as your destiny is concerned. They may argue before God that you don't deserve her, and God will turn her heart to another man, and you will still make the painful sacrifice. On the contrary, if you sacrifice her willingly, and make the necessary atonement, and if she is the wife God created for you, God will always find a way to send her back to you,' Uyanna explained. The fear of poverty and the possibility of getting Nneka back made a great impact on Ezenwa and influenced his decision. Uyanna had never been wrong, Ezenwa thought.

'What shall I do?' he asked his grandfather.

'Is she the most valuable thing you have?'

'Yes,' Ezenwa replied sorrowfully.

'You must stop seeing her. If she comes close to you, run away. It would be very painful. She would cry and threaten to kill herself. And I must warn you, once you start, there is no going back. The only thing that can break this demonic covenant is something as valuable as the thing for which the covenant was made.'

Ezenwa groaned, got up, ran into his room, threw himself on his bed, and wept bitterly. He cursed the day he met Bambam. He cursed the day he took that vengeance on Bambam. Uyanna was right. The fruit of vengeance is always bitter.

Ezenwa did not eat any food for three days. His father and mother were perplexed and wanted to know the cause of his grief. But neither Ezenwa nor Uyanna was willing to divulge anything to anybody. Nyadiba visited him regularly. Ezenwa received him coldly. Nyadiba knew he was in distress. Ezenwa's usual ebullience was absent in everything he did and said. It would not have bothered Nyadiba more than it did if Nneka had not come to his house one morning, distressed, and weeping uncontrollably.

She had waited for Ezenwa to visit her as usual, but after six days, she did not see him. She came to his house to know if all was well with him. He received her, but coldly, without any enthusiasm. His grandfather was present. Uyanna stared at her pitifully, and tried to cheer her up. She was so confused and dejected that she did not ask Uyanna any of the questions she had compiled to ask him. Everything Ezenwa said and did appeared strange and despicable to her. And when she wanted to go, he did not accompany her as he used to do. He had never been so hard on her like that. Whatever was the problem must be grave and could cost her his friendship, she thought. However, she went home alone.

Disconsolate and downcast, she had cried all night. Her parents saw her, knew that she was in great distress. They inferred that it must not be unconnected with her love life. In such circumstances, she would be discreet and taciturn. So they did not ask her any question.

The next day, desperate to salvage her love, she went back to Ezenwa's house, disdaining every embarrassment, with effrontery, in the presence of his parents and his grandfather, she knelt down humbly and begged him to forgive whatever she might have done wrong. It was a scene so pathetic and emotive for Ezenwa. Every tear that fell from Nneka's eyes was like a stab of a knife in his heart. Every plaintive gesture she made was like a twist of that knife in his heart. He clenched his teeth to restrain himself from crying. His father and mother did not care much about Nneka's despondency, but the sight of a beautiful girl like her, knelling before their son, very early in the morning, and begging for forgiveness of what she did not do, was the most pathetic sight to behold. They begged her to get up and ordered Ezenwa to console her. He nearly did but for a glance from his grandfather. Uyanna winked disapprovingly.

Ezenwa shook his head and said, 'I am sorry, I can't do it. I have no explanation. Even if I give any explanation, you would not understand.' Nneka wailed the more. Ezenwa's father wanted to force reconciliation out of his son, but Uyanna forbade him, and consoled Nneka himself. Nneka left Ezenwa's house, frustrated and heartbroken. Yet with hope, she went to Nyadiba's house and pleaded for his help, lamenting.

Nyadiba was astounded by her story. He hurried to Ezenwa's house, but met a different Ezenwa from the Ezenwa he had always known. Ezenwa ordered him out of his house too.

Nneka's condition deteriorated day after day. She refused to come out of her room, and rejected every food her mother brought to her. What piqued her most was her mother's admonition. She continued to blame her for rejecting Patrick.

Before the holiday ended, Nneka became thin. Although her charm was still with her, but anybody who saw her would know that something awful happened to her.

Academic activities resumed in the university. Bambam had graduated. Nneka returned to the campus alone for the first time. She had not lost the hope of regaining her boyfriend. She had been thinking and reflecting, trying to know where she had erred, but she could not remember ever offending Ezenwa in any way. They had gone home for the break together, and he had been amiable all the way. What fiend manipulated his sensibility? She thought. For a while, she wanted to believe that he was under his grandfather's machination. But she dispelled the thought immediately. Uyanna was a noble man. She knew from his assertions that he was incapable of fostering disunity. No, it could not be Uyanna. Never in her life had she envisaged a circumstance that would make Ezenwa turn his back on her. She had never had a foretaste of rejection in her life. Wasn't she the person who had been rejecting suitors? Hadn't Ezenwa himself been afraid that she would jilt him one day? Each time she remembered this, she wept. A week after their resumption, she made one more effort to restore the bliss she had once known.

It had rained heavily that day. She dressed in the most attractive and provocative dress she had. She sat down on her bed and waited for the rain to stop before she could move out. After about two hours, there was no reduction in the torrent, and she did not want to postpone her plan, else she would continue to think about him every time. It had been difficult for her to sleep at night. Her room mates knew she was grieving, but did not know why, and she was unwilling to tell them.

She picked her handbag and descended the steps hurriedly. There was no cyclist waiting in front of the hall. Who would wait under such downpour? She waited for a while to know if any cyclist would appear by chance. But when it became obvious to her that there was no chance of seeing one, she walked out into the rain, and started trekking down to Ezenwa's house.

Ezenwa was lying down on his bed, musing and sighing, when Nneka came. Since the day Nneka pleaded for forgiveness in front of his parents, no day passed without drawing tears from his eyes. He ate little and drank a lot of water.

Nyadiba had visited him many times, and had never stopped trying to reconcile them. Every effort Nyadiba made was futile. He did not know the cause of the estrangement, and there was no way to find a solution if he did not know the cause. Ezenwa, against all entreaties, refused to divulge anything to him, and never accused Nneka of any kind of impropriety. At a time, Nyadiba started thinking too, that one of Uyanna's errand spirits had taken control of Ezenwa's senses.

Nneka tapped lightly on Ezenwa's door. He jumped up from his bed, opened the door, and saw her drenched by the rain. Her countenance was doleful and penitent. He shut his door immediately and started wailing. Nneka became confused. She thought he was ejecting her, but what she saw in his eyes was acute melancholy and nostalgia. If he did not want her, why should he cry whenever he saw her? She knocked persistently on his door, begging him to open the door. She almost succeeded when he stopped crying and touched the bolt on the door, then heard his grandfather's voice within him saying, 'you have given yourself willingly to demons, these demons would tell God that you are unworthy of her, and turn her mind to another man. Unless you make this sacrifice, they would control your destiny, give you only what they want you to have, and take from you whatever they like. She belongs to you now, and if you don't sacrifice her, they would take her from you and give to their faithful servants. But if you sacrifice her, and she is out of your hold, then she does not belong to you, and they cannot get to her. Like that, her love would never be severed from yours.' He removed his hand from the bolt, fell down on the bed, and started crying again. As he cried, he swore never to succumb to that expendable weakness, that weakness that imbued him with fear, that fear that made him seek protection of the Scorpions.

Ezenwa's voice tormented Nneka. She sat down in front of his door and started crying too. But when she became convinced that he was not going to allow her into his room, she went away more sorrowful than when she arrived. Every painful encounter with Nneka furnished Ezenwa with hope of regaining her. Uyanna said it was a sacrifice. He had better be right, else Ezenwa would hang himself if he lost her.

What worried Nneka most was that she did not know why Ezenwa cried, so she became afraid that it could be madness. Never in her life had she seen such behaviour. She had confined everything to her heart, but as this fear tormented her, she started looking for a friend to confide in. Nyadiba and Anita were as frightened as she was, and offered no help. Their fears, instead of assuaging, augmented her own, and for this, she was forced to confide in Camilla.

Camilla listened attentively to everything Nneka said from the beginning to the end. But before Nneka ended the story, trickles of tears started dropping from her eyes. 'Stop crying,' Camilla said. 'Time would erode his essence in your life.'

'But he is suffering, he was so lean. It seems he had not been eating,' Nneka argued.

'Don't worry about that, continue praying for him. Prayer is the only thing you can do for him now. If he hates you, nothing would make him love you again except if God wants it to be,' Camilla told Nneka. She was very happy for such unflinching devotion Nneka had for Ezenwa. Nneka accepted her advice and started praying. She increased the number of hours she spent in the church, and cared less about her appearance, though it did not affect her beauty. Carelessness rarely affected natural beauty. But her gleam depreciated.

The fear of cult boys did not exist in her life again. Unsolicited visitors did not disturb her again. Many people, especially Joy, thought that she had joined one of the fanatical Christian denominations, and started avoiding her like a plaque.

Some members of the Red Scorpions visited Ezenwa many times to know his problems, but each time, he rebuffed them and refused to talk to any of them. Naturally, this would have attracted some kinds of punishment, a kind of bodily torture to teach him some lessons in obedience and fidelity, yet he was neither afraid nor perturbed by these consequences. He was prepared to take any torture as long as it would restore Nneka to him.

One day, the girl whom they called his Scorpion mother saw him on the road and commented that the mark of ownership she made on his forehead was diminishing rapidly in clarity. Ezenwa remained silent, but was inwardly happy. That was what he wanted, disentangle himself from their influence.

After the first semester, Ezenwa recovered his former ebullience and started relating with Nyadiba as he used to do, but refused to meet Nneka. This brought back a little happiness into Nneka's life. At least she was convinced that his problem was not cerebral malfunctioning, or any other kind of derangement. She continued to explore every means at her disposal to redress whatever might have gone wrong in their relationship. But by the end of the year, Ezenwa had still not spoken to her. She became convinced that he did not want her in his life again. She got hold of herself, and decided to avoid every kind of contact with men as long as she lived.

She told Camilla that she wanted to be a nun. Camilla accepted her with joy, and started preparing her for the convent. Neither Ezenwa nor Nyadiba knew about this until after their ultimate examination in the university.

When the result of the examination was published, Nneka passed with exceptional excellence. Her result was the best result in the Department of Microbiology since the inception of the university; thanks to Ezenwa's inexplicable estrangement, and Camilla's patience and advice. Ezenwa heard about the feat she performed, and rejoiced too, but made no attempt to go and congratulate her until he got back to his village.

Uyanna saw Ezenwa and smiled. 'I cannot see any mark on your forehead, I cannot see any demon behind you. You are completely free my son. You have suffered, and your suffering has bought your freedom. You can go now and tell her what happened, and apologise to her. She had the worst of it,' Uyanna advised Him. Ezenwa jumped up with joy, rushed into his room, dropped his bag, and ran all the way to Nneka's house. He lacked the words with which to apologise, but he knew that with time, she would understand. If she knew it was for her sake, an effort to be with her forever, she might understand and forgive him.

Her house seemed to be closer. He was there just in a matter of minutes. He knocked loudly and repeatedly on the gate. Without waiting to be admitted, he pushed the gate and burst into the house. Nneka's mother was sitting in front of the house. Ezenwa, still panting, greeted her, 'good evening.'

'Good evening,' she replied with every viciousness she could summon. Ezenwa felt it, but could do nothing. She too would understand when the time comes.

'Is Nneka at home?' Ezenwa asked.

'Which Nneka?' she asked scornfully.

'Nneka your daughter,' he replied demurely.

'She doesn't live with us again,' she said unenthusiastically. Ezenwa flinched. His heart started palpitating rapidly. Where could she be? He knew she was not married.

'Where is she?' he asked.

'She is now in a convent. She wants to be a nun,' she explained. 'See what you did to my only child. I hope you are happy now.' Ezenwa gaped at her as if she came from another planet. It took a long time for the impact of her words to dawn fully on him. He opened his mouth, but was lost for words. His eyes became misty with tears. Nneka's mother looked on silently. Ezenwa made a move to go, but dizziness swayed his head, he stumbled and fell. That was when Nneka's mother knew the gravity of the information she had just given him. She shouted and rushed to help him, but he got up before she came to him, and sorrowfully went away, staggering, falling and rising. Nneka had gone and gone forever.

Uyanna was sitting in front of his house as usual when Ezenwa returned. A look at Ezenwa's face warned him that something awful had happened. Ezenwa glanced at him and looked away. He did not want to set his eyes on his grandfather again, and would never talk to him again. Nobody would have convinced him that his grandfather would deceive him. With all the interest Uyanna had shown in his friendship with Nneka, Ezenwa had no reason to suspect anything fallacious in his advice. Now, he had developed misgivings about Uyanna and his necromancy. His mother had been warning him, but he opted to trust the old man instead of his mother. His mother had told him so many times that the day Uyanna would disappoint him, it would be too late to make amends. Now, his mother's prediction had been fulfilled. If he had listened to her, Nneka would have been sitting by his side now. But that would never be again. Nneka had made her decision, and nothing could bring her back. Ezenwa felt he would be better dead than alive without Nneka. How would he live? Where would he start? Where would he end? Every time he thought about her, scenes of their life together unfurled in his memory. He remembered the last day she came to his room, drenched in the rain, crying and begging him to allow her into the room. He started wailing aloud.

Ilodinuno was astonished by this grotesque alteration in Ezenwa's life. He tried to console him too. His mother was immensely worried. What Ezenwa was going through was a kind of frustration that could lead somebody to commit suicide. They made effort to stay close to him, and whenever he went out of the house, his brother walked behind him, to prevent him from committing suicide.

Uyanna made futile efforts to convince him that all was not lost. Ezenwa neither listened nor spoke to him. With that, a gap developed between them. Though Uyanna loved Ezenwa still; wasn't he his grandson? But Ezenwa would have exchanged Uyanna for the devil if he could. He neither greeted nor replied to the old man's greetings. His father, Iroegbu, attempted to pacify him with gifts and promises, but the injury was too deep to be healed with words. And the gap widened between Ezenwa and Uyanna.

Ezenwa was very glad when he was called for the National Youth Service. It was an opportunity to be away from his grandfather and from everything that reminded him of Nneka.